N[illegible]RM
N[illegible]

CW01636694

An absolutely gripping British cri[illegible] twists

JUDITH CUTLER

Fran Harman Mysteries Book 5

Originally published as *Double Fault*

JOFFE BOOKS

Revised edition 2024
Joffe Books, London
www.joffebooks.com

First published as *Double Fault* by
Severn House Publishers Ltd in Great Britain in 2013

This paperback edition was first published
in Great Britain in 2024

© Judith Cutler 2013, 2024

This book is a work of fiction. Names, characters, businesses, organizations, places and events are either the product of the author's imagination or are used fictitiously. Any resemblance to actual persons, living or dead, events or locales is entirely coincidental. The spelling used is British English except where fidelity to the author's rendering of accent or dialect supersedes this. The right of Judith Cutler to be identified as author of this work has been asserted in accordance with the Copyright, Designs and Patents Act 1988.

Cover art by Nebojša Zorić

ISBN: 978-1-83526-676-2

To my friends at Cirencester Tennis Club — Adam Swann, a wonderful coach who makes me feel better than I am on the tennis court, Douglas Emmett, who makes me feel better about life in general, and the whole roll-up squad, who turn up to play in all weathers and are never less than cheerful and supportive.

PROLOGUE

She watches the black-jeaned figure trudge along the main road towards the industrial estate. He's still on their side of the road. Any moment now he'll have to pick his way between the jam of cars and buses, his beige hoodie ducking and weaving as he slouches, resentful hands in low-slung pockets.

His father grunts. 'If those bloody jeans were any lower they'd fall off.'

'It's the fashion, isn't it? And it isn't as though he'll look out of place there,' she says.

'What sort of place is it that lets its trainees turn up as if they're off to a party?' he retorts. 'No, not a party. Whatever kids call them these days.'

'It's a youth project: of course they let them dress to express themselves. It's not as if they need to be clean — refurbishing the place is going to be dirty work.'

'And later on, when some do-gooder's paid for all the expensive kit, then they're all going to make hit records,' he jeers. 'Hang on, I've lost him.'

'We shouldn't be doing this anyway. Spying on him.'

'We're not spying on him. We're making sure that for once he's going to be where he says he is: not wagging off school, not missing job interviews, not skipping medical appointments. We're going to see him

into this last chance saloon. And I tell you straight, if he messes this up, he's out.'

She stiffens. 'What do you mean, out?'

'Out. Out of the house. I wash my hands of him.'

'He's our son! Our only son.'

'And whose fault is that?'

She closes her ears, and concentrates on the little figure in the distance. He still hasn't crossed the road. She flicks a glance at her watch.

'Late for bloody work again, are we?' he asks. 'Dearie me. A meeting with the head? A problem pupil? Well, I've said this before, and I'll say it again, if you'd stayed at home and looked after him, he'd have turned out better than this.'

'And where would we have lived? And what would we have eaten?' It's the nearest she'll get to reminding him that since year one of their marriage she's out-earned him. She isn't even a high-flyer — a fairly low-flyer, compared with all her friends, in fact. But he's still very much earthbound.

'You'd have been there. Look at him.'

She blinks hard; her contact lenses are troubling her. All she sees is the morphed figure of a child becoming a man, but not quite making it. Her baby. Trying to cross the road. And her not there to hold his hand.

CHAPTER ONE

If this was retirement, why had he ever hesitated? What could be better than nipping out to the tennis club he'd joined a few months ago and having a workout in the surprisingly warm Easter sunshine?

Smiling to himself, Mark parked at right angles to the high mesh fence surrounding the courts and the clubhouse itself. He'd manoeuvred cars for years under the beady eyes of colleagues and couldn't break the habit of perfection. He grabbed his bag and headed for the clubhouse, where people were already doing their stretches on the decking. Clubhouse! It was actually a one-room wooden pavilion, not much larger than a shed, though it did boast running water and electricity. The only sanitation was a Portaloo round the back. Apparently that had been a recent acquisition: until then members had had to retire discreetly to the woods which the site backed on to.

He greeted several people by name and got waves and smiles in reply. A friendly place. An ex-county badminton player, Fran would love playing here, once she was fully mobile again.

Tennis clubs had an image problem, didn't they? Or was that just when he was young? It was supposed to be awfully nice people with cut-glass accents and no brains consuming Pimm's and cucumber sandwiches and deigning to hit the occasional ball so long as they didn't break sweat. *Jeunesse dorée*, retired colonels and all that, not to mention Miss Joan Hunter Dunn.

If this club had been like that, he wouldn't have become a member — firstly because he wouldn't have applied, and secondly because he'd probably have been blackballed. Retired public servants would never make the social elite. But he rubbed happy shoulders with a retired plumber, a woman who had once been make-up artist to the stars, a couple of accountants, a nurse and an ex-teacher. There was also a taciturn man who he'd bet was — under a different name, of course — a career criminal. A lot of people simply turned up to play, asking no questions and volunteering nothing about their own pasts. And here they all were, in the grounds of a stately home, Hogben House. Not that the present owners, people called Livingstone, had anything to do with the club: they simply leased out the land and complained if the floodlights were used after ten o'clock.

Apart from the Golden Oldies, seniors who had special sessions on Monday mornings and Thursday afternoons, there were some really good young, fit players who played for the club in the local league. And he wouldn't talk down his fellow seniors, ponytailed Tony, for instance, who was just arriving on his menopausal man motorbike, his racquet sticking up out of one of the panniers like a stubby aerial. Many made up for their comparative lack of mobility with low cunning derived from sixty years of hard-won experience.

Not him. He'd hardly played since his teens, and had only recently taken it up because everyone said it would be good for him after his breakdown. It was — even when it had been so cold that he'd had to play in two tracksuits, a woolly hat and a pair of gloves. Today it was a different matter — he'd already stripped down to shorts. Even his level of play exercised muscles his gardening didn't, and got him talking to other people, not just to robins and blackbirds nagging him to unearth more worms. And yes, he loved it with a passion. Better than the gym any day of the week, especially in this idyllic setting. At his back were mature woodlands; in front of him were the eight courts — in two groups of four, separated of course by more fencing, making a big rectangle — and an expanse of cow- and horse-filled fields as far as the eye could see. On quiet days, with the wind in the right direction, if you had good ears it was possible to detect the A road that ran along the valley, but apart from an artistically placed church tower — not their own village's St Anselm's, but one he'd always intended to visit when he got round to it — there was no building to be seen. Even the Hall was tucked away behind banks of mature trees. Which begged the question of how the owner knew if the lights were on, but he let that pass.

Shrill laughter came from the furthest courts, swarming with kids: Zac French, the young man they'd recently appointed as coach, entertaining a load of kids. Zac had once been a Wimbledon junior champion, and was now leading the men's team in a charge up the league. The women members might pretend to swoon over his dark good looks, but more importantly everyone liked his friendly openness. He'd got a wonderful track record of teaching, not just the very youngest toddlers to the stroppiest adolescents, but even old-timers like Mark — his hour's coaching every Friday morning was a revelation.

Now, helped by some talented club teenagers, boys and girls, Zac was running what was officially called an Easter tennis camp for four- to eleven-year-olds. Why a camp, Mark wondered dourly. The kids stayed in the pampered luxury of their own homes, brought in and ferried home every day in the sort of vehicles he'd always loathed, huge 4x4's, tinted windows and all.

A swish new Audi unloaded a couple more of his fellow Golden Oldies, one, George, waving mockingly at Roland, just parking his bike.

'Bloody hell, what a racket!' George, a lanky left-hander with a killer serve, pulled a face as he realized he'd made a pun. 'They're worse than that Russian girl — you know, the one who can't hit a ball without screaming. It's time umpires awarded her opponents a point for each bellow, if you ask me. That'd soon shut her up. Sharapova! A screamometer, that's what they need. And as for that other woman . . .' He fished behind his ears, removing hearing aids. 'It's still too bloody loud to think.' All the same, he replaced the aids.

How soon would Mark need them himself? Wearing glasses — for reading, driving, whatever — was universal. But deafness carried a stigma, didn't it? All the same, even when he jacked up the TV volume enough to make Fran squirm, there was a lot he missed, especially in US-made programmes. Perhaps Fran was right: perhaps he should at least ask his GP about having his ears syringed.

Most of the dozen or so Golden Oldies now milling round the clubhouse were smiling tolerantly if not fondly at the seething kaleidoscope of colour — the kids were too young even to nod in the direction of the whites or navies which the club technically preferred. The boys tended to sport expensive Premier League replica shirts, while the girls predictably opted for candy-pinks, even to the extent of little frills round the socks topping their sequin-trimmed trainers. And all of them, every last one, squealed or yelled whenever a ball came near them.

The Golden Oldies' unofficial leader was Dougie, short and wiry, a doughty Yorkshireman in his late seventies with an understandable tendency to believe all southerners soft. Stepping forward, he raised an apologetic eyebrow to a newcomer — probably in his late fifties, still with a full head of hair — hesitating on the fringe of the group, and reached to shake his hand. Stephen. No surname. But none of them bothered with surnames, which pleased Mark after his skirmish with the media a few months back. Like himself, Stephen was clearly at the younger end of the retired spectrum, and gave up any attempts to say much about himself as Zac started a deafening race to see who could collect the most tennis balls.

'It's kiddie-time today,' Dougie bellowed. 'Normally we can use all eight courts; today — as you can see — we only have four until Zac's finished.' He dodged a wayward ball. 'It'll all be quiet by three, when the parents roll up and take them home.'

'*A consummation devoutly to be wished*,' Mark put in, wincing at another salvo of noise.

Dougie nodded. 'Now, this is how it works. Mixed doubles only. We play five-game sets, rotating the serve.'

'Five?' Stephen repeated. 'Surely a set is at least six?'

'Not with us Golden Oldies,' Dougie said. 'Everyone gets to serve once, and one person twice. If we've got even numbers, with no one sitting out, we play seven-game sets.'

'But—' Stephen objected.

'That's just how it is,' Mark murmured.

Ignoring the interruption, Dougie continued, 'We each take a playing card—' he brandished a dog-eared pack — 'to see who we're partnered with and who we're playing against. The two red aces against the two black aces and so on. Everything at random. Nothing fixed in advance.'

Stephen's smile lightened his otherwise melancholy face. 'So it's a matter of chance who gets landed with me — it's so long since I held a racquet I don't even remember which end to use. I was hoping for some coaching . . .' With a rueful grin he looked towards Zac, a lighthouse above a sea of bobbing heads. 'When the schools start again, maybe . . .' His face serious, he suddenly shot a question that clearly took Dougie aback. Mark too, actually. 'All these kids — are we supposed to have Criminal Record checks?'

'Oh, Zac'll have had all the checks going,' Dougie said easily. 'In any case, his own kid's here today. Libby. That pretty little lass there. In pink. Oh, not the wishy-washy pink the others are wearing. Petunia, isn't that what they'd call it?'

Or Gucci hot pink. Although she was hardly tall enough to wave even the smallest racquet, clearly Livvie — Dougie's hearing wasn't as acute as his brain — had her own ideas about colour.

Mark risked a glance at Stephen: yes, he was just as aware as he was that Dougie had missed the point of the CRB question.

Soon, having pulled out cards from those spread face-down in Dougie's hand, they were settled into four groups of four, with three people sitting out: one was Jayne, a willowy ex-city lawyer who resented every day her father's devotion to a busty Fifties star for the spelling of her first name. Younger than the others, she'd joined the club with her ex-husband, a man some twenty years her senior, who'd shocked all the members by leaving her for a woman of his own age and promptly succumbing to Alzheimer's. While the players warmed up, she rather ostentatiously retreated into the world of whatever she'd put on her iPhone and, donning dark glasses, lay back in a deck chair on the clubhouse decking as if hoping for an early tan. George, who could be relied on for help with computers, folded himself onto a nearby bench to watch the players. Dan, with a face like a borzoi and a distinguished RAF career, released his dog from his car. He was presumably going to take it for a swift walk through the woodlands behind the clubhouse, safe in the knowledge that all wheeled transport was banned — even, or perhaps especially, the lowly rollerblade. Anachronistically, the estate manager liked to patrol on a particularly tall horse, though it was perfect, of course, for spotting miscreants.

There wasn't much love lost between the club and the Hogben estate, for which Dougie blamed the man who'd recently bought it and who was apparently determined to wring every last penny from it. The house itself was used for shooting fairs, country fairs, wedding fairs. However, looking around him, Mark wondered briefly if the owner might have made more profit out of funeral fairs.

Where the income went, no one had any idea. Certainly it wasn't on the roads that curled through the approach to the club, which had potholes so deep that in rainy weather Mark had been known to park up a couple of hundred yards from the club field.

He was partnering Alex, an ex-teacher whose Mary Quant bob looked as if it hadn't moved on since she first had it, although her hair was now white. He'd have preferred another partner, one whose game he could predict. All too often Alex couldn't get the ball over the net; other times she'd reach and return balls that their opponents would have thought certain winners. They were joined on the court nearest the clubhouse by Henry, a square-built American with an income from no one quite knew where, and John, a taciturn retired GP with varicose veins.

Play!

He was to serve first, looking into the sun — no fun with the light-induced blurs and squiggles that seemed to linger in his eyes longer with each passing year. Even dark glasses and a baseball cap didn't seem to help. The effort to get the ball over the net without a humiliating double fault always took all his attention. It was enough to block out all the kiddie-noise. As they changed ends, they all agreed that coming out of a game that required all their concentration was like emerging from an acoustic tunnel. They went back into it as Mark focused on receiving from Henry, who dished up gentle dobblers and lost to love. Then it was Alex's turn to serve. While she retied her shoe, he had leisure to look around a little. Outside the netting, but still safe in the car park, one or two of the children were trailing from the far courts towards the rear of the clubhouse, as if to the loo.

By this time Alex's serve had gone in — a surprisingly long, wide one, making the receiver put the return shot straight on to his racquet for a nice volley down the centre. Her next serve was an ace — she seemed as amazed as anyone. At this point, two kids decided to return to the far courts via those the Oldies were playing on — bad etiquette which was swiftly corrected. The kids moaned but eventually, in the face of implacable opposition from Alex, who'd clearly retained some of her classroom skills, they bowed to the inevitable and headed back via the car park. Calm was restored.

On their way they passed Livvie, heading on her own with great assurance for the clubhouse.

The set was theirs, four-one. As they gathered round to congratulate each other and wait for Dougie to hand out the cards again, Mark glanced at the clubhouse, but there was no sign of Livvie. No doubt she'd toddled back to her father, who was organizing another ear-splitting ball harvest. But he couldn't see her on those courts, either. Like the others, he obediently took a card and settled to play, partnering John, and playing against George and Dan. A different group now sat out, to be joined by latecomers.

After a tough game, which he and John lost three-two, he joined Jayne when the next draw was made. By now, half a dozen people were waiting for a game, and two or three had already called it a day.

They were changing sides after the first game when on impulse he asked Jayne if she'd seen Livvie.

'Livvie? Oh, yes, she decided to remove Roland's bike chain, and then didn't like having dirty hands, so she started to wipe them on her skirt. Quite! I ended up scrubbing her hands with Fairy Liquid to try to get the grease off. The skirt too — she was terribly upset about the stains, and was trying to take it off. I had to take the washing-up bowl out to her — she's too tiny to reach the sink, and in any case she insisted she had to be where Daddy could see her. Fair enough, I thought. I got most of the mess off — enough to calm her down a bit. Then Dougie called me on to court to warm up and I left her on the decking having a drink of juice. Why do you ask?' she added suspiciously. Lone men weren't supposed to ask about vulnerable children, were they? He'd have been suspicious himself.

But Mark wasn't so much suspicious as anxious by now. 'Because I can't see her anywhere.'

'Oh, she's around somewhere. Come on — your serve.'

But his heart wasn't in it, and it was only because Jayne played so well that they won the game. George's turn to serve. But there was another interruption, as a lad of about ten marched straight off the kids' courts through theirs towards the clubhouse. George's instructions were short and to the point. The boy's response was even shorter — did his mother know he used such vocabulary? George and the boy argued.

Mark itched to intervene. Ever the policeman. Instead he had another look round. Still no sign of Livvie. Anywhere.

'Jayne, I'm really worried about that kid. I'm just going to check the clubhouse and the loo. Back in a sec, OK?'

It felt as if it took for ever to break into the discussion on the decking. Dougie was holding forth about something, and two women were arguing with him. When eventually he got a word in they all denied seeing Livvie. Just to satisfy himself, he checked the Portaloo behind the clubhouse: all too clearly, some of the youngsters hadn't worked it out properly, and the place was awash with pee and worse. Not the place for a child at all. In the clubhouse itself there was nothing but the kids' detritus: miniature hoodies, plastic lunch-boxes and even the odd teddy. The small sheds next to the loo where the coach stored his equipment were completely empty. Back to the clubhouse. On the decking in front was a soapy, oily puddle, which must be where Jayne had tried to clean Livvie up. George and Dan looked at him with complete disbelief as he ran straight past them, down to the kids' area. Jayne yelled something about manners, but he kept going towards Zac.

Already parental monster-mobiles were arriving to clog up the car park — yummy mummies, by and large, who descended from the vehicles to check each other's weight loss and yack into their phones without ever watching what their child might be up to. In his bones he knew he wouldn't see what he wanted to see — an oil-stained shocking pink dress. Flinging open the gate between the two sets of courts, he barged his way through the clamouring kids — they all needed Zac's attention. Now! Not when Zac'd finished speaking to someone else. Now! Now! Now! Out of the corner of his eye Mark could see an irate mother homing in on the poor young man, presumably to rebuke him for ignoring her little lamb.

'Zac,' Mark yelled, his deeper voice booming under the starling shrieks, 'where's Livvie?'

Zac casually spread his hands, attention still on the kids.

'I can't see her anywhere, Zac. Anywhere.'

Zac stared at Mark, taking in all the implications of what he was saying. 'Livvie?' He swivelled round, calling out, 'Livvie! Come here! Livvie!' He turned back to Mark. 'Oh my God!'

Fran would have done something physical — a reassuring hug that somehow wouldn't have slowed her down. All he could manage was a swift pat on the shoulder. 'It'll be all right, Zac, I promise.' That was more Fran-like. 'Stay here and keep these kids with you. Just do it. I'll do the rest.' For half a second he hesitated. What if he was overreacting? But he knew deep down he wasn't. The search had to start immediately. The Golden Hour was vital. And, he told himself, as he ran faster than he knew how to his car, even if the child had just been playing hide and seek, there wasn't a policeman in Kent who wouldn't prefer a false alarm to a real abduction.

He fished out his mobile. Yes, he'd still got the direct line number he needed. No signal! He circled round, desperate to find coverage. At bloody last! Missing children were absolute priority these days — local radio and TV broadcasts would be interrupted if the police team in charge thought the threat of abduction serious enough. And not even abduction — a simple wandering off could lead to disaster just as easily.

The call was answered first ring. Thank God for the years of practice in giving succinct details. His ex-colleagues were as fully briefed as he could manage by the time the call was over.

Pulse racing but now, he realized, with stress, not with the effort of running, he pulled his car across the car park exit. No one was to leave — or confuse matters by coming in — until Livvie was found. After all, she might well have simply got bored and climbed into what she thought was her father's car to take a nap. Or she might have wanted to pet that dog of Dan's. Unsurprisingly, Zac, a model of calm in normal circumstances, had abandoned his charges and was running round frantically, terror less than a heartbeat away, dragging car doors open and yelling Livvie's name at the top of his voice.

Being penned in drove the mothers into collective hysterical anger, some bizarrely threatening Mark with all sorts of legal action. But by now he'd been joined by Jayne, who'd swiftly understood what he was doing; she produced her iPhone and offered to take contact details of anyone who genuinely had to leave.

'Otherwise do what Mark says: stay where you are until the police arrive. Heavens, woman,' she snapped at a virago of a Mercedes 4x4 driver whose language would have shocked a street kid, 'imagine if it was your child that was lost!'

Mercedes Woman refused — unbelievably citing the Data Protection Act — to give any personal information and threatened to ram Mark's car unless he moved it. He raised his hand like an old-fashioned traffic cop. It was amazing how quickly the lingo returned: 'Just return to your vehicle, madam, and secure your child inside it until further notice.'

She opened her mouth, ready to continue her rant, but gratifyingly closed it and did as she was told, even though she mouthed off about crazy old men as she walked away.

Boosted by the trivial victory, he raised his voice over the hubbub with sufficient force — at last — to sound authoritative. 'I want all you mothers to collect your child and then go to your car and wait for further instructions.' When a couple hesitated, he snapped, 'Now!' But his voice was kinder as he continued, 'And you kids who are waiting to be collected, get back on the tennis court and stay with Zac's helpers. OK, guys?'

The teenagers in charge looked stunned, tearful. But one girl put up a hand as if she was back in the classroom. 'What do you want us to do?'

'Resume the drills, anything to keep the little ones together. Don't let any of them out of your sight. OK? Excellent.' He cupped his ear — two or three vehicles, by the sound of it, were already on their way. He grabbed Zac by the shoulders and made him listen.

The dear old blues and twos. Thank God.

CHAPTER TWO

Sergeant Tom Arkwright, about to become an inspector over in Tunbridge Wells any moment now, but currently one of the most valued — and certainly the most loved — of the members of her Major Crime Review team, stopped hurtling two at a time down the stairs so that Fran could make her way up them, considerably more slowly. The moment she saw him she snatched her hand away from the rail, but then she grimaced: he knew she needed its support.

'Don't look at me like that,' she said, the affection in her voice taking away any possible rebuke. 'It's only this gammy leg that's kept me on the payroll, I reckon.'

'And got you that commendation,' Tom said, turning so that he could walk back up with her. When you were in your thirties, a few stairs here or there didn't matter.

'Commendation, schommendation.' She was pleased he didn't think he should offer her his arm. He had made sure, however, that she was on the side with the handrail, which she needed by the time she reached the last three steps. 'I bet they were within a whisker of making me redundant, but when you're run over in the course of duty and the media get hold of the story, it doesn't look good if they put the skids under you.' They wouldn't even have dreamed of it in Cosmo

Dix's day. Dear Cosmo, king of Human Resources, but an absolute emperor when it came to PR. But he'd seen, as he sepulchrally said, the writing on the wall and had started to work in what Fran suspected was a voluntary capacity for a mental health charity.

As if he had all the time in the world, Tom leaned against the wall and said, 'I should think not! All the times you warn recruits about doing no harm, especially to themselves, and you nearly get yourself killed trying to save that woman's life—'

'All I did was act on instinct. I wasn't heroic. I didn't calculate risks. And I seem to recall also telling youngsters there are times they have to put themselves in harm's way!' They might have been aunt and favourite nephew. 'Hell, if I'd used the sense I was born with, I'd hardly have volunteered to break a leg, *at my age,* would I?' she added with a grin. 'With the wedding in the offing, too?'

'All the same, your instincts were better than most folk's would have been. And after the chewing over the media gave your old man, a bit of kindness from them to you was worth having.'

'Humph. Any kindness was courtesy of young Dilly Pound, that nice girl from TVInvicta News.' She paused meaningfully: briefly it had been clear that Dilly would have preferred to hook up with Tom rather than the official fiancé she eventually married. Why not? The clean good looks and gym-honed figure would have attracted any young woman, and yet they made women her age disconcertingly maternal. 'Another three months and another nine days' wonder featuring someone else, and I shall be out on my ear, believe me. I just hope I can protect the rest of the team. Though I suppose old cases never die . . .'

'Most people would be glad to go—'

'It's a good job you didn't add anything else, young Tom. References to age are my prerogative.'

He chuckled with her. They were so secure in their friendship he never bothered calling her *ma'am* except in public, though he rarely called her Fran within possible earshot of the others in the team. 'Would I dare? But you've done your thirty years of service, you've got a good team together who are more than capable of reviewing unsolved crimes, and now you've finally moved into your new house and you've got the wedding to think about — well, take the redundancy or retirement package, whichever is better, and run, that's what most people would do.' He was about to say something else but didn't. He would in his own good time, Tom being Tom.

She leant against the banister-rail, easing the weight off the injured leg. It was only will power that had made her discard her walking stick, will power and a fear that she could still be pensioned off, this time on the grounds of ill-health. Now it was more than will power that stopped her even limping — her body had reacted with such resentment to her lopsided gait that half the muscles of her lower back had only last weekend gone into such severe spasms that she'd fetched up in bed popping heavy-duty painkillers. Thank goodness for her lovely NHS physio, Anna, who'd stretched everything back into a semblance of normality and issued her with a long list of exercises.

She managed a smile. 'I'll go when I'm good and ready, Tom. Between you and me, I want Mark to establish his routine first so we don't tread on each other's toes. He's started playing tennis, and if I was limping round the place killing time he'd feel too guilty to go without me.'

He nodded, implying a mixture of understanding and exasperation. 'So how is he? Completely recovered?'

'Yes, though he still sees the shrink once a month or so. But shedding responsibility has made him a new man. So long as he doesn't get any more stress . . .'

'Good. One thing less for you to worry about.' Checking his watch, he turned to go. Already three steps down, he asked cheekily, 'But between the two of us, how are things really between you and our esteemed DCI Murray? You're so polite to him I guess you're not the best of friends.'

'Me and Sean? Like this.' She crossed her fingers.

'My auntie says you're supposed to cross your fingers behind your *back*, Fran, when you're fibbing.' And he scooted before she could think of anything to say.

She progressed more slowly to her office. It wasn't so much her leg that protested at her little peregrinations as the muscles that her limp forced into extra work; they stiffened as soon as she stopped. The physio had assured her that this was normal, and had suggested, though possibly not seriously, that she might consider the sort of ice bath that England cricketers plunged into after a day's play. As it was, Fran did all the exercises she'd been prescribed as assiduously as if she'd been training for the Olympics.

Alice, her secretary, produced a cup of tea as soon as she'd parked herself at her desk. 'Any news?' she asked, waving a packet of biscuits under Fran's nose. With her own middle-aged tussle with calories, she might have known better.

'Get thee behind me. However will I get into my wedding dress?'

'Spanx, of course. Double layer if necessary. Any news about Mr Wren?'

In the very short period during which their careers had intersected, Mark's chief bugbear had been an acting chief constable dismissed by his many detractors as being as tiny as his name suggested. Most of Fran's generation of officers had service to others in their DNA; in Wren's case, it seemed to have been replaced by forelock tugging to politicians who insisted that cuts could be made in policing while improvements in performance were made at the same time — and all this with a twenty per cent cut in their budget. At least one honourable chief constable in another county had resigned, declaring that he and his officers were being asked to do the impossible. Fran had colleagues in other areas who'd been made redundant and then, on the quiet, been invited to reapply for lesser but vital jobs with much worse conditions of service. A chief superintendent back as office junior? Not her. OK, she exaggerated — but not her, anyway.

Alice was waiting.

'Should there be news?'

'Rumour has it he's about to flit the coop.' She flapped little wings.

'Bloody hell!' Fran was genuinely shocked. 'Why on earth? You're winding me up!'

'Honestly. Thought you might have heard something — in your position.'

And what position might that be? 'I've heard nothing. Absolutely nothing. My God, I hope it's not true.' Not because she wouldn't be delighted to see the back of him, but it could be a disaster. 'Imagine the headlines: *More Trouble at the Top Rocks Kent Force*! And worse,' she added dourly. The media would rehash all the stories: the old chief's major error of judgement resulting in the death of his deputy — drama there in itself. And then the business of Mark and his daughter, now officially a criminal — just what Mark needed now he'd finally achieved relative anonymity.

'If the chief goes, isn't the usual policy for everyone eligible to have a temporary upgrading?' Alice asked, with a look Fran didn't quite understand. 'I mean, I'm surprised they haven't got a new deputy or assistant chief, at least.'

'Budget — top brass costs more. In any case, what's *usual* these days? What's your money on the Home Secretary discovering a force doesn't need a chief constable at all? Or will it be the new elected Commissioners that discover that? Hell, don't get me started on how much money that little venture into democracy is going to cost!' She took a deep breath and continued, with an ironic smile, 'Or maybe we'll be privatized — yes, one or two forces are in discussions with the management of security firms. And there's also talk of us sharing resources with another force when there's a major crime,' she added, dropping her voice confidentially.

'Yes, Essex,' Alice agreed casually, as if the top-secret information was general knowledge.

Without missing a beat, Fran continued, 'In the meantime, we just do our best — which in your case, Alice, involves removing those biscuits from my presence and passing me those files . . .'

The old chief constable had always wanted Fran to revamp the Major Crime Review Section — in other words, checking on cold cases to see if, possibly with the aid of new technology, they could be solved, even decades after the event. Wren seemed to like the idea, and had asked her to mentor a DCI on secondment from the Met, Sean Murray. She'd never understood exactly why he'd been parachuted in, but since the senior ranks were so depleted by resignation, sickness or even maternity leave, she hadn't argued. When she and her leg were seriously desk-bound, she'd got him to chair team meetings, take on her role in visiting crime scenes in person, and even handle the press a couple of times. However, he'd not won many hearts there, and she was looking out for a media relations course to make him more user-friendly.

More friendly full-stop.

Actually, she wouldn't argue with young Tom's private and highly technical description of him: *weird*. Sean fizzed with some suppressed anger, so potent she wondered how he'd managed to get through psychological screening. There was, however, nothing on his record to suggest any problems, either with colleagues or with the public. And she had to admit, all the reports she'd generously let him write up had been exemplary, as had the minutes she'd graciously left him to take at interdisciplinary meetings she really couldn't bear to attend.

In other words, she'd exploited him something shocking, if not badly enough for him to make a valid complaint to his mate Wren, or anyone else for that matter. After all, he was amassing valuable experience, possibly even while sneering at her lameness. As for that, and her quasi-hibernation in her office perusing old files, her response was what she'd told Mark when he'd raised eyebrows over supper: as she'd actually been part of the original investigation team for some of the cases she thought might warrant reopening, she was best placed to revisit the investigations. So while her fitter colleagues literally did the leg work, she'd spent the time she'd freed up rereading pile upon pile of case notes, and generally, with the miracle of hindsight, of course, rethinking the lines of enquiry that her bosses back then had wrongly insisted on pursuing. However much Sean Murray rubbed up the wrong way colleagues he persisted in seeing as country bumpkins, their progress had been excellent, with the end in sight for most of their investigations so far.

Now for the next one. Which should she choose? There were a couple that interested her. It would really benefit Murray to be involved in the decision.

It was well within her rights to pick up the phone and tell him to come to her office, and no one would have thought any the worse of her. But she'd always hated being on the receiving end of such summonses. Besides, the exercise was good for her. So she left the phone where it was and headed out. The sooner all the muscles started working properly the better. And limp up the aisle to Mark she would not.

She thought she heard her phone ring — but Alice would field that. She wouldn't even limp as she walked down the corridor — hey, that was good. Back straight, shoulders relaxed — any day now she'd be back to normal. Well, any week now. Hip, hip, hooray, rather than hip, hip replacement.

DCI Murray had wangled his own goldfish bowl off the main CID area. Just how she wasn't sure: it wasn't as if he had some managerial function apart from the one in the Review team. Ideally, he'd have had a room adjoining hers, but that would have meant displacing the secretarial team, and the women were so jumpy and anxious about their future she'd refused to sanction anything that would have added to their fears.

It would have been nice if he'd leapt from his chair as she hove into view, but at least he cut his phone call. It was easier to stay standing than to sit and have to get up again. 'Sean, I've been looking at the files for the early Nineties just to check if there's anything that grabs my interest. There are a couple I'd like you to look at with me.'

'Oh?' He was busy stowing files and checking his pockets, as if ready to leave. Why hadn't his mother taught him some manners?

'One involves an old people's home; the other's nothing specific. Not yet. Just a little cluster of mispers, girls based in children's homes,' she said, as if she was expecting him to take an interest. 'Kids barely in their teens. With all this stuff coming out about girls being groomed for prostitution I thought it might be worth a look. They may just have done a flit, of course, poor girls,' she shrugged sadly.

'I know they say Ashford's the fourth best UK town to live in,' Sean said, clearly not agreeing with the optimistic assessment, 'but I'd also say it must be one of the easiest to get away from. Near to the Channel for ferry or Eurostar; M20; London itself. And of course we're talking about an era with much less CCTV coverage than now.'

He was right, of course. But there was something about his tone she didn't like. So she insisted, 'All the same, when you've reviewed the care home deaths, I think the children's home deserves a new pair of eyes . . .' Yours, Sean.

He was on his feet. 'I presume it can wait till Monday.' Statement, not question, she noted. 'It's my guvnor's wedding this weekend, and I'm taking some time off in lieu — starting about now, actually.' He looked at his watch ostentatiously. Or was it insolently?

'It's usual to clear it with your line manager.' And Fran couldn't remember so much as a scribbled note.

'But he's up in London, isn't he? Getting married.' Definitely insolently.

'Since it's the Met that pays you, I suppose he is. You'll have to accept me as a pale substitute, won't you? And I have to say, DCI Murray, that I prefer to be asked, not told.' She held his gaze. 'I'd have said, as I'm sure your *real* line manager would, that it's fine to take the time. But you'll have to be in bloody early on Monday to get your head around all these cases, won't you? We'll talk about them at . . . say nine-thirty. If that's all right by your line manager. And you'll find the files on my desk when you come in.' Which meant she had to arrive at the crack of dawn to check up on him, but since she was something of a lark, that wouldn't be a problem.

As she reached the door, she turned. 'Enjoy the wedding.'

So she'd better go and look at the files herself. She took the long way round to her office, reasoning that every pace she took must strengthen the leg. As she reached her desk, the phone rang.

'Ah, got you at last, Fran! Don Simpson here,' a familiar voice greeted her. In his late forties and a policeman of the old school, Don was now running the Major Investigation Team. 'I've got something in Ashford. Are you up to coming over — or will it be just young Murray?'

'How interesting is it?' she asked offhand.

'Very.'

'In that case I'll come myself.' Which she'd always had every intention of doing from the moment he first spoke.

* * *

'How did you manage to shed Murray?' Don demanded by way of greeting. He was grey-faced, all the usual beer-induced high colour washed out of him. Fatigue? Something else? How was he going to cope with a long investigation?

'Oh, don't worry about him.' This wasn't the time or place to explode with rage, though she was sure Don would relish the story. So she concentrated on trying to heave herself out of the car without a wince or a grunt. 'OK, let the dog see the rabbit.' Being extensively briefed during the journey was one thing: being there was another.

He pointed at a half-demolished building, but for once made no effort to accompany her. She looked at him sideways. He was more ill than tired, surely. But he'd bite her head off if she asked — hers, or, more likely, some innocent junior officer's.

They were in one of the Victorian parts of Ashford, the brick buildings amazing relics when you realized they must be less than a mile from the new station that hosted Eurostar, not to mention an extensive shopping outlet. The building lurked near the nineteenth-century railway works, some still in use, others as dilapidated as this one. In fact it was probably an old railway store — the brickwork was the same. What remained was covered in graffiti, some, though Fran hated to admit it, well executed and amusing. But now it was taped off. A stationary JCB was poised in mid-strike by one wall, like a dinosaur suddenly repelled by its meal. A brawny and heavily tattooed man in his forties, presumably its driver, was now sitting half in, half out of a police vehicle, looking as if he was about to throw up. At least someone had found him a bottle of water. Hilary Baird, a sergeant in her thirties who managed to combine consummate tact with outstanding ability, stepped forward and murmured discreetly into her ear: 'Barry Grant.'

Fran had a sudden bizarre vision of herself as the Queen at a garden party.

As he caught sight of her, Grant got up and came staggering forward — perhaps he recognized her from the times she'd fronted appeals on TV. 'In there — in there!' Grabbing her arm, he pointed into what remained of the shell. 'All staring up at me! I'd better show you! Barry Grant,' he added unexpectedly, as aware of the niceties as her sergeant, it seemed. So much for stereotypes, as she always told young officers inclined to prejudices. He thrust his right hand forward.

She shook it gently, covering it with her left. 'Fran Harman,' she responded, with a sober smile. 'It's all right, Barry. You just stay here.' She might have sounded kind — hoped she did — but in reality there was no way she wanted him back in the heart of the crime scene. 'Heavens, you're frozen — I'm sure one of my officers can find you a blanket.' Shock, of course, nothing to do with the weather, which was amazingly mild. 'And I think you'd be more comfortable if they took you away from here to give us a statement.' She looked for Hilary Baird again: her innate kindness managed to extract all sorts of revelations from the people she cosseted. 'Sergeant Baird will look after you, won't you, sergeant?'

They exchanged smiles: no need to say anything at all.

As she picked her way over the rubble, Fran could see exactly why Grant had looked like a man recounting a nightmare. Four skulls turned their empty sockets towards her as if in silent reproach.

CHAPTER THREE

As he moved his car aside, Mark couldn't work out which was worse — having been recognized the moment he made the phone call or not being recognized by the uniformed sergeant who was driving the first response car. He introduced himself as the PolSA: 'Police Search Advisor', he explained, unnecessarily, of course, given who he was speaking to. Mark didn't correct him, having embarrassingly missed his name. The acting chief inspector he'd spoken to on the phone, Ray Barlow, arrived next, wide-eyed behind his spectacles and with a rather too respectful smile and shake of the hand. But Mark didn't have time to indulge his own emotions now. Zac, who was grey with terror beneath his year-round suntan, was running towards them. His account was so incoherent Mark was glad he'd been able to establish the facts first. A motherly plain-clothes officer, who might as well have had *family liaison officer* stamped on her forehead just over a rather too ready smile, emerged from another vehicle and ushered the poor sod away from the action, in which he'd clearly wanted to be involved. Photos, she'd want, important information about Livvie's medical history — anything to make the search process easier.

'So, guv'nor,' acting DCI Barlow summed up, using his fingers, 'we've got members; kids who were assisting the coach; kids being coached; and kids wanting to go home.'

'Right. And, once I'd spotted the problem, no one was supposed to leave till you got here. That being said, half a dozen mothers have come and gone so far, leaving all their details with a highly competent woman called Jayne — over there, the one with the sunglasses in her hair. I'll get the members to get their heads together to work out exactly who was playing on the other courts.'

'And you say you've done a preliminary check of the premises?' the uniform sergeant demanded, as if doubting him. And why not? Just an old guy with winter-pale legs, embarrassing in shorts.

Mark said quickly, 'Yes. Nil return.'

'Thanks, guv'nor,' Ray Barlow said. 'Look, I may be the one nominally in charge but Jules Warden here is the expert. He'll want the info to help lay out his plan of campaign.'

Jules, every inch a TV-issue cop, nodded. 'Look — Mark, is it? — sorting this lot's going to be like herding cats. Could you collect the senior players, since you obviously know them, and keep them together? Tell them what we're up to? And maybe recruit a search party? Thanks.' He turned away to tackle the next imperative.

Mark nodded. 'Just one thing, Ray: I'm not the guv'nor any more, though that doesn't mean I won't work my socks off to find the kid. Oh, I forgot to say, there's a fence with a couple of palings pulled aside so people can get access to the grounds of Hogben House if they try hard enough — or are very small. Woodland,' he added, pointing.

Jules must have picked up the last words and absorbed the implications. 'Get your team of tennis players to check the woods, then. Usual routine. As soon as the rest of our team arrive, we'll take over.'

As he hesitated, Ray nodded. 'On my authority, if you insist, guv.'

Most of his fellow Golden Oldies had already formed a knot by the clubhouse, though he could see that one or two more had slipped away quietly since play had stopped. Damn and buggeration. But thank God for the efficiency of Jayne, who seemed to have established him as leader and herself as deputy. She said grimly, 'That new guy, Stephen, said he'd got a dental appointment and had to go. He's given me his address and phone number, so I suppose it's possible to check,' she added. 'Assuming he's telling the truth, of course.'

'Excellent. Anyone else missing? Roland? Hey, he's not taken his bike, has he? Shit and corruption!'

'His details will be on the membership list,' Dougie said repressively, looking at Mark as if he didn't like the transformation he'd seen. 'And you've got a copy of that.'

Best to play the incompetent penitent. 'At home, of course. I suppose no one's got a copy here? No matter. What the police will need is a list of everyone who turned up: I can't remember, nor when everyone arrived or left. We'll probably need a group effort on that. But later. The important thing is finding Livvie. Now. The police are afraid that she may have wandered off into the woods back there,' he said, as if it wasn't his own fear. 'Actually, I'm *hoping* she's wandered off there and that if we get together a search party we'll find her and no tears shed. Have any of us beside me got their mobiles handy?' A murmur told him that about half had, albeit in their cars. 'Because what I was thinking we might do was go off in pairs, calling out for her. Stay within earshot of the next pair — so keep calling out for Livvie. OK? If you find anything, anything at all that might have any connection with her, stay put and phone. This is my number.' He dictated it. 'But don't — you know—' He stopped abruptly.

'We've all watched TV, Mark,' Jayne said. 'We know about not disturbing crime scenes.'

'Assuming we find a crime scene. Pray God we don't, that we just find the child safe and sound,' Mark said. 'If there's no mobile reception, of course, split up — one stay with whatever you find, the other come back here. Call to your neighbours so they know what's happening. Dougie, would you do this with your playing cards to speed things up?'

As if glad to be back on familiar territory, Dougie obliged. No one mentioned there might be another reason for Mark wanting them in random pairs — that he didn't want any hint of possible collaboration. In — in whatever . . .

'Which way shall we head?' Jayne asked.

'Towards the house, first. I'll get one of my officers to wait there to tell you what to do next.' Hell and damnation — had anyone noticed the slip? He'd better not make the same mistake in front of his former colleagues.

He didn't. He hung back behind the knot of officers Ray and Jules were briefing until Ray clocked him. The circle widened to admit him. In his turn — after those reporting zero from the car search — he reported what he'd done.

'So we need someone to be ready by the house. Mark — is it OK to call you Mark? — will you go down there with Constable Kennaway? OK, Seb? That way you'll know if we've got the full complement as they check in. I've got local radio on to it already. All the guys checking CCTV have been alerted.'

'Helicopter?' Mark prompted.

Barlow caught Jules's eye. 'Seems the new guv'nor hasn't authorized it — and the latest diktat is that every major bit of expenditure has to be run past him first. And he's off on some Home Office jolly.'

Mark was ready to scream. 'The ACC, then. Shit, they've not appointed anyone yet, have they? Bloody budget cuts!'

'And the appointments' budget's been frozen, according to today's news, Mark. Pity, I'd have thought your Fran was a shoo-in.' There was a bit of a question in his statement.

Hell — what if she'd been approached and turned it down, afraid for his sensibilities?

'And the lead detective superintendent's off sick,' Ray added with a final burst of despair.

'Tell you what, Ray, if anyone would stick their neck out to get that chopper up and flying, it'd be Fran.'

Ray shook his head doubtfully. 'But she's with the Major Review team, isn't she?'

Which was true, but there might be a subtext. People at Ray's level sometimes feared the rough side of Fran's tongue. 'Doing one job's never stopped her interfering in another, has it?' He reached for his phone.

* * *

So what had landed in Fran's lap? She was clearly at a crime scene, as preoccupied as he'd have expected. She'd been all too willing to rock the corporate boat and scramble the chopper, but had had to cut their conversation short. At least she'd managed her now standard valediction: 'I love you.'

PC Kennaway, a young man who clearly thought looking bad-tempered gave him professional gravitas, didn't seem best pleased to be landed with someone who ended a phone call with the words, 'And I love you too.' But at least his first question was sensible: 'How far is it to the house you mentioned? Walk or drive?'

'Drive. There's a sort of porter's gate that Joe Public use — they're allowed to walk round, keeping to the paths, between ten and four. Hence the unofficial access via the broken fence.'

'Gotcha. So would anyone open the main gates if we asked them nicely?'

'I wish I knew. I don't know how much of the time the new owner spends here — Fran and I aren't on visiting terms, Seb. But road's quicker.'

'Not if it's all like this track,' Kennaway said through gritted teeth, as he tried to drive faster than the potholes encouraged. He ended up swinging the car from side to side like a rally driver, doing his best to dodge the worst.

Mark hoped he wouldn't throw up.

* * *

'Sodding locked!' Kennaway declared. 'Clever electronics, too, so I can't just bust them open like I could a padlock and chain.' Furiously he jabbed at the Entryphone again, but to no avail.

'Leave the car here — right across the gates just in case, eh?'

Kennaway obliged, leaving the lights flashing lest anyone think they might be on a social visit. 'But how do we get in?' His eyes took in the ten-foot walls topped, like the featureless gates, with spikes.

'I told you. There's a little side gate for public access. We'll nip through that — it's not four yet so it should still be open.'

It was, opening on well-oiled hinges, though Mark suspected Kennaway would have preferred to kick his way in. To their right stood the house — something of an architectural hotchpotch to Mark's mind, with a plethora of Victorian accretions. No wonder the National Trust hadn't shown any signs of wanting it. Putting aside his pride in the purer lines of their Georgian rectory, he led Kennaway away to their left, where a gravelled patio looked out to the estate. A path broad enough for a car wound towards the woods. Another, marked STRICTLY PRIVATE, headed off to the right, in the direction of what Mark presumed would be the formal gardens.

'They should be coming from the woods,' Mark said, possibly unnecessarily.

'Yes. I can hear them.'

Did he shoot a suspicious glance in Mark's direction? Not just old and white-legged but deaf too? Possibly. As to the legs, he'd completely forgotten his tracksuit, still stuffed into his tennis bag on the edge of the courts. Probably it would have to stay there a while, as part of a possible crime scene.

Thank goodness his eyes were better than his ears. Now he could see some of the search team clearing the woods, heads down. No one waved or shouted. Even Dan's dog looked dejected, tail drooping.

'So what do we do now?' Dougie asked, still leader.

Seb opened his mouth and closed it again. Afraid he was going to suggest they ought to go and reclaim their Zimmers, Mark jumped in. 'You've done north-south: have any of you got time to try east-west?'

'As long as Libby's missing, we've got all the time in the world.'

'You mean Livvie?' Kennaway snapped.

Dougie blinked. 'In any case,' he added more pragmatically, 'we've got to get back to the club somehow, to put together that list you wanted — people's comings and goings — which means more walking anyway.'

'Plus,' added Jayne, 'I don't suppose we can move our cars until the police say so. So walk we can and walk we will. When we've done the east-west search, we regroup back at the clubhouse — yes?'

'First one there get the kettle on,' someone ventured — but no one laughed.

Kennaway turned to respond to his radio.

Mark said, 'I'll walk with you, if that's OK.' He turned to leave, but Kennaway wheeled round and raised a finger in the air. 'Just one moment, Mark. I'd rather you came with me, if you don't mind. After all, you were the last person to see her, weren't you?'

'No. That'd be me,' Jayne said.

Kennaway visibly dithered. How the hell would he make it to sergeant if he couldn't make decisions?

'Shall I take Jayne's place, then?' Mark asked reasonably, raising his voice as a helicopter swooped towards them. Good for Fran. But his smile withered and died. The chopper wasn't the police one; it was a private one. Mark had a suspicion that it would make the police search even more complicated.

There was only one person aboard, and his expression, as he disembarked and strode towards them, was hardly welcoming. Kennaway's apparently habitual scowl was overlaid by something like terror: perhaps he'd once been caught scrumping and had a lingering fear of bad-tempered landowners.

So Mark stepped forward himself, a formal smile on his face and his hand outstretched. The words came out regrettable, unbidden. 'Mr Livingstone, I presume.'

CHAPTER FOUR

'You think there may be more bodies — skeletons — there?' Fran asked the pathologist, white clad like the rest of them. Already big screens had been erected round the site, and she'd requested a temporary roof. The less media intrusion the better at the moment, especially if the child Mark was worried about was still missing. They'd want everyone's attention on that, not on those already beyond help.

'I think it's entirely possible. It looks as if they were bricked in with a false wall. It's a good job for those working on the wall that the cavity was the right humidity.'

'Because if it had been damp, there might have been adipocere formation, right? Grave wax?'

They exchanged a smile. For all she was old enough to be his mother — just — Dr Hemp liked to treat her as a favourite student.

'Right. It might have preserved the body in its original shape, which might have made things easier for me — and I suppose for you. At the other extreme, if the space was very dry?'

She frowned as if puzzled, but they both knew she was pretending. 'Then the body might become mummified in a shrivelled, leathery state. The poor JCB operator was scared enough as it was.'

'He'd only just started,' Don put in. 'As you can see, there's a good two thirds of the wall intact, so we'll have to brace ourselves for more.'

Hemp's frown was genuine. 'Probably youngsters, like these?'

As Don nodded grimly, Fran clapped her hand to her mouth — couldn't ever stop herself doing that when kids were involved. 'Youngsters?' she repeated.

'Mid-teens, I'd say at first glance. I can be a bit more precise later.'

'Cut off before they'd even lived.' At last she nodded. 'Before we bugger about with the rest of the wall we'll remove these first. Give them a bit of dignity.'

'We might have to use a different JCB operator,' Don put in with a sour grin. 'Poor bastard.'

'We'll take it down brick by brick, however long it takes,' Fran said, more sharply than she meant to. Her hip was hurting badly, and it was only the need to maintain team morale that kept her from popping more painkillers and going back home to her bed. Team morale? Her morale too. Better to be doing something useful than reflecting on the frailty of human life. 'OK, where are we?' She didn't need to consult her notes to recap: 'We have this building which was used for some twenty years as some sort of youth drama centre. Council run, right? Its clientele had more or less abandoned it for other purpose-built centres in the town, and four years ago the council were glad to close it down: it drank money and was, frankly, an eyesore. Right?'

'Right,' Don said.

'Can you get someone to check the misper records?'

Don looked at her oddly. Sean Murray would have been doing it if she'd had the sense to pull rank. 'I'll get someone on to it, Fran.' He spoke to a constable she didn't know, who nodded and headed briskly away.

'Thanks. Hell, Don, it'll be sad news for some families but at least it's news. Closure. An end to not knowing.' She clicked her fingers in irritation. 'I've got the paper files on Nineties mispers on my desk at this moment, as it happens.'

'Actually, Fran,' he said, almost hesitantly, 'this might be as much a job for your review team as for MIT.'

'Of course. We'll cooperate in any way we can. Joint Incident Room for a start. It'll be good experience for Sean Murray.'

Don looked around him ostentatiously. Murray, of course, was nowhere to be seen. 'A shout as big as this is all hands on deck time, isn't it, Fran?'

Don had a history with her protégés — seemed to find fault with all of them. He'd recently had an unseemly professional tussle with a woman DCI she really rated and she'd had to bang heads together. She hoped he wasn't going to embark on a similar feud with Murray — her own dislike of the man was bad enough, and until his behaviour earlier, she'd have bent over backwards to support him, even in the face of just criticism. 'He's tied up with something else,' she said flatly.

'He never seems to be there when you need him. Can't we get rid of him and have someone else?'

In other words, someone who pulled his weight. She couldn't agree more. All the same, she said, 'Don, the way things are, who knows what we can and can't do?'

'Ah, you've heard the rumours about Wren. Good riddance if you ask me.'

'Depending on what sort of chief we get next.' A mutual frown put an end to speculation. 'OK, so we're going to need a team of forensic archaeologists, aren't we? And I've a nasty feeling we're going to have to fork out for some overtime, Don — Joe Public won't like the thought of what all this plastic sheeting is hiding.'

'Quite. Best flip a coin to see which one of us hangs round to watch them at it, then, Fran. Head or tails?'

'You choose, Don. And organize the archaeologists. I'll authorize any overtime necessary. But first I just want to call Mark to see how the search for that missing child is going on.'

No news. 'We've criss-crossed the woods behind the club three or four times,' Mark said bleakly. 'Nothing. She's just disappeared. I was there.'

Fran felt as sick as he must. But she went into bracing professional mode, as if he were one of her team. 'So were a lot of others, Mark. Including her father. But you were the one who noticed and did something. Weren't you? Hold on to that. What next?'

'We've got together a list of anyone at the club even for a few minutes this afternoon. Some of us are going over to that caravan site down the lane to carry on searching. Others — well, some of the guys are in their eighties, Fran, and a lot of folk have other commitments.'

He was trying to justify staying on with the other searchers, with an implicit apology for not having her supper on the table, wasn't he? 'Of course.' She wanted to tell him not to overdo things himself but buttoned her lip. 'Look, I'll be late home myself. Shall I bring something in for us both? About eleven?'

'Something sinful, please. Look, my battery's low. Don't worry if you can't reach me.'

She would, of course. 'See you elevenish. Love you.'

'And you.'

He must be worried to have managed that.

* * *

The arrival of the archaeologists, led by a sturdy middle-aged woman called Dr Evans, with a chic hairdo completely at odds with the rest of her laid-back appearance, seemed a sign of progress, especially when they deployed themselves like a well-oiled machine. Even their lightest touch brought the rest of the brick and plaster cascading down. Those responsible for recording and bagging the debris seemed to be the ones working hardest. As usual Fran was moved by the respect almost bordering on reverence with which the whole site — the archaeologists' term, not theirs — was treated.

At last the fourth skeleton had been taken away. Dr Evans eyed the rest of the wall and then looked round for Fran, who made her way over with an appreciative smile. 'You people have done a wonderful job.'

'It helped that the brickwork was so friable. But we'll need better lighting and scaffolding before we tackle the rest of the wall.' Evans looked at her watch. 'Maybe an early start tomorrow, when you've got the scaffolding set up?'

Fran nodded. 'It'll suit me fine to keep the media in the dark just a few hours longer.'

'You know they like to have news yesterday.'

'We've got a kid gone missing. I want the public's attention focused on finding her just now.'

'Of course.' Evans touched her arm. 'Well, it's all covered decently. We've definitely cleared this section, so you can feed them that as and when. And it's truly much better to work in optimum conditions.'

'Not to mention absolute safety. Do you have a scaffolder you regularly use, or do I have to try Yellow Pages?'

'We've got a good bloke — I'll call him now. Assuming you can pay him overtime?'

She could. And could then go home. She phoned Mark but got nothing. His battery must have died. The landline went straight to answerphone. So he was still searching. Her stomach clenched, but not for him, for the child she didn't even know: eight hours was a long time — well past the Golden Hour in which they always hoped to get a result.

The inestimable Sergeant Baird had returned from ferrying and debriefing Barry Grant some time ago; now she turned to Fran, who had joined her in the car. 'Back to Maidstone, ma'am?'

'I'm Fran at this time of night, Hilary. I'm not sure yet, actually, where I need to go. I can't seem to raise Mark to come and do his chauffeuring duties,' she added apologetically.

'Mr Turner? Well, you wouldn't, not if he's still tied up with the search for that missing child. You know they extended their search to the caravan site just down the road?'

Fran nodded — old news.

'Well, now they've moved on to the cricket field area.'

'Better get me out to Great Hogben, then, Hilary.'

Baird was manoeuvring the car carefully. 'Actually, guv, I wouldn't say this in front of anyone else, but do you think it's a good idea? Your leg . . .' Not to mention the poor back. 'Trying to walk on rough ground in the dark — it's dead risky, isn't it? You'll get all the latest information if I take you back to Maidstone.'

'I might get a flea in my ear: you probably heard about the chopper.'

The sergeant threw back her head and laughed. Then she stopped. 'If they'd found her, I'm sure you wouldn't. But since they didn't . . . But last thing I knew, Mr Wren's meeting was running on and he was still in London. He's not a great one for coming in at weekends, so you might get away with it.'

'Hang on — whatever happened to Friday?'

'Maybe the meeting will overrun even more . . . In any case, if he bollocks you, you can always threaten to go to the press. A missing child pretty well trumps everything, even budgets, doesn't it?'

'It should do. So why did no one think of going all-out twenty years ago when those kids went AWOL?'

'Kids? God, I didn't realize . . .'

'According to the pathologist. Teenagers, he reckons. Three boys, one girl. Yes, back to my office, Hilary — if Mark's still out hunting I might as well do some hunting from my desk. But ten-thirty's my witching hour: I need to have a takeaway on our kitchen table by eleven.'

* * *

If Fran felt done in, Mark looked it. He was still in his tennis tracksuit, but had added a fleece: they'd switched on the central heating but it was only just beginning to take the chill off the kitchen. It might have been a gorgeous day, but the starlit night threatened a frost. He'd become such a serious gardener he insisted on nipping off to close up the greenhouse and then to swathe some of his favourite shrubs with fleece. Only then did he consent to have a hot shower while she reheated their comfort food — highly illicit fish and chips. By then, with a bottle and a couple of glasses in front of her, she could admit that her back hurt enough for both legs to be propped up.

'Two old stagers,' he grumbled, pouring red wine. 'Heavens, is that really only one portion of chips? There's enough for an army.'

'How long is it since even a single chip touched our lips? Well, then — and the fish is supposed to be good for us.'

He made a great show of tucking in.

She did the same. It might have been sawdust for all the pleasure she got from it. She looked at him under her eyebrows. 'It's no good, Mark — we have to break the no-talking-shop-at-home-rule tonight, don't we? Missing kids, dead kids — we need to get stuff off our chests. You first. So long as you don't start blaming yourself.'

'I blame all of us there — but actually no one. I don't even blame Zac. The last words Livvie said to Jayne were that she had to stay where her father could see her. And there were always responsible adults around. When we'd finished searching the woods we spent ages together making a great chart of who was there, the time they arrived and left, who they played with, who they sat out with. With some folk unable even to remember which side of the court they're supposed to be standing on . . .' He paused for her to chuckle dryly.

'So how does Ray Barlow — it is him who's in charge, isn't it? — feel about things?'

'Desperate, I'd say. Not secure in his role, since he's only acting DCI. Your chopper was a master stroke, by the way — it made him think someone thought the situation was as serious as he did. He's done everything by the textbook — we all have — but she's . . .' He swallowed a mouthful of food with obvious difficulty. 'She's probably dead by now, isn't she? And we'll find her body in a ditch.'

She poured him more wine. If she filled her own glass again, she'd never be up at five, would she? But she ought to say something, something positive, with luck.

'Unless she becomes another Madeleine McCann,' he added before she could think of anything.

'But this is UK policing, not Portuguese. And we've all learned a lot from that case,' she said, finding a few words at last. 'Damn it, you were one of the ACPO team who drew up the code of practice. An immediate response; a dedicated team; designated and trained peripheral staff. If things get tough we can always call in the national team. What's happening now?'

'People are scanning every single CCTV image from the surrounding area — it would have to happen where there's virtually no coverage, of course. Some are rechecking those shot earlier; others are on the current ones — in case someone concealed her but thinks it's OK to do something about her at night.'

Sean Murray's words popped up unbidden. 'Kent's an easy place for people to get out of,' she half-echoed them, soberly. 'Europol notified yet?'

'I don't know.' He grimaced. 'Not my job any more, is it?'

'Give me a couple of minutes — I'll get on to Jean-Paul. Privately — so no one thinks I'm checking up on Ray.'

'At this time of night?'

Jean-Paul le Tissier was an old contact, but also an old flame. No need to rub Mark's nose in her past, which was occasionally more brightly coloured than his.

'I could text him?' Which told him she still had his private number. But then, they were both senior officers, who occasionally needed to be able to make contact out of hours.

The message sent, she turned to the table, which Mark had already cleared, to lay it for tomorrow's breakfast.

'I've got an early start, I'm afraid,' she said, unnecessarily. She almost added, *What about you?*

But he replied to the unasked question. 'I should be out there, looking. But I promised I'd look after Mark junior, remember. Working parents, Easter holidays,' he added, not quite managing to grumble. In fact, his son's return into his life, complete with two kids that they both adored and a wife they'd soon come to love, had made what could have been a stressful retirement a delightful one.

'Are you planning to work on the model railway layout?'

'Something much grander. We're off to Swindon, to Steam. The big railway museum. Fran, how can I go? In the middle of all this?'

'How can you not? Unless Ray Barlow specifically asks for you — and then, who looks after young Marco? And Phoebe?'

'In any case, what could I do for Ray? Be on the end of a phone, maybe . . .'

Fran's phone rang. It seemed Jean-Paul kept late nights. For a few minutes he and Fran were all charming formality. And no, no one had requested help, but now they had it. In Gallic spades.

Mark had headed upstairs while she took the call, his back suddenly bent, as if under a physical burden. She watched, heart in mouth. One thing they hadn't talked about was how he felt taking orders from a comparatively junior officer. True, he'd been in charge of policy rather than hands-on daily investigations, but it must be strange to be sucked back into a world he'd left so abruptly. She couldn't have done it.

As he slipped into bed beside her, his body no longer young, but lean and muscled after all his work in the garden, not to mention, of course, on the tennis courts, he answered the question she didn't dare put.

'I thought I'd hate it. All the time I was with people I'd seen come up through the ranks, I kept thinking, I should resent this. But I didn't. I just felt — I don't know, call it pride, that they were doing the job so well. Putting into action the guidelines I'd helped set down. Satisfaction. Like when young Marco gets the hang of wiring points.'

She squeezed his hand. 'I'm glad.'

'I cocked up big time at one point, though.' He told her about his meeting with Livingstone. 'Talk about rubbing Joe Public up the wrong way.'

'He must have heard the quip a million times.'

'And does that make the millionth and first any better? I scooted, I tell you — left it to young Kennaway to get permission to search the outbuildings.'

'Which I'm sure he got. Well, if that's the worst thing you've ever done . . .'

But he was already falling asleep, and loving tenderness was replaced by an urgent need to roll him over to stop his snoring.

CHAPTER FIVE

'Ray! Sorry, I was miles away! Years, anyway.' Fran returned with a bump from the nineteen-nineties, as represented in her pile of files. Automatically she checked her watch. Six a.m. She didn't remark that Barlow was in early — she'd be surprised if he'd been home at all.

'Can I pick your brains, Fran?'

'If you can find anything there at this hour, pick away and welcome.' But she had to be careful. The poor man had already found an ex-ACC on his team. He might not want too much input from the man's fiancée, for all he'd worked for her for ever. 'Move that box of files and sit — first time in eighteen hours, I'd guess?'

He sank into the chair, smothering a yawn. 'Can I be absolutely straight with you?' He waited for her nod, which she hoped didn't show the apprehension she always felt when asked that question. But when it came, it wasn't so bad. 'Have I done something to offend the old guv'nor? He was brilliant yesterday, but he said he couldn't come in today.'

'Ray, he'd have given his teeth to. But he promised ages ago to look after his grandchildren — two who didn't go to the tennis camp yesterday. Probably the only children in Kent who didn't, from what Mark said.'

'You're sure? Must have been weird for him being a civvie, having to take orders.'

'I never knew a senior officer with less side than Mark. Even when he sported lots of braid, and saluting and deference were in order. He's just like us, Ray — a pro. I'm sure you're right about it being strange for him, but he's one of those people put on this earth to make life better for others, you know. He'd do whatever was needful. And he was full of praise for you and your team.' Ray needed to know that — waiting to be confirmed in your post was no pleasure. It was as if you were somehow on approval and could be parcelled up and sent back.

Ray smothered another yawn. 'So he wasn't offended?'

'Just frustrated he couldn't do more. Or do anything today. He'd have been good on one of the public response phone lines, wouldn't he? As for tomorrow, I'm not sure if he's been booked to look after Marco and Phoebe or if he's free.' Saturday — one of their parents should be on duty, surely. But despite what he'd said a few hours ago, she didn't feel she had the right to commit him to anything. 'Somehow I don't think I'll be available for grandmothering duties, do you?'

'Not with those skeletons in Ashford.' He laughed grimly. 'But you wouldn't mind if I asked him?'

'Ray, it's between the two of you. Not forgetting how you feel about having an old hand on your team. Which is?'

'Embarrassed, at least to begin with, I suppose. But then he was worth his weight in gold.'

'Good. But there's something else, isn't there? Some problem?'

He shifted in his seat. 'I just wondered how Europol got involved. I just never thought . . . and yet I've got some French guy offering us CCTV footage of French ports and stations.'

'If I wasn't too old to blush, I'd be blushing now. It was nothing to do with Mark. It was me. I just called in a favour from an old mate. You know how the French like to do things their way: well, I cut through the paperwork. I should have asked you first, but it was almost midnight and I was hoping you might be getting a few minutes' kip — which, by the look of you, you weren't. So don't begin to think that Mark or I went behind your back because we didn't trust the way you were handling the investigation.'

'Thanks, guv.'

'You're more than welcome. And if there's anything else I can do, just ask. But I ought to be over in Ashford to see if we've got any more skeletons. I know Don Simpson's in charge but the Review Unit has some input,' she said, getting up and reaching for her jacket. The forecast might be for even warmer weather later in the day but Mark had been right about the overnight frost — and there was no sign of it thawing yet. 'Have you had any sleep at all?' she shot at him. 'I know I'm not your line manager but I can tell you that you look like death warmed up. I know we all want to work on a case like this till we drop — heavens, I used to do it myself — but often the best breakthroughs come after even a couple of hours' sleep.'

As if tacitly accepting her advice, he fell into step with her as she walked to the car park. It wasn't Hilary Baird driving her this morning, but a constable so slight and bony you'd never have him down as opening bowler for the county police cricket team. Abdul Aziz, known to his mates as Dizzy. He'd driven her in from the rectory as if he was driving a hearse, not like a lad desperate to join the elite team of drivers whizzing VIPs round the country and making sure they were kept out of harm's way. This morning she'd been glad of his silence, working her way through texts and emails as he drove. She had to admit that having a driver gave her another hour of working time each day, but she hated the lack of independence, not to mention the appearance of elitism. In such desperate financial times, too. Mark usually did the honours, but after all his exertions yesterday and with his day with the kids coming up, she'd decided to accept what she was entitled to, just as she'd had to yesterday. But the sooner she could get behind the wheel the better. Another couple of weeks at most now, even if that felt like years.

Ray was about to say something when his mobile rang.

You didn't stand on ceremony when you were on a case like this. 'Go on, take it,' she said, huddling into her jacket.

He'd turned away but now, with a grin, he faced her, tilting the phone so she could hear the voice at the other end. Mark's! So much for his having a lie-in.

'Ray, I don't want to teach my grandmother how to suck eggs, but a thought's just struck me,' Mark was saying. 'Livvie was very proud of her appearance. Very. I know it's a long shot, but what if she was so disgusted by the oil on her dress that she took it off? Or covered it up? I heard some mother yelling at her child yesterday that she was sure she'd taken a waterproof to the court and the child insisting she'd left it at home. What if the mother was right? What if the child had taken it and Livvie had borrowed it, as it were? Everyone's been alerted to look for a child wearing petunia. What if she wasn't?'

'Thanks, guv'nor. Mark. There'll be a note somewhere of the mother's complaint: I'll get someone to check with her now and get a description of the coat — assuming it isn't actually at home, like her daughter said. I'll get back to you.' He cut the call immediately.

Fran sighed. So much for Ray's two hours' sleep. But given this new lead, she wouldn't protest. But he turned to her with a huge grin. 'Looks as if having a kip gave Mark a good idea. I'll get the team up to speed with this and get my head down. Promise,' he added, as if she was his mum.

* * *

'Thought you'd still be tucked up in your nice warm bed, Fran,' Don greeted her, with an obvious effort. A sheen of sweat made his face paler, greyer. Worse than yesterday. But Fran knew him well enough to know he wouldn't welcome a direct enquiry. It must be business as usual until it obviously couldn't be any longer.

She patted a folder by way of reply, adding, as he raised his eyebrows interrogatively, 'I knew you'd want to be here when the archaeologists started again, and I thought you ought to see some of this.'

'This is the twenty-first century, Fran. Texts and emails and — oh, yes, even a little thing called a phone.' He fished an indigestion tablet from his pocket and chomped.

'I know, I know . . . I know you can even send me live footage as it happens . . . But they can't replace my eyes and ears and — I don't know — my copper's nose, can they? Anyway, since I am here, these are more details of kids who went missing in the early Nineties. And several photos of each that aren't on the computerized files. The facial reconstruction people might find them useful confirmation — and vice versa, I suppose. They were all investigated as mispers — but to my mind the investigations were desultory at best, especially compared with today's procedures.'

'I gather there's no news of that missing kid. Jesus — it makes you feel sick to think of it,' he added as she shook her head. Was that sufficient explanation for the tablet? She caught him in a wince. But he straightened quickly.

Just as she did when another back spasm bit — which it did now.

'Quite. Our work here's important but Ray Barlow's is beyond urgent, isn't it?' There was a short silence. She didn't think he'd been offering a prayer as she had, but was sure he was wishing at least as hard. She coughed, and pointed to the half-demolished wall. 'There seems to have been a general assumption that because most of these kids were either school drop-outs or unemployed kids not in college—'

'NEETs,' Don supplied. 'Except they're always bloody scruffy.' His attempt at a belly laugh made him wince again. And she thought he rocked slightly.

She pretended she hadn't seen anything, and continued her sentence: '. . . they probably mooched off to London without bothering to give anyone precise details of where they were heading. They all had one thing in common, however — they were supposed to be part of the group turning these premises into the youth club it became. No-hopers, was how the youth leader described all of them — or variants of the term. Other kids confirmed that their missing colleagues didn't like the hard physical work or the fact they had to be there nine till five, and had likely done a runner.'

Don, ever hard to impress, looked interested. And then swayed. Visibly. But he took a deep breath and dared her to comment.

'The person who's the common factor is the youth leader, of course — a guy called Malcolm Perkins. Known to his friends and the kids as Mal, sometimes Big Mal.'

'Any criminal record?' he managed.

How long could they continue this charade? Would she have to order him off the site? 'Nope. Generally considered a good bloke by the kids and indeed by their parents. Tough but fair. Services background. Left with an exemplary reference.'

'Left!' Don raised an eyebrow. 'Was this Perkins ever questioned as a possible — let's put it bluntly — mass murderer?'

'Nope. But it'd be nice to talk to him now, wouldn't it?'

'You're telling me. I suppose you and your magic papers don't know what happened to him?'

Fran grinned. 'I did try Googling him, actually. But Malcolm Perkins isn't such an unusual name, and I didn't have time to chase them all down.'

'More of a job for a junior officer — young Sean, for instance.'

'Come on, a DCI is hardly a junior officer! I've got someone good on to it, Don. As to the question you've been too polite to ask straight out — *why are you here?* — I lived through these investigations when I was a youngster. I know the shortcuts some of the SIOs took. I didn't like them at the time and I like them less now. I'll delegate when I want to delegate, Don. As in the case of chasing Malcolm Perkins.'

Raising a hand to acknowledge her point, if not apologize, Don asked, 'Anyone else on your radar?'

'One name came up — one of the lads supposedly working on the project. He was supposed to have a temper and a half. Strong, too — had once played football for his school before he found training too much of a fag. A couple of the lads and several of the girls questioned said they were afraid of him.'

'Was he a bully or something?'

'Not as such: they said something was always simmering under the surface. But — no, take it.'

Don turned aside to speak into his phone. As he did so, the wind caught some of the pages Fran had given to him, fanning the faces of what they both clearly now thought might be victims.

She put out a finger to stop them moving further.

He ended the call. 'What's up?' Pocketing the phone, he shifted the file so they could both look at the face. His frown matched hers. 'Looks familiar, somehow. Just for a moment. All that hair, though—' He covered the flowing locks with a big, square hand. 'No. No one I can place. Can you?'

'No. With or without hair. Just something about the eyes. Christopher Manton. The angry one. But then he disappeared too. So perhaps his strength was no use to him in the end. Maybe he's over there, poor kid.' She nodded at the remaining section of wall, now covered with scaffolding. The first archaeologists were swarming round.

'Or maybe he did it and scarpered,' Don said, clutching his gut but gritting his teeth as he continued. 'Thank God for DNA: at least we should be able to identify them all fully and comprehensively. I'll get someone to run to earth the latest addresses of the parents. Are you hanging around, Fran, for a bit?'

'If you've got something pressing, yes, I am.'

'The wife's been on at me to get a doctor's appointment — and I thought the first in the morning shouldn't have much of a wait. So I let her talk me into it.' This from a man who always joked about dying in harness.

She looked him straight in the eye. 'Good. Before you pass out in front of my eyes. Go. Now. And if the doctor wants tests or whatever, you bloody take time off, or I'll know the reason why. Get it? I'll give your apologies if that damned budget meeting goes ahead. And tell you what, young Dizzy can drive you. Don't argue.'

Terrifyingly, he didn't. Neither did Dizzy.

The archaeologists weren't quite under way. She had a moment to take a phone call. 'Ray?'

'Mark was right, Fran. The mother didn't much appreciate one of our constables turning up at feeding time, I gather, and *he* didn't appreciate having kiddie porridge slung all over him, but the raincoat was definitely missing. Cue for one of those *you-said-I didn't-say* arguments, I gather. But no coat. That's the main thing. At least she gave us a picture of her own child wearing it, so we know the make and colour and everything. So we're doing another trawl through CCTV we've already had checked for one outfit to see if we've missed her in another.'

'That's brilliant. Brilliant. I'd phone Mark with the good news but I'll have to leave it to you: I've a horrible idea another skull is just appearing . . .' She was lying, but this wasn't a fingers-crossed-behind-the-back lie — just a white one to get him in touch with Mark. Could hierarchies persist in the mind even when the top dog had retired? It seemed they could, in Ray's mind at least.

It took only a few minutes before her lie became the truth, however. Twice over.

'It seems weird, them being buried vertically — like some nod towards an ancient religion,' she said to Dr Evans, whose colleagues were watching the pathologist examine two more skeletons.

'I don't think I know any burial practices like that, not in the UK,' Evans replied slowly.

'OK, let's go with my original theory: that they were killed at the end of the working day and sort of slotted in the gap that was left between the wall proper and the false wall.'

Evans said aloud what Fran wanted her to say: 'So you're talking someone big and strong who can stay late without it being remarked on. And tidy up any damaged brick or plaster work. So it's got to be a trusted worker or more likely the site supervisor.'

'Or both.'

'Bloody hell. Pardon my French. Like Hindley and Brady. Sorry, other way round.' She gripped Fran's forearm. 'And what if one of them killed the other when the last slot was filled, to guarantee silence? Sorry, you're the detective.'

'Not anymore, not really. I'm the manager who enables everything to happen. And also the sounding block for professionals such as yourself. Though I have to say the last bit sounds more fantastic a theory than I'd encourage any of my team to come up with. But not impossible. At least we don't have the scenario of someone killing all the others and then bricking himself up in the last space.'

'That sounds more like grand opera than life. No, I don't think even I would go there. Is it you who gets to go to the post-mortem?'

'Not in this case — it's actually Don Simpson's baby, so he'll get to go.' When he got back from the doctor's. She frowned. Don had to be at death's door to take sick leave; whatever fear had driven him to the GP must be serious. 'If not, his DCI.'

She looked at her watch. Hell. Wren had a budget meeting scheduled for half an hour's time. Heart sinking, she phoned Alice. 'I don't suppose Mr Wren's still in London, is he?'

'You suppose right. Get yourself down here, Fran — and I'll have a nice soothing cup of chamomile tea waiting.'

CHAPTER SIX

Dead teenagers, a missing child, and then all the usual crime you expect in a big county, home to countless career criminals, who preferred to be known as businessmen, and to all sorts and conditions of immigrants, legal and illegal. And that was just the high-profile stuff they had to deal with. So why were they sitting round trying to work out where to shave yet another slice off the budget? Another diktat from the Home Office, presumably. As her colleagues, minus Don, argued, she idly sketched an ivory tower. And then she heard her name mentioned.

'The chopper, sir?' she repeated innocently.

'It's hardly the news one wants to hear when one's taking note of budget imperatives, Ms Harman.'

'And a missing child is, sir?'

'Have you any idea how much it costs to use the helicopter and crew for just one hour?'

'Have you any idea how much a child's life is worth?'

'There's no need to take that tone with me, Chief Superintendent.'

'I was merely responding to your rhetorical question with one of my own, sir. As the most senior officer handy, I was addressing not a budget imperative but a policing one.

As I was sure you would have done, had you been here. I understood that no one was allowed to disturb your top-level meeting. What else could I do?'

Clearly no one present would have done anything else.

Ray Barlow, obviously just as frustrated with the waste of valuable time, flashed a grin at her. But his cough was obsequious and apologetic — symptomatic of an officer who was still only on a temporary promotion. 'The media response has been very favourable, sir. Often in these cases we're accused of doing too little, too late. And as I'm sure you've noticed, the team's media officer has managed to keep the story right up on the front page, despite Fran's skeletons. Which would have been major, major news any other day.'

'I'm sure it will, any moment now, when we get round to telling them about the skeletons, of course . . .' Fran smiled grimly.

'You are implying that you haven't issued a press release, Chief Superintendent?'

Before she could respond, giving reasons she was sure they'd all appreciate, someone chimed in, 'Sir, might we have an update on the search for the child? I'm sure we'd all be grateful. A girl of four just disappearing into thin air . . .'

Diverted, Wren nodded. '*Maidstone's Maddie* is not a headline I'm enjoying. Nor the questions asked in editorials — *have the police learned nothing from Portugal?*'

Ray blushed to his ears. 'First, sir, I must emphasize that we followed procedure to the letter. I've had very profitable informal contact with the MIT already, but now I'm requesting more formal assistance.' He looked across at Fran.

Fran stared. Where on earth could they find all the officers that implied, particularly if Don was half as ill as he looked?

'The sooner the better,' Wren snapped. 'Even if you have to put your skeletons on a back burner, Harman.'

'It'll be hard to, sir. Although we've not made a formal press announcement yet, I gather we've already started to contact the families whose kids disappeared at the salient time to warn them there may be news. They're bound to talk. Meanwhile, we're pursuing the person who seems to Don and me the likeliest suspect. While we absolutely don't want to get Livvie out of the headlines, something as big as this is bound to attract attention, sooner or later. What I'd like to do is bring the editors together and ask for an embargo, just for a while longer. I don't know if they'll cooperate: you know how the media love a serial killer.'

'I'd rather we didn't use that term at the moment.'

From the back of the room, a voice asked, 'How many skeletons to date, sir?'

Wren looked at Fran. She took it as permission to respond. 'Eight.' The ensuing murmur suggested her colleagues thought she'd been right to use the term. She waited just long enough before adding, 'But we think that that's all. As I say, we have a prime suspect, the man who was the youth worker at the time. But there is someone else in the frame. Whether he stays there depends on the DNA results.'

'DNA tests on eight bodies . . . It would keep Livvie in the headlines if we didn't prioritize them, perhaps.' They could all see him doing the mental arithmetic and not liking it.

'Don's not the sort of person to let grass grow, sir: I should imagine tests on the first four, the ones uncovered last night, are already underway. And I don't see how we can prioritize some and not the others.'

'So what do I have to cut to pay for them?' Wren snapped. 'None of you realize that the budget isn't bottomless. A few hundred here, a couple of thousand there — it all has to be paid for somehow. Possibly by making officers redundant. Not just people you know. People in this room.'

Fran blinked. The threat felt personal, and not just to her. But she threw down a gauntlet she knew she might regret. 'Sir, I'd be happy to fall on my sword — I'm sure the few of us older ones still left would, too. But every team needs a leader. We've got temporary appointments, teams left to run themselves, people taking two roles. If jobs are to be done well, we need the resources — and they include officers with experience, sometimes, and certainly with authority.'

More murmurs: the mood of the meeting had certainly swung in Fran's favour. But she was taking it in the wrong direction. And then she got distracted further. Her phone throbbed. Dizzy Aziz? Headed SOS? 'This looks urgent, sir. May I take it?'

He probably assumed she would with or without his permission, so he graciously gave it.

Her face must have told her colleagues there was a problem. 'Don Simpson, sir. Running MIT,' she added, in case he couldn't place such a senior officer. 'Appendicitis heading briskly for peritonitis. They're operating as soon as they can.' She looked around. While most of her colleagues looked genuinely worried for Don, a good few were clearly already considering staffing implications. As it happened, she was too.

And so was Wren: 'I assume that since you're involved in the skeletons case, you can take over Don's role.'

'I've run two major sections at once in the past,' she said frankly, 'but that was in the days before staffing was cut to the bone. Still, we do have DCI Murray, even if he's only on secondment. Would it be possible to give him a temporary upgrading so he could run the Major Crime Review section? He knows the team and how they work. And although DS Tom Arkwright's due to take up a promotion in Tunbridge Wells in a couple of months, perhaps he could be persuaded to take up a temporary upgrading here. He's been with the team from the start and is utterly reliable.'

Wren nodded. 'Excellent heads up, Fran. We'll have a conversation after this meeting. Twelve?'

Whatever happened to *Good idea — let's talk later*?

A uniform superintendent asked, 'How about recruiting back on short-term contracts some of the officers already made redundant? Other forces have done it. And asking others back in a voluntary capacity? I'm sure they'd be glad to help out in the Livvie search.'

Ray Barlow said, 'I've already had extensive help from the old ACC.'

Why couldn't he keep his trap shut? Big mistake, unless Fran was very much mistaken.

'Mark Turner? Hell, man — what if the media get hold of that? Can't you see the headlines? *Disgraced ex-cop back with the force!* Get rid of him, now.'

Wren had every reason to dislike Mark, she had to accept that. No one would want to come into a new post to find the popular choice had turned it down and had swiftly become a mouthpiece for the resentment about mandatory cuts sweeping through the whole service. Then to have the same man behaving oddly in the extreme and resigning with maximum speed — it put the force in a bad light. But their resources were now so depleted that she might have hoped Wren would put aside his natural resentment and embrace the return of a highly experienced officer working as a volunteer.

How many pairs of eyes were on Fran? But she wouldn't allow herself to catch any of them as she took a calming breath. 'With due respect, sir, I hope that's not going to be minuted,' she said quietly. 'Mark left because he was having a stress-induced episode.' Loathsome term but useful. 'He saw retirement as the only option. Personally I'd rather he spent his time looking after his grandchildren and playing tennis, and I have a deep-rooted objection to anyone being asked to do highly skilled work for free, but surely a volunteer of his calibre is worth ten pressed men.'

Ray decided to risk his career. 'Mark chaired the APCO committee that instituted the nationwide policy that is now driving the investigation; he reported the child as missing before anyone else realized there was so much as a problem; he's come up with two good leads and provided vital international help, thanks to a contact.' He shot the swiftest glance at Fran. 'Given the present situation, I'd say his presence was worth the tiny risk that the media might not approve. In any case,' he continued slyly, 'TV Invicta might put a different spin on it — *Have-a-go-police-heroine's husband back in the saddle.* That sort of thing,' he added with a blush, as he recalled they weren't yet married. But he came up with one more argument. 'And who, really, is to know? He's offered to join the team taking phone calls from the public: he'll be completely anonymous.'

A uniform superintendent mimed applause. 'There is just one thing, sir — while all this talk goes on, we're not doing what we're paid to do: fighting crime. There's a child to be found. There's a mass murderer wandering the streets. What are we doing sitting on our fannies chewing the fat? You want cuts? It's your job to make them. Or to fight shoulder to shoulder with the other chief constables and resist them. That's up to you. But if you'll excuse me I've got a major traffic incident on the M20 to sort out.'

The meeting didn't so much break up as disintegrate.

* * *

Five past twelve, and here she was, waiting like a naughty schoolgirl outside the head's study. She expected, and probably deserved, a bollocking. But she might, if she were quick enough, wrong-foot him. And she knew from Alice that he had to be out of the building by twelve-fifteen at the very latest.

At last she was admitted to the Presence. She made no effort to sit — no point. Even while Wren was drawing breath, she said, 'DCI Murray's upgrading, sir?'

Taken aback, possibly by her lese-majesty, he said, 'It was a surprising suggestion.'

So he knew — of course he did — that she and Murray disliked each other.

'Never look a gift horse — or an intelligent officer — in the mouth.'

'What are his feelings?' he asked, closing his laptop and stowing it in a very nice leather case. Designer, by the look of it. Somehow she didn't think he'd got it at discount at the Ashford Outlet.

She'd have loved to ask if he'd remembered to encrypt the data. 'I've not been able to consult him. He's taken time off in lieu to go to a Met colleague's wedding. His former guv'nor.'

‘What? With all this going on? And you *let* him?’

Tempted though she was to point out that Sean was Wren’s protégé, not hers, it would not have improved the situation. Nor would reminding him that Murray had been wished on her without any consultation. As for Murray’s ongoing relationship with the Met, that had been Wren’s decision, too.

He picked up his case.

Fran answered his question: ‘Technically his line manager’s in the Met, of course, and he’d already granted him leave. No reason not to — he wasn’t to know we were about to have two major cases on our hands within five minutes of Sean’s leaving the building. If you were to consider his temporary upgrading, you might want his position to be regularized, so he’s answerable to someone here. I know you’re in a rush, sir — shall I contact HR and get them to do the necessary? And for Tom Arkwright, of course.’

What he’d have said had his secretary not popped her head round the door to tell him his car was waiting, she didn’t know. ‘Yes, I’m on my way,’ he snapped. But it was clear that whoever was expecting him was of more importance than a stroppy DCS, so she could walk away congratulating herself on having — at least temporarily — got away with it again.

Human Resources were having their own crisis, by the look of it, but at last she got someone to fish out the appropriate contract details and email them off, together with a short explanation. Once she knew the offer was official, she thought she might do the friendly thing and phone her congratulations through herself. His phone rang out, not even going to voicemail. OK, a text, then, asking him to make contact immediately to hear good news. There. She’d better learn to think of it as good news herself. As for Tom, she’d test the waters before offering him the step up. After all, he had a perfectly good promotion in the pipeline, and since his relationship with Sean wasn’t much better than her own, he might prefer to head off into the glorious sunsets of Tunbridge Wells.

* * *

'Acting DI sounds good,' Tom said, summoned to her office with a request to pick a sandwich for them both en route. 'Of course there's a downside, or you wouldn't have asked me quite so cautiously.'

'The downside is that I wouldn't be your boss any more. Not directly. You'd be answerable to Sean Murray; he's being offered a temporary upgrading too. You'll have heard on the grapevine about Don Simpson.'

'About young Dizzy Aziz carrying him like a baby into the doctor's surgery and then into A and E? Blues and twos and topping a hundred, Fran.'

In other words, topping a hundred and twenty. 'That bit hadn't reached me. Good for Dizzy. So Don's going to be off for the duration, which means I take control of MIT as well as keeping an eye on our Review team.'

He looked at her sideways. 'Will the leg be up to it?'

'The medics say I should be able to drive in ten days or so,' she told him, lopping four days off their estimate. 'Meanwhile, I've got Dizzy or Hilary.'

'So you have. What's your advice, Fran?'

She pulled a face. 'Two months' salary at the new level, then you move anyway? Money in the bank and CID status to take with you? But I'm not sure what sort of a guv'nor Sean will be: you might prefer the status quo and less hassle. Perhaps,' she said, by way of explaining Murray's abrasiveness to her, 'he's just one of those blokes that still don't like being answerable to a woman.'

'The women at my level certainly don't like him. Look, can I think about it over the weekend? Not that I shall be gallivanting round the country, unlike others I could mention. I shall be working, of course,' he added as he left. 'You need someone to keep their eye on you.' A waving hand was all that was left of him.

CHAPTER SEVEN

The door had scarcely closed and her grin still hadn't faded when someone else knocked: Ray Barlow appeared first, followed by one of the most glamorous young women in the force, Donna Stewart. Unlike Ray, who always looked in need of a good night's sleep, Donna clearly spent a great deal of time in the gym and was generally known as Madge — as in Madonna. She was one of Don Simpson's best DCIs, though one whom he often seemed to sideline.

'It seems to me, Madge, that you're more than capable of keeping the search going for Malcolm Perkins and Christopher Manton. Right? Any problems, raise them at each day's briefing meeting, or with me if they're urgent. Until the DNA evidence comes through with ID for each skeleton, there's not much you can do on that front — but I want you to keep me informed each time you get a new name. I met some of the parents at the time, and though my training in breaking crap news is out of date, it might give them some sense that Kent Police care if they dredge up the officer they knew then, to meet them once again. And I know it takes time, and I haven't got time to scratch my head, but that's what I want to do if I can.'

Stewart nodded. She sucked on her coffee as if it was a high-tar cigarette. 'Any chance we could get the press office involved now? We've all been working very discreetly, but there's no way we can sit on a secret like this.'

'Not if it means losing Livvie from the front page,' Ray said. 'And Wren seemed happy with the idea.'

Fran glanced at Madge, who said mutinously, 'No one consulted us. Or even mentioned it as an option.'

'I'm sorry: I should have done. I'll just check with the press office what's going on. Excuse me . . .'

The answer came quickly.

'Yes, the chief is fixing a meeting with media contacts. Or rather he's getting the press office to. But the press office think we're asking too much to maintain the situation for more than another twelve hours. Twenty-four maximum. So is it realistic to think we can achieve anything on the Livvie front, Ray?'

'I've — we've — done everything. Searched everywhere. Spoken to everyone.'

'By which you mean? Look, put it all on that expensive new screen over there for me so we can download it on to our computers. Madge, I know you've got a million and one things to do too, but I'd welcome your input. New ears, new eyes. Once you've got all the data, if you don't feel able to see anything, buzz off and deal with your own jobs. In the meantime, help yourself to some of this cake.' Tom Arkwright's auntie's legendary Dundee. So legendary neither of them needed to ask where she'd got it. 'You too, Ray — eat as you talk if you want. And then I want you to go and get a couple of hours' kip. You too, actually, Madge, if there's nothing pressing. OK? Good. Fire away, Ray.'

He listed the areas they'd searched: the club area; the caravan site — under and inside each caravan; the cricket club — the rudimentary pavilion; under the covers and so on; Hogben House . . .

'That's now owned by someone called Livingstone,' Ray said.

She grimaced. 'I gather poor Mark made a bit of a gaffe there.'

'Easy enough to do: I nearly did myself, to be honest, when I met him later. We've been in every room, from the attic to the cellar. He's been very helpful and obliging.'

'And you don't trust him,' Fran said obligingly.

'I wouldn't go that far. But the man's got a chopper — he could have spirited the kid away in that and no one any the wiser.'

'Has he flown it since the alarm was raised?'

'No.'

'And before the alarm was raised?'

'He says not. He says he just landed and was — er — greeted by Mark and Seb Kennaway.'

'Airport and other records?' Madge put in.

'Confirm what he said. But if you only flew a little way, would you bother telling anyone?'

'I suspect you'd lose your licence if you started bending the rules,' she said.

Fran nodded. 'Did any of the Golden Oldies or the kids hear a chopper at the relevant time? No? Well, there is something else to think about: if he took off from his own pad, he'd have to get Livvie that far. So he wouldn't have much time. Are there any signs that she might have gone that way?'

Clearly there weren't.

'Or that someone could have taken her that far?'

Madge put down her slice of cake. 'That implies a conspiracy, doesn't it, ma'am?'

'Does it? It wasn't uppermost in my mind but you might be right. I think we need to look at the possibility of someone seizing the child and getting away more quickly than on foot, though not necessarily by chopper — which I'm sure you've been doing, Ray.'

He nodded, but rubbed his face as if trying to recall what he ought to say next. 'Thanks to Mark's quick thinking, only a handful of mothers and members left before we arrived. All have been traced. All their vehicles have been subjected to forensic examination. All their properties ditto. All their alibis — and criminal records. All good upright citizens. Except one woman guilty of shoplifting from Harrods.'

Fran snorted. 'Just good aspirational crime, then. OK, let's put cars to one side for a moment. Bikes and motorbikes. The child got her clothes dirty playing with a member's bike, as I recall. And he left early — right?'

'Right. Roland Anderson. He came back through the park, as it happens, to join the search — seems someone phoned him. Before you explode, ma'am, it seems they were just trying to get as many helpers as possible. And he's been more than cooperative. As soon as he realized there might be a problem he spoke to one of the team and then to me. Seems he was one of those people responsible for running Criminal Record Board checks in some Midlands diocese before he came south.'

Madge raised a finger. 'So if anyone knew how to rig the system, he would.'

'That's exactly what he said himself. He's quite distraught.'

'Keep his name right away from the media, if you can,' Fran said. 'Think of what happened to that poor guy in Bristol when his lodger disappeared — he was absolutely hounded by the press. I know he got a good fat wodge of damages, but his life was destroyed and worse still it hampered the search for the actual killer. We don't want either happening here.'

'Of course not.'

'Meanwhile, let's think positive. We've no body yet. That's good. Possibly.'

'Are you thinking kidnapping? We've had no ransom demands.'

'You don't necessarily get them if the kidnapper wants to keep the victim,' Madge said. 'Natascha Kampusch, for instance. Or those American girls, who had to bear the kidnappers' children, for God's sake.'

'Those girls were older, of course. But it might be worth talking to a senior officer in the Austrian police, Ray. And anyone else with experience of abducting and keeping victims.' She stopped short.

'Like whoever bricked up those kids in the youth club,' Madge finished for her.

Ray shook his head. 'Wrong age group. With the building work there was lots of opportunity. Lots of potential victims. Which, before you ask, is why on my advice the club cancelled the rest of the tennis camp. Apart from having no coach, of course.'

'Quite. How many circles of hell must Zac be trapped in?' There was a tiny silence. Surely, however, it was better to look for a solution than to dwell on someone's private agony, so she squared her shoulders and asked briskly, 'Is there anything in Zac's past to make him a target? Any rivals when he was younger?'

'Zac's a quintessential nice guy. Everyone speaks highly of him.'

'I bet,' Madge said dourly, 'that everyone who knew our killer said he was a nice guy.'

'But there's no suspicion Zac harmed Livvie!' Ray objected. 'Couldn't have — all those witnesses!'

Fran raised a hand for silence. The bickering stopped. 'If Zac was a top tennis player he must have had rivals, people he beat, people with grudges. And though he's a nice guy now, he might have been mean and nasty when he was younger: champions have to be pretty ruthless, you know.' She tried to recall what Mark had said about him — there'd been nothing but praise, had there, for his teaching skills? 'Have you talked to him about that?'

Ray managed a weary smile. 'Fran, we've followed the guidelines to the last full-stop. Zac, Bethany — that's his wife: the family liaison officer's worming everything she can out of them. Not easy when they're frozen in terror. It's a good job their little boy's too young to understand what's going on.' He added, 'As for the youngsters who'd been helping him out with the tennis camp, they're traumatized too, of course.'

'There's no suspicion any of them could be involved?' Madge asked. 'All CRB checked?'

'They'd be too young, according to Mark, to need checks,' Fran said.

Nodding his agreement, Ray continued, 'At best one could have been an accomplice, but at the time of the incident, they were all on the courts in full sight of each other and of Zac. Not to mention any mothers who'd come early to collect their brats. Fran, I need a miracle here.'

'We all do. Urgently.' If she told them she'd spoken to the priest who was going to marry Mark and her and asked her to start praying, they'd think she was fit for the funny farm. 'Apart from those we know about, those you've interviewed, none of the players went missing at all? Even if they said they were just using that Portaloo that Mark loathes so much?'

'No. And none of them has any sort of record. There is one guy who turned up out of the blue and promptly disappeared: we've still to trace him. Not much to go on. Just the name Stephen and an appointment at the dentist. Someone's still checking all the dentists in Kent for a patient called Stephen. Trouble is, no one can recall the make of his car, let alone the reg.'

Fran gave a sour laugh. 'Why am I not surprised? Mark says some of the members can't remember which side of the court they're supposed to be on. OK, finding him is clearly a priority.' Unlike Mark to forget a thing like that, all the same. She'd call him the moment she could. 'Get on to the media, but make it clear we only want him as a witness, not a suspect.' She drew breath. 'I'd say our main lines of enquiry must be means of transport and means of concealment. And, tell you what, Ray, I'd suggest you ask Mark to come straight here as soon as he's returned Marco and Phoebe to their parents.'

'Have done already, guv'nor. But I don't think you mean as part of the phone team, do you? More as a witness.'

'Actually, as neither. You know how you natter at the end of the day about this and that. I'm sure he's casually dropped out stuff that might just have a bearing, and maybe if you and he just sat down over a coffee . . . You never know: the brain often throws things up when it's not trying. Like the make of Stephen's car.'

Madge asked, 'Guv'nor, what did you mean by *means of concealment*? A very large tennis bag? That sort of thing? Or more like the false wall we've got at the youth centre?'

'A tennis bag — hell, even one of those monsters the pros use for tournaments would be hard put to hold a child. Wouldn't it? I'll check, all the same. As for walls, we've tapped on every single bloody wall at Hogben House,' Ray said, sounding defensive or exhausted. Or both. 'Twice. And checked every single rubbish and recycling bin. And all the outhouses.'

'I'd expect nothing less,' Fran said, with a warm smile. 'Look, we could start going round in circles, we're all so knackered. Heads down for a couple of hours, both of you — I don't need to write it as a formal order, do I? And then Ray and I can talk to Mark, and you, Madge, just keep pegging away. Talk to Tom Arkwright about his search for Malcolm Perkins. The sooner we find him the better — but just for the time being, we won't go for media coverage. Twenty-four more hours really hammering at the kidnap case. Then we'll have to let rip on the wall.'

Madge amazed her by throwing back her head and laughing. 'You've reminded me of a play I saw at Stratford. Where they talk to the Wall? Two bumpkins.'

'*Midsummer Night's Dream*,' Ray said. 'A level. Two lovers. Pyramus and Thisbe. Shit. What if any of the kids behind that wall were lovers?' His face went stiff. He asked, as if he needed reassurance, 'Fran, do you ever find yourself thinking of victims just as part of a case, not part of a family, as statistics, not individuals?'

'It's all too easy. But I'd bet my pension you don't think of Livvie as a statistic or part of a case. Now shoo, both of you. Snooze time.'

'For you too, guv?' Ray asked, over his shoulder.

'Long enough to make me bright-eyed and bushy-tailed when we talk to Mark tonight,' she promised, ostentatiously pushing aside a pile of files on her desk and putting her head down on her folded arms. But only for a second. Madge was back as quickly as she'd gone.

'Message from the pathologist, guv. He's about to start work. Obviously Don can't go along, but I thought you might want to. Unless you want to delegate it?'

'If you don't mind driving me back here, I'd be happy to come with you,' Fran said, hoping her yawn hadn't shown.

* * *

'So the good news is that at least the kids you've looked at so far, Joe, were dead before they were walled up,' Fran summed up.

Dr Hemp nodded. 'Strangled, almost certainly. Skeletons don't lie. And it makes sense: the killer wouldn't want bloodstains around, not if there were still other young people around on a regular basis. You can explain away one missing worker, especially if he or she has a reputation for skiving, but you can't explain signs of violence. You let everything die down, wait for the kids to stop talking about whoever's gone AWOL. And then, when you feel like it, you can knock off the next.'

'Hmm. Though we must be talking a very tight time-frame here, if the kids were supposed to be building a wall. It's not something you do piecemeal, is it?'

'I wouldn't have thought so. Not that I know anything about building walls.'

'So we're talking someone strong?'

'Not especially. None of the victims so far was heavily built. Girls size four to six. Boys just as slight.'

'Off the record answer, please, Joe. I know you've not done formal post-mortems on all eight yet, but you'll be able to tell me this. Was there anyone strapping enough to have played football for his school?'

'You don't have to be strapping to be a good footballer, Fran. I know some of the men playing these days are mighty giants, but in those days, for all sports, slight was the norm. Think back to George Best or McEnroe or whoever your sporting hero might have been.'

Fran grinned. 'Long hair, short shorts, slender as popstars. OK. But there'd be evidence on your bones of muscle-building activity, wouldn't there?'

'Well done. In those I've examined so far, no.'

* * *

'Still two possible killers in the frame, then, guv: Christopher Manton, the young footballer, and Malcolm Perkins.' Madge loaded Fran into the car as carefully as if she were her grandmother, which had the immediate effect of making her feel about ninety. 'And no news of either so far,' she continued, setting off with the same deference to Fran's extreme age. 'Bugger it — all the electronic footprints people can't help leaving, all the surveillance we've got everywhere, you'd think it would be easy enough to find them, wouldn't you?' She gestured at the cameras that seemed to have spread to every available vantage point.

'You would. Unless people don't want to be found. And we are talking twenty years ago, at least for Manton. Perkins — remind me when he left?' Fran yawned, by way of an excuse for her memory, though she couldn't recall ever having heard a date. The case hadn't been hers, after all.

'June 1993. So he didn't make an immediate bolt. Which makes him look less like the killer.'

'Logic? I'm sorry: I'm brain-dead without my siesta,' she lied. Actually, maybe she was telling the truth.

'Because if he'd killed all the kids the false wall would hold, you'd have thought he'd go looking for others and other places.'

Fran felt sick. Nothing to do with Madge's driving, which still, like Dizzy's, would have done an undertaker credit.

'After all,' Madge continued, 'all the evidence suggests that once a man — and of course, it usually is a man — gets a taste for killing, he's not going to stop just because he hits a tiny snag. He'll find another source of victims, another place to stow them.'

Fran said quietly, 'We'll just have to hope the reason we can't run Perkins or Manton to earth — whichever one did it, or both in cahoots, of course — is that they're dead.'

* * *

Mark sank into her better visitor's chair as if it was as comfortable as a bed.

'The reason people have children when they're young,' he said, 'is that they've got enough energy to keep an eye on them. And keep up with them. And answer inane and/or very sensible questions.'

'But you were on the train most of the time — six hours doing nothing but relax,' she pointed out, tongue in cheek. She dunked a tea bag for him, and passed him a chunk of dark chocolate.

'So I was!' He slapped his forehead. 'And there I was forgetting the time at Steam! Not to mention the trip round some of the old works, now masquerading as a shopping centre. OK, an outlet, like Ashford's,' he conceded, 'so at least the clothes and shoes Grandpa had to buy were discounted. I got some more tennis shoes for myself,' he added brightly, before recalling why he was in Fran's office. 'Not that I can ever imagine playing again if we don't . . .'

'In that case, we'd better find her, hadn't we? And PDQ. Go on, have some more — choc's supposed to be good for the heart, isn't it?'

'I don't notice you pigging it down.'

'With the wedding coming up? No, thank you.'

'Marco tells me he's read on the internet that people who eat dark chocolate are slimmer than those who don't.'

'Perhaps they don't eat anything else. OK. When you've wiped that bit off your mouth — just there — then we can talk to Ray. He's desperate for a breakthrough, and you've become a sort of talisman. I think he's right, actually — that you'll have absorbed far more club gossip than you think. And also that your recollection of the scene will be sharper than most.'

'I'm an ex-cop, Fran, aren't I? Emphasis on ex. Not a thrusting new boy, with eyes like gimlets and ears like radar scanners. Which reminds me, I'm going to have to do something about my ears. I kept missing bits of what the kids were saying. Phoebe particularly — she's much squeakier than Marco, whose accent's becoming more British by the day.'

'While Phoebe still sounds like an all-American girl. Those braces on her teeth can't make it any easier, poor kid.'

'Right — Bugs Bunny with a mouth full of toffee. But I hope it'll be worth it,' he said dubiously. 'Think of those celebs with the widest mouths you can imagine stacked with rows of incredibly white gnashers. They look deformed, some of them.'

Before she could respond, Ray Barlow phoned. Did they want to talk in his room or in hers? Hers, she rather thought.

CHAPTER EIGHT

'Cannabis Cop at Crime Scene! Crazy Ex-cop on Kidnap Case!' Mark inserted quotation marks with his fingers. 'You must be out of your minds, both of you. The media would have a field day. Don't you see? That was why I said I'd do back-room stuff. The moment I turn up at the club, someone in that posse of reporters will spot me and for want of something better to write about will go for my jugular. Again. And yours too. *Livvie Cops Stumped: Nutter on Case.*' He sat back in his chair, folding his arms implacably.

Ray Barlow smiled, just as he had in response to similar imaginary headlines conjured by Wren. More mildly, he suggested, like Mark hooking his fingers into quotation marks, *'Have a Go Heroine takes over Livvie Case. Top Cop in Wheelchair visits Site.'*

'*Wheelchair*,' Fran squawked. 'I don't even use a stick these days!'

'Joe Public doesn't know that,' Ray said. 'OK, how about a compromise? Elbow crutches? Just the one?'

She zipped her mouth. There was no need for them to know the pain trying to rely on one crutch had caused. Perhaps twisting her body for such a short time wouldn't have such a bad effect as prolonged use. Maybe she should consider the wheelchair after all . . .

'They'd be so busy snapping you and hanging on your every word,' Ray continued, 'that they wouldn't notice anyone else. Come on, Fran, you know you've got the pizzazz to carry off a solo performance and distract everyone's eye. Mark and I would just slip in as part of your entourage and not a soul would notice.'

'Sand to Arabs, fridges to Eskimos,' Mark murmured. 'All the same, Ray, I truly don't want to risk it.'

Ray looked him in the eye. 'May I be blunt, Mark? When you were ACC not a lot of us in the force would have recognized you if we'd met you in the supermarket in civvies. I'm truly desperate here. Or I wouldn't ask. Would I? My judgement on the line too. And Fran's.'

'He's done every last bit of forensics, Mark,' Fran put in, getting bored. 'It isn't as if he's not tried to do without this.'

Mark clearly wasn't going to give in easily. 'What about the raincoat? Has that made any difference?'

Ray shook his head. 'Mock-up pictures of Livvie wearing the raincoat have been out with each regional news bulletin. It made the national headlines with the BBC and ITV; Channel Four are leading with something political but have promised coverage. But none of the CCTV in the areas has helped. It's as if some giant bird swooped down and took her off.' His grin was tired as he added, 'And no, we've checked with the aviation authorities — Livingstone's chopper was where he said it was at the salient time. And I think even your Golden Oldies might have noticed one landing on your courts.'

Mark opened his mouth and shut it again. Then he said, 'We might have noticed a high-wire act, or a trapeze artist too. Even Tarzan, provided he'd worn his leopard skin. Though with all the noise we'd probably not have heard his classic call.' He demonstrated, if quietly.

Undeterred, Ray returned to his original wish. 'How about going in white coveralls, Mark? Complete with head gear? I wouldn't recognize my dad like that.'

Fran pulled herself to her feet and went walkabout, as if exercising her leg. In fact, she was exercising her mind. Letting it go blank. Or not. Leaning against the desk, she waited as Ray asked, 'What noises might you have heard, had it not been for the kids? Say you turn up early for your lesson with Zac. No one but you there.'

'Not a lot, as I said. The ears are going,' he told him apologetically. 'So I don't get much birdsong these days.'

'My dad went to Specsavers,' Ray said. 'Lost his upper frequencies, apparently. How about things that are lower frequency?'

'You mean such as cars and such? I can hear chainsaws in the woods, sometimes. The plop of other people's tennis balls.'

'Before anyone else turns up.'

'Pigeons. The odd cow. The loo emptying people. They always seem to arrive the same time as I do. But not, sadly, yesterday afternoon. Sad in more than one sense: because it might have been a lead and because the whole loo — well, you wouldn't have used it if you didn't have to, not after those kids and their poor aim had sprayed it.'

'They take away the whole unit and replace it, do they?'

'There's some pattern. Mostly they just empty the sump, or whatever they'd call it. Every so often we get a freshly sanitized one. Perhaps not often enough. Suffice to say when it's bad, like it is now, I'd swear some folks nip over or through the fence and use a tree. No names, no pack drill.'

Ray leafed through notes. 'No mention of the loo anywhere in anyone's statements, as far as I can see at least. No, some lads used it. I don't see how it would help us, unless, as you say, the men who service it came during the game. Which you confirm they didn't.'

Fran started prowling again. 'I heard you say, Mark, when you phoned Ray, that Livvie was a fastidious little girl. Would she have used the loo if it was foul?'

'All the other kids did. I presume she did too . . . Ah.' He looked at her and held her gaze, before turning to Ray. 'Any trace of her on the fencing? A hair, anything?'

'Would you excuse me, guv, if I called the forensics people?'

Mark nodded. Neither Fran nor Ray showed any sign of registering his gaffe.

'When you talk to them,' he said, pausing as Ray started to dial, 'you might want to get them to see if they checked for any traces the far side of the nearest tree. I know she told Jayne she had to stay where she could see her dad, but I don't know any little girl who'd lower her knickers and pee where she could be seen. Or perhaps not the nearest tree. That'd smell too.'

Ray, already talking, raised a thumb.

Fran wandered to the window. 'Nice bright evening. Remember we planned drinks on the terrace after work each day?'

'We've managed them at weekends. Sometimes. OK, once or twice. When that wind wasn't blowing. Yes?' Mark asked Ray, now finished with his call.

'They'll be checking within the hour. Fence and unofficial latrine. I've asked for a much wider sweep, too.'

'Tell you what,' Mark said, 'I'll take up your offer. What's one white suit more or less? So long as Fran does her one woman show for the media.'

'No wheelchair, mind,' Fran said, as if it had ever been a serious suggestion. She reached for her jacket. She added as if she was happy with the idea, 'But an elbow crutch if you insist. By the way,' she asked, as Mark passed it over, 'what sort of car did that guy Stephen drive? The one with the dentist's appointment?'

'A red Audi Three; not lipstick red, more towards the maroon end of the spectrum.' He gave a bemused look as Fran and Ray high-fived each other, and Ray reached for his phone again.

Fran leant towards Mark, and asked quietly, 'Have you had time to phone Zac and his wife? As a friend, of Zac's at least?'

'With the kids hanging on my every word? Actually, while they were off spending their Easter money, I did try.

But I couldn't get past the Family Liaison woman — she sounds a veritable Gorgon.'

She could always offer to pull rank with the FLO and make sure Mark got through. But how would he feel about that?

'I did insist she let Zac know I'd phoned and tell him to call me whenever he wanted,' he continued. 'But since I'm neither flesh nor fowl — well, it's like this walk in the woods tonight, isn't it? I'm in a very grey area.'

She couldn't deny it. But as she reached to squeeze his hand, Ray ended his call and there was no chance to continue their conversation.

* * *

Fran wasn't known for giving impromptu press conferences, usually preferring to leave her front-line colleagues dealing with the case in question to front them. But today she would give a bravura performance, if her silence as they left her office was anything to go by.

'I can almost hear the wheels turning,' Mark said, touching her temple as they walked to the car park. 'Go for it, sweetheart!' He kissed her lightly on the lips, probably lese-majesty, of course, but what a man might do to the woman he loved. Although Ray was happy for him to travel with him and Fran, Mark was firm in rejecting the offer, and with a wave of the hand moved away to join the forensic team, with whom he'd be travelling.

He'd just be looking, not touching, he insisted. On Ray's orders someone gave him a clipboard so he'd look ultra-useful. He'd probably just doodle, something he'd seen Fran do profitably over the years. The more florid and complex the doodle, the more convinced you were she couldn't even be listening, let alone concentrating, and the more likely she was to come up with exactly what you needed. Pray God it worked for him this evening.

Fancy remembering the car like that. Funny thing, memory.

Smiling wryly, he nonetheless kicked himself for his earlier refusal to come along — he should have trusted Ray to manage the press, who were penned at the end of the long, potholed track to the club. Even keen snappers, perched on stepladders, with cameras capable of shooting images in the dark wouldn't be able to spy into the crucial area. Since the track curved back and forth and was lined with clumps of mature trees, not yet fully in leaf but dense nonetheless, their ultra long-focus lenses would be useless. The personnel carrier swept past them. Just to make sure no one would be able to see him, let alone register his face, he bent down, as if to pick up his dropped pencil.

The wooded area itself was as brightly lit as you could wish for — with, unfortunately, concomitant deep shadows. He stumbled a couple of times as he headed for an outpost where he could watch but not disturb his colleagues. A path, much better maintained than the track they'd just bumped along, wound alongside the fence, but was always more than seven or eight metres away. It was iron hard, and much easier to walk along than plunging through than the undergrowth — what they called a bridle path. When he was a kid, he'd thought it was spelt *B-R-I-D-A-L*, and wondered why brides needed separate routes when they were heading to church. In any case, all the brides he'd ever seen had been in limos with white ribbon. And then someone had told him it was a path set aside for horses. He smiled back at his younger self. And frowned at his older one. He reached for his phone. No damned signal, of course. But there'd be one somewhere in the car park. After all, that was where he'd been when he'd first called for help. Or he could borrow a colleague's radio. Correction: *former* colleague's radio.

* * *

From the corner of her eye, Fran saw Ray turn away from the press melee, taking a call. When he jammed a finger in his spare ear, she looked harder. Yes, something was up. She was too far away to work out what was going on. Afraid that if she lost concentration she might say the wrong thing, she raised her spurious crutch like a conductor's baton. 'Ladies and gentlemen, we need to get on with our search. Time is of the essence, remember. But I'll brief you again as soon as I can. You know that. Do your best to elicit your readers' and viewers' help, please: it could be vital.'

Though questions were still crackling through the air as if part of a dying fireworks display, she turned away, remembering to put the crutch to the use for which it was intended. She managed what she hoped was a convincing hobble, praying she wouldn't pay for it later with more back pain.

Taking Ray's arm, poor old lady that she was, she propelled him fiercely out of earshot of the reporters.

'I saw your face. What is it?'

'Mark's had an idea. I'm not sure. But it's worth a shot, I suppose.'

'He is an ex-cop. And cops are renowned for their hunches,' she said dryly. 'And the idea is?'

'A horseman. He says the estate manager patrols the grounds riding a horse to spot miscreants on wheels. Before you ask, there was no sign of any horses in the stables at Hogben House. I've just checked with the people who did the search there. But I'd like to check all stables within riding distance of the clubhouse. Assuming we can locate them.'

Fran pulled a face. 'Around here I'd bet there are more fields devoted to feeding horses than to feeding people. So, lots of stables. What's your feeling about using those guys to put out an appeal?' She jerked her thumb in the direction of the lingering reporters.

'What's yours?'

'Let's talk to Mark. If the estate manager's the only guy he's seen riding in this area, an unexpected visit to his house and his stable might be my preference. And if that fails, and he's clearly as white as the driven snow, we go very public indeed and get each and every stable checked. Do we have the estate manager's address? Not to mention a name?'

'Ross Thwaite.'

'Doesn't sound local.'

'Does he have to be? These days you're college-trained, aren't you, not stepping into your father's hobnailed boots.'

She nodded. 'Of course. Well, let's go visiting. Actually, let's pick up Mark — he deserves a bit of glory, assuming there's any on offer. If not, he can get egg on his face with the rest of us.'

Ray gave a clipped order — the personnel carrier would bring back Mark, solo and no longer clad in white. 'But we can't have him take part in any raid, Fran, can we?' His voice had a pleading undertone — after all, he was only temporarily promoted, and naturally didn't want the slight inconvenience of being caught in control of an unauthorized civilian to mar his chances of having a permanent upgrade.

Mark too would have been horrified at the prospect of her cavalier and uninsured breach of regulations. 'Absolutely not. Don't worry, Ray — we'll play this by the book. How many do you want in your posse?'

'I thought enough to surround the property. A real tight ring. Enough to cut off any escape should one be attempted. But I'd like it to be a silent presence. Fran, I keep thinking of cellars and false walls like your youth centre. I keep hoping. Though by now the poor kid's more likely to be in the bottom of a well. Or a mine shaft. The Kentish coalfields . . . I don't know.'

'We're a bit far west and south for the mine shaft option, thank God. As to wells, I simply don't know how many there are round here. They must be marked on large scale maps . . . No. We'll keep hoping she's alive. We've not got enough officers to search for both a living child and a body, so let's focus completely on the former. Ah, is that Mark's transport of delight? Good.' They exchanged a wave. He headed towards them but hung back, as if afraid they didn't want him as party to their discussion. 'Can we just double-check we've got the right address, Ray? We don't want to get it wrong and give the game away.'

'Double-checked, guv.'

'Thought it would be.' She shot him a swift, apologetic grin. 'And remember, it's just an enquiry, for the moment at least. And a very polite enquiry, too. No searching for anything except a child. Don't lay a finger on his computer or anything. Not yet. A treat in store, maybe. So you and Jules in the front, Mark and me tagging along in the back. And no blues and twos, just as fast as you can safely go.'

'Don't want to lose any more top brass, do you?' Mark added grimly.

* * *

Ten minutes later, the team deployed itself in total silence around a rather smaller Kentish cottage than she thought a man with the title *estate manager* deserved. There was a lean-to that might have been doubling as a stable.

Jules pulled up about ten yards down the lane. Had Thwaite looked, he'd presumably have thought one patrol car innocuous enough. People carriers might have alarmed him, so the two that had rendezvoused with the fast response car lurked hidden round a convenient bend further down the lane. Although at first they'd agreed that Fran would speak to Ross Thwaite, and Ray would take an immediate lead if things got remotely physical, Mark now chipped in with a suggestion. 'Fran, you're supposed to be lame, remember. He might even have seen you on TV with your crutch. In any case, anything above sergeant grade might arouse suspicion. Jules led the search of Hogben House itself — he's the PolSA, after all. Instead of leaping round like Superwoman, let him do his job. Him and Ray, maybe?'

Fran gave him a mock salute, turning to Warden. 'OK, Sergeant Warden — hell, no wonder you prefer to be called just Jules — do your stuff. Loft to cellar. Even the old outside privy, if there is one. The well. The water butt. The bloody bird feeder . . .'

'I'll go and brief the rest of the team,' Ray said. 'And join in the fun, if there is any.'

'I don't want fun, Ray: I want a result.'

Saluting, Ray trotted off briskly. A couple of minutes later, he joined Jules as he walked up the cottage path. He closed the gate firmly behind them.

'You were right, Mark. It would have been completely OTT for me to pop up on his doorstep — given altogether the wrong impression. Ah, here they go.'

A man in T-shirt and tracksuit bottoms stood framed in the doorway, backlit, so they couldn't see more than his silhouette, which was neat enough to suggest he used the gym or the rural equivalent of long walks and chopping wood. He shrugged and gestured — they could go in. Jules soon emerged, and waved a casual arm: he was quickly joined by what must have looked to Thwaite like a couple of bored cops anxious for their Friday night down-time, Ray mucking in to the rear.

'It's no good, is it?' Mark groaned. 'Livvie's not in that cottage or Thwaite wouldn't be so insouciant. I've wasted everyone's time.'

'Let them check the stable first,' she murmured, tempted though she might have been to agree with him.

It only took a few minutes for Ray and Jules to emerge, accompanied by Thwaite, shrugging on a body-warmer. He led the way to the stables; all three went inside.

All three emerged. Thwaite shook hands with the officers, who headed for the gate, again closing it conscientiously.

'We checked everything bar the horse's hooves,' Jules sighed. 'Sorry, guv,' he added, to both of them equally. 'Horse called Snowdrop, by the way, on account of a white blaze here.' He touched his forehead. 'Rather sweet, for a grown man's mount.'

'Lots of other horses, lots of other stables,' Fran said briskly. 'Rather you than me getting up close and personal to the gee-gee,' she added. 'Nasty big things, with metal corners and sharp teeth.'

'That one was OK,' Jules said mildly. 'My kid sister could ride it and no worries.'

Fran said, aware she sounded tetchy, 'So do you want to go public about searching stables, Ray, or get folk to grass up their neighbours? Shit. Sorry about that. Horses . . . grass,' she added, noting the complete absence of so much as a groan.

'Both. I'll draft something and let you see it, shall I?'

'Just draft it and put it out. I'm going to take some of my own advice and go and put my head down. And since we're only a couple of miles from it, it might just as well be on my own pillow.'

CHAPTER NINE

Fran groaned as Mark, too weary to do more than swathe her in a towel, heaved her out of the hot bath he'd insisted on running for her. Before the water could fully drain, however, he put the plug in again. 'Save water, save time.' He stripped off and got in after her, wincing from the heat but refusing to add cold water. 'I just hope the smell of lavender will have faded by tomorrow.'

'You'll smell truly glamorous. It's not just lavender but sandalwood and rose,' she added, with a pale grin. The towel was big enough to double as a bathrobe, so she huddled into it and pulled the elegant little Victorian chair towards him. Then she changed her mind. Hanging up the towel, she grabbed her robe and slipped out of the room. He might have been drifting into sleep when she returned with two tots of his favourite malt, though he wasn't sure if he could even have spelt its name at the moment.

She handed him his glass then settled on the Victorian chair. 'I've got to implement the Child Rescue Alert system, haven't I?' she said quietly.

'What? You haven't done that already? Why on earth not? You're short of officers, and yet you — good God! You've got a national network at your disposal!' Before she could reply, he said, 'You've been sparing me, haven't you? You saw how much I enjoyed playing cops and robbers again and didn't want to spoil my fun. Bloody hell, Fran, I was one of the people who helped establish the system, helped staff it! For just such an occasion as this!'

She blinked. 'I thought it was doable in-house.'

So he was right. She had been trying not to hurt his feelings. But she looked so weary and — yes — in so much pain that he bit back his fury and let her carry on, which she did with more confidence. 'More importantly, Wren's brought morale down to such a low level, a bit of in-house success would have done us all good — might have saved a few jobs, too. More cuts, that's all he ever says. More like a parrot than a wren. But the thought of round-the-clock coverage from forty-odd trained call handlers on duty nationwide, not just volunteers like you who could do a daily double shift at most — it sounds like heaven. And all those extra resources from CEOP's Missing, Abducted and Trafficked Children Unit dropping like manna from heaven. I'll go and text Ray to tell him what I'm doing and then call the night team.' She put her glass down on the windowsill and was limping out when he remembered another issue.

'How are you going to break it to Wren? He's not the sort of guy to like a fait accompli.'

'You're right. If only I had enough time to sell it to him as his own brilliant idea.' Her smile was malicious. 'I could phone him now. No? OK, a text to him too.' Off she went.

Whoever had called the organization the Child Exploitation and Online Protection Centre might have thought of something that made a better acronym. But it was a brilliant agency, with every officer hand-picked and totally dedicated to preventing children falling victim to everyone from real-life rapists to anonymous muck grooming kids online. Pity he couldn't be part of the investigation anymore, though. A great pity.

'Done,' she said, waking him up again. She sat down, but didn't pick up her glass again.

'Did you see Zac's appeal on the news?' he made himself ask. 'Zac and his poor wife?'

'Nope. It'll have been recorded for me — you'll be able to see it tomorrow too. You could save Dizzy Aziz a job and run me into work — hell, where's your car?'

'In your spot in the car park. It parks itself there automatically.'

'As it should — all that training. Dizzy it must be. Hey, did I tell you about his heroics with Don . . .'

He didn't care a toss about Don or anyone else, for that matter. But they needed to plaster over what could have been an awkward moment. More than awkward. How dare she put an enquiry at risk because she was worried about hurting his feelings? And then he remembered that it hadn't even been her enquiry till less than eight hours ago. He looked at her face, drawn and grey above the rosiness of her bath-warmed body. How was she going to survive at this pace? Last time she'd been so overworked, she lost the plot a couple of times and he'd come close to having to discipline her.

And not like that either. Of its own accord, a small smile twitched the corner of his mouth, though he suspected there'd be no bedtime games tonight: it would be all either of them could do to stay awake long enough to get into bed. But he ought to make some response to her little anecdote: 'A hundred? Bloody hell! That probably means nearer a hundred and twenty — maybe even a hundred and forty — if I know him.'

She put her fingers in her ears, managing a comical grimace. 'He admitted to a hundred. At least they got there in one piece. But I've not even phoned the hospital. Hell, Mark, what this job does to us . . .'

'Put it on the list for tomorrow. You might even snatch a few minutes to visit him. If you need to justify taking time off to Wren, Don was running the case you had to take over, and you need to pick his brain.'

It was her turn to heave him out of the bath, and to produce another of the huge, fluffy towels that had been one of her real extravagances: heaven knew how much energy washing and drying them consumed. At least, since he'd been house-husband, they'd rarely used the tumble dryer. He'd sited their whirligig washing line to catch every last gust of wind, and was more assiduous than he cared to admit in checking the online weather forecast for the area. Not just to see if he'd be able to play tennis, either.

* * *

Neither the bath nor the whisky had done its job. Despite having drifted into a doze in the bath, he was now as wide awake as it was possible to be, and furious. Furious with himself; furious with Fran. In whichever order.

Now what?

His therapist had given him a range of relaxation and visualization exercises, and his GP had offered tempting sleeping pills. He knew exactly where they were, imagined the delight of sloughing off his worries — and then reflected on the inevitability of waking Fran when he went to get them, no matter how quietly he padded to the bathroom. More to the point, she'd have to be at her desk by seven at the latest the next morning, and someone needed to make sure she didn't sleep through the alarm and that she went off with more than black coffee inside her.

So the relaxation exercises it had better be.

Feet, knees, hips, back, shoulders, arms, fingertips. All as floppy as he could get them. Except it was supposed to be *let* not *get.* And the brain was supposed to sink into all this floppiness, not dart between theories about what had happened to poor Livvie. What if it had been a woman, not a man who'd taken her? But surely all leads, regardless of gender, had been followed up.

Why hadn't the locals come together to form giant search parties, as they had with other missing children? Look at the response to the Machynlleth abduction and murder, where everyone and their dogs had turned out to help. In this case there'd been a real lack of community involvement. Had Ray approached community leaders?

He snorted, enough to make Fran stir. What was a community in commuter-belt Kent? A herd of women in big cars? No, herd wasn't right. What might the collective noun be? A chatter? A text? A pamper! He must remember that one and see what Fran thought.

And who would be this pampered community's leaders? The nail experts? The yoga gurus?

He would suggest that he and Ray go through all the tennis club members' details tomorrow — something might click.

Such as Stephen driving a maroon Audi. Where had that come from?

And what on earth was lurking at the back of his mind? Something someone had said that had struck the most distant of chords. Only one thing to do — what he'd made himself do times beyond number when he'd been an operational officer: go to sleep knowing it would come to him in the morning.

If only. Then he'd counted lamp-posts on a motorway. Now, how about the leaves on the greening branches of the beech at the end of their lawn . . .

* * *

If ever there'd been a morning for dawdling over warm croissants with fresh butter and apricot conserve, this was it. The sun had already warmed the little patio by the kitchen, and when he stood at the edge he could see skeins of mist down in the valley, separating the tops of the trees from their roots with a ghostly swirl.

He filled the bird feeder: how long would their winter lodgers stay with them? He thought he could count on the self-interested robin, but what about the goldfinches? At least he knew the collective noun for them: a charm. He smiled at them as they swooped between Niger seeds and sunflower hearts, jostling with each other as he withdrew to what they considered a safe distance. He imagined them congratulating each other on having trained him so well, producing food before they even needed it, and moving the feeders to a spot with plenty of leafy cover. They'd liked the sunnier spot better, he fancied — but they'd been exposed to the sparrow hawk, which had come in with terrifying killing power and taken three or four in succession. The goldfinches might not have noticed the depletion in their ranks but he had. Now the feeders hung just a wing-beat away from the trellis up which he'd been trying to coax a *Clematis Armandii* until the frost had killed it as swiftly as a pair of secateurs, though it was supposed to be hardy, evergreen indeed. At least the honeysuckle and wisteria had clung on, and while it had been just the skeletal stalks — there must be a proper name for them, but he couldn't recall it — that had provided a refuge, now buds promised thick foliage for later.

Perhaps the finches would stay, and bring their young broods. Perhaps the next generation would do the same. He liked the idea of perpetuity.

The seed put away and his hands thoroughly washed, he loaded the toaster. He hadn't got his home-made wholemeal loaves, with lots of extra seed, to produce the best toast yet — it was inclined to be chewy — but at least Fran consented to eat a couple of rounds as she was ferried about the countryside. He knew she mustn't take her painkillers on an empty stomach. Today he'd join her as she edged into the car driven by Dizzy. And surely something would trigger the memory of something important that was said last night that still, maddeningly, eluded him. But he'd better not hunt for it; far better to talk to Dizzy about the prospects for the forthcoming cricket season.

Or was it? The conversation, meant to be a casual enquiry from a front-seat passenger whiling away the time — the real guv'nor sitting in the back, working — took a more serious turn than he'd been expecting.

'Thing is, Mr Turner — OK, Mark — I've got this chance of turning professional. Cricket,' he added, as he checked his mirror, signalled and manoeuvred as if Mark was a driving examiner. 'Warwickshire.'

'I thought you were keen on training as an elite driver, driving royalty and so on,' Mark said. 'Fran was saying you'd come out top on all the courses you'd been on.'

'I was. And I did. But how long before they privatize protection driving? Get G4S or someone to ferry them. OK,' Dizzy admitted, 'they might lose a few passengers or turn up late for a royal visit, but that's privatization for you. There's a lot of us thinking of jumping before we're pushed,' he added glumly. 'At least I've got my bowling to fall back on. If I make it big time, it's a good career. If I don't, then at least I've tried, haven't I?'

'Of course you have,' Mark agreed brightly. With a change of voice, he added, 'Is morale really that bad?'

'You want to talk to the Police Federation rep,' Dizzy said. 'Sir. Mark. Not just my level. Higher ranks, too. After all,' he added reasonably, '*you* left.'

'But I'd served my time and I wasn't well.'

'And you get a pension, don't you? They're saying we'll have to work years longer and get much less when we go. And a good cricketer — a really good one — can think of hundreds of thousands a year. Only for a few years, I know, but even so.'

He ought to counsel him against giving up a safe career for a job with such a short shelf-life. He ought to remind him about the training he'd had so far, all the opportunities ahead of him. What about the respect of the community, the knowledge that you were making a difference? Weakly, he remarked, 'The Bears are a really good team, aren't they? And all those changes at Edgbaston . . . I've only seen them on TV, of course. It looks a truly wonderful ground.'

'Actually Sussex have started sniffing round too.'

'Have they? Great. Which would you prefer?'

'Whichever offers me the best terms,' the kid said soberly. He must have had all the talk of respectable careers up to his ears. And then some.

'You've got to want to work with the people there, too. Check the set-up. Talk to people.'

'Already doing that, guv.'

'Excellent. Now, your first game at Lord's, I want tickets — right?'

'Right. First game or first test match?'

Careers counselling over, how would he spend his day? Drifting up to the incident room where, thanks to the influx of CEOP's MATC unit staff, he would be nothing but an unemployed loser, didn't feel like a good option. But neither did returning to the rectory to garden till he dropped, and then retiring to channel-surf the Saturday afternoon sports options. The idea of turning up at the tennis club in hopes of finding another spare player was repugnant, although Zac had used the club website to thank people for their support and encourage them to return to the court.

Perhaps, perhaps, he might just do that. Just in case any of his friends might react to a familiar face by recalling something that an official questioning had scared away — like whatever he needed to remember had completely gone.

But Dizzy had slowed the car to an impeccable stop, and Fran had finished texting and emailing and was ready to be eased out of the car. On the plus side, she leant much less of her weight on him than she had been — she was definitely getting better.

'It's a good job the media can't see you as agile as this,' he said with a grin.

'I must keep the crutch handy, just in case you need to go into the woods again. You look as knackered as I feel. But there's no reason why you shouldn't get some sleep. Take the car and go back home for a bit.'

'While you run round in circles doing something meaningful,' he snapped.

'While I'm closeted with Wren, who didn't like my bringing in CEOP, any more than you disliked my not bringing them in.' Fran could still manage an ironic smile. 'Hell, Mark, there's nothing I'd like more than your input in every single meeting going today. And I know Ray relies on you utterly. So don't take out your retirement blues on me, please.' She linked arms with him. 'Come and have a coffee.'

'Don't bloody patronize me. You're not ACC yet,' he said, probably loud enough to be heard by Dizzy and any other passing officers. He flung her arm away and fished the car keys from his jacket. 'Any errands you need running? Any shopping? I'm supposed to be doing the Sainsbury's run today, aren't I?'

CHAPTER TEN

'You look as if you've lost a fiver and found a rusty button,' a voice greeted him, as he stood among plants he didn't recognize, which was, he supposed, his fault for going to a nursery specializing in recherché flora at sky-high prices. But since one of the owners had landscaped much of their garden, he felt he couldn't betray him by nipping off to a garden centre chain and buying boxes of bright petunias. In any case, it was too early to risk planting petunias, or any of the other bedding plants he'd find at places where he'd found tomato seedlings in January. If their plants wouldn't have grown, their profits certainly would.

He picked up an attractive shrub but registered how much his impulse might cost and put it back again as he turned to the speaker.

'Caffy!' His pleasure was genuine: he'd first met the young woman when she was part of PACT, a team of restorers and decorators who'd rescued their rectory. The acronym stood for Paula and Caffy's Team but was more appropriate than most.

She jerked a thumb in the direction of a tiny café offering none but healthy options. 'They need your money: organic produce is one of the first things people cut back on in a recession.'

'Even in a niche location like this?' Naturally he had fallen into step with her.

'You colonize that table and I'll get you — tea? Or would you prefer coffee?'

'Tea, please. Green.'

He returned with a tray on to which a couple of slices of rich fruit cake seemed to have migrated of their own accord. Having heard Caffy denigrate cupcakes for comprising everything that was bad for one, from the colouring to the refined sugar and saturated fats, he thought he'd better play safe.

'We've not seen you for a bit,' he said mildly. Most builders disappeared as soon as their work was done, but Caffy wasn't most builders. She'd become far more than simply a valued professional. She'd become a nurse, mentor and — yes — very dear friend, declaring early on, much to the chagrin of his old boss who wanted to be his best man, that she would be his best woman. When he'd been at his most depressed, at times when most of his former colleagues had found it hard to approach him, Caffy had turned up at odd hours of the day and made him do things. Walk. Do a bit more digging. Paint another wall. Join the tennis club. He could understand the impulse that had driven a former pop singer and his lawyer wife to take her into their home, where she now had her own apartment, and to treat her as a daughter, for all she must be in her early thirties now.

Best not think about daughters, with his own, much the same age as Caffy, now doing time for drug-dealing, and for some reason that no one, even her husband, could understand, denying Mark access to her children, though he'd have thought that without a mother, they could have used a grandpa.

Despite his sudden surge of gloom, Caffy's smile made the whole room glow. 'I've been on a fabulous course about restoring old buildings.'

'But you know all about that. Unless our rectory rebuilt itself.'

She grinned and poured the tea. 'But that's only Georgian, and truly Paula was the expert there. No, this is much older vernacular architecture. You know the craze these days for inhabiting everything in sight — did you see that piece in the paper about a couple who'd turned a public lavatory into a bijou residence? Well, some people are trying to restore absolute ruins, and English Heritage want to make sure the work is done appropriately. So we've had a wonderful time in hard hats and goggles, scrabbling round where even rats wouldn't attempt to run.' She paused to sip tea and test the cake, which earned a nod of approval. 'So what's this about the missing child? It's your tennis club, isn't it? You must ache to be properly involved.' She shot him a look under her eyebrows. 'You're not taking it out on Fran, I hope?'

How did she make such leaps? 'Not until this morning, when she started being kind to me.'

'When all you were doing was being kind to her?'

'Not quite. In fact, last night I nearly gave her a dressing down for not doing her job properly.'

'Did I hear that right?' She looked genuinely shocked, but more than that. Angry for Fran and disappointed in him. Clearly she was biting back words he deserved but didn't want to hear.

'I know. I forgot I wasn't the boss any more. I forgot she'd only taken the case over a few hours earlier because the person running it had asked for help. I forgot she was running someone else's case too because he'd ended up in hospital.'

'What did she say?'

'I think she was too tired to notice.'

'You know Fran better than I do but I'd be very surprised,' Caffy said dryly. 'So, apart from bollocking people from the sidelines, how are you involved?'

He felt on safer ground here. 'I was the one who called the child in missing,' he said, picking at some cake. He explained, at last concluding with a sigh that hurt: 'Poor Livvie: if only I'd kept a better eye on her—'

'And was she yours to keep an eye on? Any more than she was any other player's? Not to mention her father's. What do the other players say, by the way?'

'Apart from the first afternoon and evening when we searched for her, I've seen none of them. I was thinking about going along to the club — but I'm not sure . . .'

'Why not? Are you afraid one of them will suspect you? Or worse still, will one of them whom you like betray him or herself as the abductor?'

Would anyone except Caffy insist on the grammatically correct *him or herself*, instead of the easy option of *themselves*? But would anyone except Caffy have a copy of *Sir Charles Grandison* sticking out of her bag?

'I suppose — I did think one of them might speak more freely to me than to my col — to the police. So I did wonder about popping down for a game. I could knock up on the tennis wall if there was no one else around.'

'But you don't like the thought of enjoying yourself when everyone else is either working till they drop or sick with worry. Makes sense. But so does a bit of exercise and a bit of conversation that might prove useful. No?'

'I'll think about it.'

'Which means you won't. So you could think about doing something that Fran would really appreciate, as a sign of contrition.'

He grimaced. 'I've already done the shopping. But that was more an act of revenge, somehow.'

'Trolleys at dawn!'

He managed a pale smile. 'Funnily enough, I gave one guy a mouthful because he'd parked in a disabled space — yes, he was in running gear — and then I had a real go at a woman on her own in a Chelsea tractor who thought the size of her vehicle entitled her to park in a parent and child slot. Badly.'

'So you feel better now?'

'Caffy, I feel like a total shit. And the worst of it is, I've probably made Fran feel like a total shit too. Which she isn't. She's working so hard she'll end up like me if she's not careful. Or as ACC,' he added, horrifying himself with his honesty.

'One of which you could deal with, and one of which you couldn't. Well, what if she did end up taking your old job? Come on, would the world end?'

'She'd probably have more to do and less to spend. Oh, and more silver braid.' He managed a shamefaced grin. 'She'd probably be given a new office, a new desk and a new, but unbelievably uncomfortable, chair. And she'd hate the job. She's a doer, my Fran. She doesn't like sitting back and giving people orders. Though she does that well,' he conceded. 'The giving orders, not the sitting back, of course.'

'So you're afraid that she'll take a job that will make her unhappy? Or is it that seeing her in your job will make *you* unhappy?'

'It'll be a different job, I should imagine. Far more responsibilities than I ever had. Sacking people, for a start, to balance the budget. She'll hate that.' But they were both aware he hadn't answered her question.

Caffy nodded. 'I guess she'll work that out for herself. And I guess she's already worked out that you'd hate her to replace you. She's no fool, you know.' She looked at her watch, a surprisingly delicate one given her job.

Surprising himself, he leant over and touched it. 'I've always wondered about that.'

'A bloke who thought he loved me gave it to me. And I thought I loved him. But it didn't work out.'

'That guy from the Met? The one who couldn't deal with your past?'

'Yep. The guy who couldn't face sex with an ex-prostitute.'

Seeing the watch suddenly as a manacle, he said, 'But you still wear his watch?'

'It's just a timepiece. Anyway, I was looking at it, Mark, not because I was bored with your company, which I never am, I promise, but because I ought to be on my way. I've—' He'd never seen her blush, but she was blushing now. 'I've got a date. A bloke I met on that course. Alistair.' The blush deepened as she allowed herself the pleasure of speaking his name aloud.

'Something my therapist said once: *never let the past you can't control get in the way of the future you can.*'

She nodded, clearly puzzled.

'You should take off that watch,' he said. 'Use mine instead.' As he spoke he unfastened it and handed it to her.

Passing him her watch in exchange, she leant over and kissed his cheek. 'Like some other therapist said, and this guy probably comes with a capital T, *Go and do thou likewise.*'

Although he hugged her and waved her on her way with as much love and hope in his smile as he could muster, his heart constricted. What if this new bloke also wooed her and won her and then let her down?

And then another clause arrived unbidden in his head, 'Just as you're letting Fran down.'

Sitting staring at the nursery car park wasn't going to help with anything. There were some things that Fran positively loathed — putting out the kitchen waste for compost, for instance, though for some reason she was much better at emptying the wormery than he was. Hospital visiting was another, and Don Simpson a third. He'd bet good money though that, despite all the other pressures, she'd carve enough time to go and see how he was. He didn't like hospitals any more than she did, and Don wasn't his favourite cop either. All the same, after a domesticated detour back home to stow the groceries, he'd go, and a text from him telling Fran what he was up to would give two messages, the obvious one and the covert one that he was sorry for his tantrum and was doing penance. His reward was a text with no more than a smiley face.

Looking like a policeman — yes, his mirror told him daily that he might have shed the life but not the skin — he marched into the hospital as if he owned it. None demanded his non-existent ID. No one even hinted that visiting didn't start for another couple of hours yet.

'Hello, guv'nor! Didn't expect to see you here!' Don Simpson, overflowing from a regulation vinyl-covered armchair, put aside his *Daily Mail* and gestured to the stacking-chair at the end of his bed. Although he was still wearing a hospital gown, he was also sporting an unexpectedly handsome dressing gown, black embroidered with birds. Chinese, perhaps.

'Well, the queen couldn't come, so you got the Duke of Edinburgh instead,' Mark said, realizing his would-be joke didn't sound so funny when spoken aloud. He dropped a pile of puzzle books on the bedside table: Don was renowned for his Sudoku and codeword skills.

But Don took it in the spirit in which it was intended. 'Ah, Fran won't have time to scratch her arse at the moment, will she? Those skeletons of ours, and now the missing kid — yes, I saw her on the news this morning. And in the papers, of course: good coverage, as you'd expect. She seems to be running the whole shebang. Sodding manpower cuts.' He shifted uncomfortably.

'In a lot of pain?' Mark asked.

'Not too bad. Just these chairs are meant for someone half my size. They say I'll probably be going home tomorrow. Oh, no, guv, they don't keep you in a minute longer than they can help: the longer you hang around, the greater your chances of MRSA or whatever. I've waved goodbye to the appendix, and the antibiotics are working nicely. Tell you what, I owe that lad Dizzy. Drove like the bloody clappers. I didn't manage to look at the speedo, though.'

Mark opened his mouth to regale him with the conversation he and Dizzy had had earlier, but Don was speaking again. 'The tiniest wound you ever saw. Hardly any pain. And my temperature's down.' In hospital mode already.

'I'm glad to hear it. Fran will be too.'

'How's she coping with all the pressure?'

Did he look as surprised as he felt? Don wasn't known for his tender-hearted perceptiveness. 'You know Fran,' he replied. 'She's trying to keep your case under wraps as long as she can — she doesn't want the media to stop focusing on Livvie. We need to find her fast.'

'Find her body, you mean, poor little mite. But Fran's right about those kids — a few hours' delay won't do them any harm. At least she's got good blokes in Ray and — though it grieves me to say it — young Murray.'

Mark frowned. 'I don't think he's involved.'

'Why the fuck not? He's a right royal pain, but he's bright enough. Not like Fran to keep him away from this sort of action.'

'I've an idea he's on leave this weekend,' Mark said. Or had he heard wrong yet again? He added, 'I didn't take much notice of staffing in your case, being so involved with the other. So I may be wrong.'

'Leave! When I'd already phoned him and told him to get his arse down to Ashford double quick? You're joking. When Fran came down, he wasn't with her, but I assumed she'd got him to do something else nice and boring while she came herself. She likes to be at the pointed end, doesn't she?' He shifted in the chair again. 'Won't like being ACC, will she?'

Thank goodness for his conversation with Caffy earlier. 'Do you think Wren would back her?'

'Ah, but they say Wren's going. He was only a stand-in, after all, and not a very good one, if you ask me. A manager.' He made the occupation seem a cross between a mass murderer and a predatory paedophile. Then he realized who he was talking to, and added hurriedly, 'Not like you, guv: we could see from your face what you felt about meetings. Him, now, he loves them. Never happier. Unless he's buying himself new kit for his office. Has Fran told you about the space age coffee maker?'

Suddenly Mark found the visitor's chair as uncomfortable as Don found his. 'Of course, there's no saying Fran would take the job even if Wren wanted her in it,' he said. 'What would people like you say?'

'What we said when you got promoted: a good cop wasted.' He grinned. 'OK, in the middle of all your management crap, you found time to do some real things. We could see you were still a cop at heart. All the changes you made were for the better. Even when you lost focus with that business of your daughter, you were still three times the cop Wren's ever been, or ever will be. Like I say, he's just a manager, and not a good one, either. At least if we had Fran up there, we know she'd fight to make a difference like you did. Mind you, we wouldn't give her more than — what? — three months before she threw in the towel. Or killed Wren.'

'But if he's going anyway—'

'Even if the chief was the Archangel Gabriel himself . . . Anyway, who's to say the new commissioner, when we get him, will choose anyone better? And what a waste of money that business is,' Don declared, getting thoroughly into his stride. 'They say the whole process will cost a hundred million pounds — and then we have to pay the commissioners a hundred K on top of that. Per annum. And their so-called advisers, too, whatever they might be when they're at home. How many constables would we get for that? You tell me!'

'Four a year, I reckon,' Mark said. 'Don't think I didn't raise my voice against the proposals at every single meeting I had. The last thing we wanted I said, was politics getting involved with policing . . .'

CHAPTER ELEVEN

'At least we've got a voluntary embargo on the skeletons story, though it's taken me forever to persuade Wren to back us — and almost as long to persuade the various editors,' Fran said, sinking into her chair and waving Ray into the better visitor's chair. Tom Arkwright was young and fit enough to perch: besides which, he'd not been working half the night, had he? And he had the benefit of that auntie who sent him cakes as if she meant single-handedly to keep Royal Mail financially viable. Or was it Parcel Force? It depended on the weight, didn't it? Today's, which Tom was just about to cut, might just merit the latter: it bulged with cherries.

Ray, looking peaky, stirred extra sugar into his double espresso. 'But we can't hold them off forever.'

'Another twenty-four hours, that's all. By which time young Madge may have come up with some useful information, so we give them a story, as well as bald facts. OK, give me some good news. Either of you. Both of you for preference.' She nodded at Ray to start.

'First up, we're still checking every single stable in Kent, livery or private. Could take weeks. Nil returns so far.'

'I'll talk to the chief about choppers with heat-seeking equipment if we have nothing by tonight.'

'I can just see his reaction to that!' Ray said.

'He can react all he likes so long as we get one.'

'Are you going to do your usual thing, guv,' Tom put in, 'and get permission after you've done the necessary?'

Ray pursed his lips at the lese-majesty, and jumped in quickly. 'Thanks to Mark remembering the make of car, we've traced that guy Stephen. Stephen Harris, as it happens. Not that it's done us much good yet: he was at the dentist's exactly when he said he was. Which was a good hour. He had a scale and polish from a hygienist, and then the dentist himself gave him a check-up. CCTV cameras on the car park confirm his arrival and departure. And he's lucky. He lives in a flat with CCTV back and front, and there he is, letting himself in and not emerging again for about three hours. Then he left for what was presumably a celebratory curry, and again the restaurant confirms he was there.'

'And he doesn't ride, I suppose?'

'Claims he's only ever been on a fairground horse, and that was when he was six.'

'OK. What about the estate manager guy?'

'Ross Thwaite. We're still keeping an eye on him. But he's done what you'd expect — taken his car out and done a supermarket run. Asda. And then he went back home and he's digging his garden.'

Fran was galvanized. 'Is he, by God?'

He gave a sour smile. 'But not deep holes. Just turning the ground to plant out some seedlings. Cabbages and such.'

'OK. But keep an eye on him — OK? And let me know anything, absolutely anything, that's untoward. Have the CEOP team made any progress?'

Ray spread his hands. 'I can't understand it — there's been a really poor response from the community.'

Tom asked, 'What community? It's not like Yorkshire where we all know one another. There's the natives, going back for centuries, resenting the rich commuters and their wives in posh cars who don't belong anywhere and don't know anyone. No cohesion, no pulling together, that's the consequence.' He sank the knife viciously into the cake.

Ray took a thick slice. 'When my mum cooks these, the fruit always sinks to the bottom. Anyway, to be honest, trained or not, there's none of the CEOP experts better than the old guv'nor for winkling out useful information. If only we could give the public just one more thing to go on. Oh, there is something you should know: there's some right bastards out there on Twitter saying young Zac must have done it himself. Something to do with him making the appeal. They say the police always get people they suspect to go on press conferences so the press can ask the questions we can't because we're restricted by PACE. Bastards.'

Poor old Police and Criminal Evidence Act: it got blamed for everything. But it was necessary, no doubt about that. Usually. 'Bastards indeed. But since we sometimes do, it's hard to argue. All the same, get our geeks on to the tweets. If anyone goes beyond the line, I'd like them nailed. Very painfully indeed. And I'll refer to them in tonight's media statement. Do you want to push off now or have another slice of cake?' She pushed it over, taking a slice herself. She thought about Spanx but bit in regardless.

Before he could reply, the phone rang. Since she'd explicitly asked not to be interrupted, she snatched it up crossly.

'Reception, ma'am. There's a Mr Turner asking to see you. I told him you were in a meeting, but he's insisting it's important. Shall I get a CEOP detective to deal with him?'

Sic transit gloria mundi, as Caffy would probably have observed. She said quietly, 'I think you might find that Mr Turner was our ACC till about six months ago. He's also my fiancé. So I'll come and get him.'

Tom was on his feet, ready to spare her old bones. But she had an idea that Mark might feel more comfortable being met by her, not by someone he might just consider to be a minion, even though he knew and liked Tom. She even left her mobile and pager on the desk.

'Sometimes I wish I smoked,' she said as she kissed him, in full view of the reception team. 'Then I'd have an excuse to come out into the fresh air on my own. As it is, do you fancy a romantic turn round the car park?'

'I might. But you might not, when you hear what I have to tell you. I know, I know, I could have phoned, but you never know who might overhear.'

'So let's stroll by all means, and hope the CCTV cameras can't lip-read.' She slipped her hand into his and set them in motion. 'Hmmm. Lovely fresh air! Well?'

'It's the elusive Sean Murray. He knew about the skeletons when he did his bunk. Don phoned him, expecting him to hightail it down to Ashford: when you arrived instead of, rather than as well as, Sean, he just thought you'd decided to sideline him.'

'What? Ouch.' Stopping so suddenly jarred her leg. 'All that stuff about a wedding was a load of cock and bull?'

'Who knows? But it seems that in the time it took for him to put down the phone on Don and speak to you, he'd made up his mind to flit.'

'And he hasn't responded to any of the texts or emails I've sent to him. Well, I thought, a wedding . . . My God, Mark, what does this mean?'

'Maybe a phone call to his Met guv'nor might prove enlightening?'

'It might, mightn't it? Formal or informal, do you think?'

'Depends whether you find him in his office or at a wedding.'

She took his hand. 'You were going to say something else, weren't you? About phoning.'

'You're not his line manager. He's Wren's protégé. Do the maths.'

'Even if that means dobbing him in to Wren?'

'In his position, I'd want to know. And take action myself. Wouldn't you?'

* * *

'I prefer a few hills,' Wren greeted her.

She tried not to let him see how appalled she was by the cliché: while the lower echelons toil, the chief constable spends his afternoon on the golf course. It was the worst sort of PR for one thing, and punishingly bad for morale, especially as she'd had to commandeer a constable to drive her. Wren's predecessor had always been where his colleagues could see him. True, he was sometimes a damned nuisance and at least one of his decisions had been catastrophic, but everyone knew he was involved, even to knowing lowly constables by name.

But here was Wren, stowing his golf clubs in the rear of the sort of 4x4 she always deplored — even though her mother, safely stowed in Scotland, thank goodness, would have been thrilled to bits if she'd turned up in such a monster-mobile. Perhaps that was the very reason why she'd stuck to a conventional car, even though a Saab was hardly bog-standard.

'Sorry to bring you out here, Fran,' he said. 'But you must admit the views are fantastic.' He gestured.

The Sene Valley course was one of the most picturesque in the country, with huge skies and views of the sea over steeply rolling hills and deep dipping valleys. Unbidden the words of a hymn came into her mind:

Where every prospect pleases
And only man is vile.

Her nod was perfunctory, until she recalled how therapeutic she found the view from her rectory. She added a smile, but despite herself her words seemed to have a hollow ring. 'A wonderful place to get away from it all,' she said. 'And in such wonderful weather, too. Mind you,' she added, 'it looks an exhausting course just to walk round, let alone playing and towing a buggy.'

He nodded, and looked at her. 'You play yourself? You and your husband might care to play as my guests one day.'

She didn't bother to mention her injured leg, since the invitation was so pallidly phrased as to be non-existent. 'Thank you. Sir, as I said when I called you, we have a problem and I need your advice. DCI Murray, sir.'

'At a Met colleague's wedding, I believe you said.' He was waiting for her gasp of admiration at the powers of his memory, so accordingly she smiled. 'Has he responded to your suggestion that he might like a temporary upgrading here?'

'He's responded to none of my attempts to communicate with him, sir. However—' Fran couldn't stop herself lowering her voice to the confidential level Mark found so hard to hear. 'However, he did receive one communication that appeared to elicit a response. Mark visited Don Simpson in hospital this morning—'

'How long is Simpson likely to be off?'

'I've no idea, sir. As far as I know it wasn't discussed, though I understand he'll be allowed home very soon, minus the offending appendix. Anyway, during the course of their conversation, Don revealed that Murray knew all about the Ashford skeletons.' In response to a brief flicker of Wren's eyebrow, she continued, 'The afternoon they were found, Don couldn't reach me on the phone, so he called Murray as my deputy. Don couldn't reach me because I was walking to Murray's office. When I got there Murray had already cleared his desk, making no reference to Don's call and the goings-on in Ashford and assuring me that his Met line-manager had granted him time off in lieu. Since I didn't know about the Ashford case, I had no reason to override the decision, though I did insist that Murray should be at his desk by seven on Monday morning.'

'Which he may well be.' Wren looked as if he'd rather be elsewhere. Much rather. Somewhere he could avoid making a decision.

'Of course. And getting the dressing down of his young life. On the other hand, sir, the texts and emails and calls he should have received by now all came with good news. Not many people I know would ignore the chance of being an acting superintendent.'

Turning from her, Wren slammed his tailgate shut. At last he faced her. 'I take it you want me to contact the Met? Just because someone's skiving off on a nice weekend?'

'Just because someone's skiving off on a nice weekend when he knows everyone else is working their arses off in a major murder enquiry?' Her phone rang.

'Yes, take it.' He sounded no more than irritated. But he added in a much more authoritative voice, 'And I'll make a call or two.'

Hers wasn't easy to deal with; the Livvie case press officer wanted someone to front another appeal. Did she have any suggestions? Should they risk asking Zac and his wife to appear again?

'Are they up to it?'

'I think they might be if you and Mark were there.'

'Mark?'

'Don't forget Zac coaches Mark: he likes him, admires the way he leapt into action as soon as he spotted something was wrong. But protocol . . .'

'Bugger protocol. Bugger procedure. On the other hand, I'm not at all sure how Mark would feel about it. He's retired, after all. Have you asked him?'

'Can't reach him, ma'am. I've texted and left messages, but had no reply at all. Could you ask him when you see him?'

As if both of them would break off what they were doing and take afternoon tea together.

'I'm unlikely to do that before midnight,' she said. 'Meanwhile, I'm in a meeting with the chief constable: talk to Ray about the idea, and maybe I can test the chief's reaction.' Or maybe not. Every instinct rebelled against the idea of involving a civilian other than the parents in the appeal. And slice it how she might, Mark was no longer a police officer. Furthermore, he was avoiding publicity like the plague. She wanted to respect that. Didn't she? Or — deep, deep down — was she still stinging from his rebuke last night and this morning's unpleasant quip about her not being an ACC yet? She hadn't deserved either. Had she? Her eyes filled with unexpected and very unwelcome tears.

'Harman? Harman? Are you all right?'

She must have jumped visibly. And to her amazement Wren was peering at her face.

'Sorry, sir. A touch of hay fever, I'd say.'

'A bit early in the year, isn't it?'

'Gorse, sir. And you should see me near a hyacinth.' She polished her nose as if she were a schoolgirl.

'Very well. Sean Murray. You told me he said he had his line manager's permission to go to his former boss's wedding.' Although he was clearly doing no more than reiterating the facts, it felt like a subtle accusation.

'I did.'

'According to Dan Philips, he made no such request. Nor, also according to Dan, is there any such wedding in the offing. I thought you would want to know so you can deal with the matter accordingly when he shows up on Monday.'

'All my unanswered messages about the temporary upgrading?'

'Which may now hang in the balance. Because Dan and his colleagues couldn't contact him either. I'm disappointed, Fran. Very disappointed.'

This sounded like a less than subtle criticism of her, although Murray and Wren had been like crossed fingers. No, she was being paranoid, surely. 'Despite our lack of personal rapport, I thought him a very reliable officer, sir. This is quite out of character.' That much was true. He'd have happily grassed a colleague up, but not stepped an inch out of line himself. 'And I'm really very worried, in view of what Don said. If he bolted, as he seems to have done, it looks as if he did so in response to the news of the Ashford skeletons.'

'We can hardly describe him as a missing person yet, can we?' Wren mused. 'All the same, I'd like you to check personally that he left the building with nothing of strategic or operational importance.'

What about Murray as a human being? But she'd try to raise that later. Meanwhile she'd better respond to a justifiable management concern. 'He'll have his laptop, sir, I should imagine. But after that Met scare — you'll recall that a huge amount of classified information went AWOL when some idiot of an officer left his laptop on a train — Mark required everyone in the Kent service to have everything of note encrypted.' And she'd obeyed the instruction, a right royal pain as far as she herself was concerned, by requiring the geeks to institute spot checks on everyone. Which probably didn't include Wren.

He nodded coolly. 'You'll let me know of any problems by ten tonight. And that includes not locating him.' He looked at his watch and seemed to consider the conversation closed.

'Sir, there is another aspect of his disappearance you might feel it necessary to consider.'

'The timing of it? Of course. You think he might be having some sort of breakdown, like your fiancé's.'

If ever a comment was below the belt, that one was. 'It's not impossible. There might be other reasons.'

He peered at her closely. 'Are you saying what I think you're saying — that he might have been involved somehow? In the skeleton case?' he added in a voice that suggested he'd mentally rephrased the question several times and wasn't sure he'd got it quite right.

She raised her hand as if to tell him to slow down. 'That might be a conclusion too far, sir. But such . . . coincidences . . . are worrying.'

'They are. Put some feelers out, Fran.'

Fran? She nearly gaped at him.

'Informal as yet. In fact, get someone to run the standard checks for a misper. Someone as discreet as they come, reporting direct to you. And keep me informed. Whatever time of night or day. Now, anything else? Yes, there is, isn't there? I'm due in the bar in three minutes' time.'

'The Livvie case, sir. The parents are happy to make another appeal this evening. But they want Mark with them.'

'Good God, why? And why have you countenanced it for a moment?'

'I haven't, sir. Since it's a matter of policy, I'm asking you. Before you ask, I've not even mentioned it to Mark yet.'

He shot her a surprisingly shrewd glance. 'You're no keener on this than I am, are you? So you won't argue for once. You know what you have to do: knock it on the head. Now.' Another glance at his watch and he was off.

With an apologetic shrug at her driver, so was she.

CHAPTER TWELVE

His good deed — his expiation, more like — over, Mark was at a loss. He should have felt a huge relief that the CEOP team had virtually taken over the Livvie case, managing most aspects of the investigation — from organizing specialized search teams to advising on the media. Virtually everything. Fran and Ray were still officially the lead officers, which was good for Ray's career, of course. As for Fran, he had a feeling she really would have liked to shrug her shoulders and let the thrusting keeny-beanies do all the boring bits — but the system didn't permit cherry-picking, and he knew she'd rather eat coal than back out altogether, even if that had been an option.

As for him, there really was no place for a retired amateur. Rather than hang around in a strop, he headed home to Great Hogben. Should he take advantage of the glorious weather and do some more in the garden? But he could almost, like a true countryman, smell frost in the clear air: planting out delicate young plants was not an option. So should he indulge the very strong desire he'd mentioned to Caffy — to go down to the tennis club? The club itself was no longer a crime scene. Some players might have been put off by the kidnapping, especially if they'd planned to bring their children to mess around while they played. Others might stay away out of a vague notion of 'respect'. But there might be a crop of rubbernecks too — and would he be setting himself up as an object as interesting as the courts and clubhouse?

On the other hand, and perhaps this ought to be the overriding argument, Ray was quite keen for him to pick up any gossip that might be going, and to talk to any Golden Oldies who might be around, about their perceptions forty-eight hours on. He'd made it clear to Ray that many Golden Oldies were on a limited — and much cheaper — membership option which meant they weren't eligible to play at peak times, including weekends, so there might not be too many about. It might also be that those who were would rather not speak to someone they might have felt was somehow playing under false colours, if not exactly false pretences.

At this point he almost gave up the idea. The club was now such an important part of his life that he didn't want to be excluded. But then again, that might happen whenever he returned. All he could do was trust to the sense of fair play that made people call line decisions in their opponents' favour or admit to double-bounces even on a crucial point.

Six of the courts were occupied when he arrived, with no one sitting out waiting for a partner. Some youngsters were playing singles — two boys, two girls. The girls in particular were embarrassingly good: he couldn't believe that one day soon they wouldn't be playing at county level at least. One man was patiently basket-feeding another girl of about nine who already hit the balls harder than Mark could. The others were just Saturday regulars of varying degrees of ability. He didn't know any of them except the two girls who, come to think of it, looked familiar.

The tennis wall beckoned. He obeyed. It was so good to switch his mind off and simply respond to the demands of a ball.

At last some shadows fell across the ground. The two girls whom he now recognized as two of Zac's team of helpers were watching him, but not surely because they wanted tennis tips. He stopped at once, catching the returning ball left-handed, which made him feel marginally better.

'Flora, isn't it? And Emily? How are you both?'

Both flushed deeply and probably painfully: they might look and play like goddesses, but they were after all no more than young teenagers with horrible hormones, plagued by shyness in the presence of even an old male like him. Still, he told himself, it was better to cause a blush than a pitying sneer.

They looked at each other, tongue-tied.

This was something he could deal with: all those years of eliciting a response from people who didn't find it easy to speak about what was important. 'You did very well with those little 'uns on Thursday,' he said. 'Kept them amused, interested — stopped any panic. Well done. Zac would have been proud of you if he'd had a second even to notice what you were doing.'

'Is he — is he OK? I mean . . .' Flora managed.

'I've not seen him. There's someone called a police liaison officer who will probably have moved in with him and his wife and son while we — while the police find Livvie.'

Flora might have noticed his slip, but she was too busy picking up on his last few words to say anything. 'Are you sure they'll find her? Alive, that is.' Her voice nearly broke on *alive*. Brave lass to ask the unaskable, all the same.

'I could do one of two things here, Flora,' he said gravely. 'I could switch on a smiley face and say *of course*. That would be treating you as a child. Or I could treat you as an adult and tell you that honestly and truly I don't know. Any more than the police do.'

Emily, who'd been gnawing her lower lip during the whole exchange, widened her eyes. 'But you *are* the police, aren't you?'

'Not anymore. I was, but then I was ill so I retired.'

'But it was you who — you know, sort of bossed us all. I thought . . .' She blushed again.

'You don't stop being bossy just because you've given up the job,' he said, almost blushing himself at the recollection of his treatment of Fran. 'And I'm afraid police officers find it extra hard to switch off. We always want to ask questions — *what if . . . what next . . . what should I do . . .*' He smiled. 'Just now I'm itching to ask you if you've remembered anything else that can help. I'm sure you told my former colleagues everything you remembered at the time, but you might have thought of things since. Things you might think are too trivial to report to anyone,' he prompted, 'but might just be a missing piece. I mean, the other night I couldn't have told the man who was interviewing me what make of car a certain person drove, but then, when I was thinking about something quite different, up the information popped.' He was talking too much, wasn't he? He'd lose Flora, if not the younger Emily, if he kept rattling on like that.

'Would something like a car be . . . sort of important?' Emily asked.

She wasn't talking about a car though, was she?

'Anything could be important.'

'Or not, of course,' Flora chimed in.

'When I was a cop I'd rather have had a hundred pieces of information I couldn't use than miss one I needed.' Somehow he must stop himself asking point-blank what one of them had seen or heard in case they froze into denial.

They nodded, still doubtful. Emily looked wistfully at their bikes, clearly wishing they'd never started this and were heading home. Or was he jumping to conclusions? In any case, he had to admit that their parents were braver than he might have been in their situation, letting them swan round on their own in a place where a sexual predator must surely be on the loose. In fact, that was the next important thing to do: get them to call home and explain what was delaying them.

A car was bumping along the track. He permitted himself no more than a glance.

'How would you know if you needed it?' Flora asked. Another blush.

'When you were a kid you must have done jigsaws. Right? Well, imagine that a police investigation is a giant jigsaw, being put together by dozens of people. That's just the police officers involved. Add in things like CCTV — more pieces being put in by more people.'

'Sounds like total chaos,' she said, as if refusing to admit she might be interested.

'Oh, it is,' he admitted cheerfully. 'Organized chaos, mostly. Now, imagine this case is the jigsaw. All these pieces coming in. More and more when people respond to TV appeals. By now the people in charge must have a huge picture spread out. But they don't have all the important pieces.'

'You don't have one with the kidnapper's face on it,' Emily put in brightly. Ignoring Flora's scowl, she continued, 'Everyone says she might still be alive, that's why she needs to be found now.'

'She might. I hope she is. All the people at HQ hope she is. They can only work at their best if they believe they'll succeed. But they all know that the missing piece of the jigsaw, wherever it is, isn't in their possession.' That wasn't wholly true, but he had to do something to prompt them. The car had parked and only one person got out: any moment now the little bubble of concentration that held the three of them together would be burst.

'So talking wouldn't be sneaking?' Emily confirmed, sliding her eyes towards him.

'No.'

'But what if we said the wrong thing? Got someone into trouble?'

'If they had done something wrong, then — well, you might have grassed them up but you might have saved Livvie's life. And if they hadn't done anything wrong, the police would quickly establish that they weren't part of the jigsaw. And you absolutely wouldn't get into trouble for saying it.' He changed his voice from calm and reassuring to authoritative: 'Now, first of all you must phone home. Or text. Must. No argument.' He raised the index finger that had silenced a thousand arguing junior officers, including, of course, Fran herself. 'How do you think your parents would feel if you were a minute later than you promised to be? And what would they say if you talked to the police without them knowing? Now, both of you.'

He gathered up the balls he'd scattered while they texted.

'Would you like to talk to a woman officer I know very well? It'd be like talking to your mum or your grandma,' he added, disloyally. Did Fran ever refer to him as a grandpa? 'I could get her to come here or go to your home, so your parents would know exactly what was going on.'

'We couldn't just tell you?'

'Of course you could. But you'd have to talk to a real police office sooner or later.' He paused, wondering what on earth his ears were telling him.

'Weird,' Flora said.' Sounds as if one's on his way now.'

All three turned. Blues and twos heralded a police car clearly not coping well with the track.

'Let's go and introduce ourselves, shall we?' he suggested with what he hoped was a convincing smile. He picked up his bag. He and the girls were falling into step when he realized all was not well. The person who'd driven up was pointing in their direction, practically jumping up and down with what looked like fury.

'Who's rattled his cage?' Flora demanded.

'Go and collect your bikes and wait by the police car. I'll find out,' Mark said, trying not to sound as grim as he felt. 'Promise me you'll stay by the police car. Get in if necessary. Go on: scoot.'

Because it was quite clear that he was about to be manhandled by the furious would-be player. Manhandled and subjected to a whole stream of abuse he didn't want the girls to hear. Though, come to think of it, he'd heard just as bad outside many a school playground.

* * *

'I don't care,' his assailant was telling the community support officer, not the fully-fledged constable Mark would have hoped for. He was lacing his comments with a lot of words Mark hadn't heard since he'd retired. 'I don't care if he used to be a policeman. I don't care if he was prime minister or archbishop of Canterbury. The man's clearly a paedophile. Grooming young girls. He's got to be the one who did young Livvie in. Look at the smarmy bastard!'

The PCSO, who had in these days of radical economies come on his own, looked from one man to another, with an occasional glance at the girls, now huddled together and in tears — and hopefully out of range of the tirade of blasphemous invective. Clearly he hadn't a clue what to do. By now all the players had abandoned their games and had formed a loose circle round the protagonists.

Keeping his voice as mild as possible so the girls weren't treated to a scene, Mark said, 'The man's got a point, officer. But your priority should be those kids. Why not lock me in your car — though I promise you I've no intention of trying to escape — and call for assistance? Ask for DCI Ray Barlow. Got that? DCI Barlow. That's really important. And make sure you also ask for a colleague trained in interviewing young people, because apart from this guy's accusation, which clearly needs investigating, the girls may have information about the Livvie case. Cuff me if you want,' he added, holding out his hands. One day he'd dine out on this, God willing.

'What about Mr — er—?' the PCSO asked.

'Perhaps he should wait in his car, too,' Mark said, suddenly desperate to laugh.

* * *

It was a long and hot nineteen minutes before Ray Barlow arrived, again on his own. With Mark still incommunicado in the response vehicle, Ray questioned his accuser, the PCSO and then the girls, whom he shepherded away from all the action. Mark couldn't have faulted him, except that it left him stranded even longer. At last he knew he must attract the

PCSO's attention: 'I'm sorry, officer,' he gasped as the door opened, 'but it's so hot in here I'm afraid I might pass out.'

His assailant told his audience that frying in hell was too good for him, but the PCSO showed a smidgen of initiative, leaving the driver's door ajar and asking the two largest tennis players to make sure Mark didn't stir. He now appeared to be taking a statement from the assailant.

Now another police vehicle approached — Mark hoped bleakly that there wasn't a major incident about to go down, or his former colleagues would be woefully short of transport. This one was driven by a woman: at last, a real constable! However, Ray waved her back as she parked, got out of the vehicle and approached him. Ray was still listening to the girls, prompting them from time to time, just as he'd done. For everyone's sake, not least his own, Mark hoped Ray would be more efficient at eliciting information than he had been.

At long last, Ray escorted the girls back to the woman officer. Emily, however, hung back, arguing so quietly Mark couldn't hear — those wretched ears! Monday, yes, Monday, he'd get them tested — but plainly refusing to do as she was told. She reminded him of a small dog, refusing to go walkies, legs braced, head back. Ray summoned the PCSO, who then dragged his reluctant way to Mark. Pushing his head down needlessly hard to prevent him hitting it as he got out of the car, he then grabbed him by the arm — rightly, as Mark forced himself to admit, lest his prisoner tried to make a run for it — and frogmarched him into Ray's presence.

Ray was clearly almost wetting himself in a desire not to laugh. 'Ferris, I believe you haven't been formally introduced to our former Assistant Chief Constable, Mr Mark Turner. Mr Turner is working closely with me in the search for the missing child, Livvie. Emily, here, and Flora had approached him with information that they thought might be useful. I'm afraid Mr Purton got hold of the wrong end of the stick. He may have overreacted,' he added dryly, still not meeting Mark's eye.

‘Not at all,’ Mark lied. He assumed the smooth PR voice that had kept him going during his spell as ACC. ‘In his position, seeing an old man on friendly terms with two schoolgirls, I’d have been very suspicious too. No need for tears, Emily — all’s well that ends well.’

The girls looked balefully at Purton, who clearly wanted to huff and puff even longer, with a lot more interesting epithets, but was disconcerted by Mark’s response, as were the previously hostile players, who continued nonetheless to mutter.

In response to a jerk of the head from Ray, the PCSO ostentatiously herded the players back to the courts, as if practising recently acquired skills in crowd control.

‘Are you really all right, Mr Turner?’ Emily called. She shook off the woman officer’s warning hand and came nearer. ‘That crazy idiot didn’t hurt you, did he? Because it was us who came to talk to you, wasn’t it, Flora? And you made us text home and said we should talk to a proper policeman.’

‘Which I guess you’ve just done,’ Mark said, with an encouraging smile. ‘But don’t tell me what you said. It’s between you and the police now, and no one else needs to hear.’ He looked meaningfully at Purton, who responded by stalking back to his car and grabbing his tennis bag. Funny: half an hour ago the two of them might have suggested a couple of sets against each other. But Purton would have to take his place at the wall or wait his turn. He didn’t feel particularly sympathetic.

‘Are you OK to drive, Mark? To follow me?’ Ray asked quietly. ‘Because I think when I brief the team you’ll want to hear what those kids said.’

CHAPTER THIRTEEN

They were just concluding a very efficient briefing on the skeletons case: Malcolm Perkins had been certified dead two months ago, after a distressingly prolonged battle with motor neurone disease. He'd never left any confession. But in the years he had managed to work as a youth worker, there had been no reports of any suspicious disappearances. Fran had managed not to snap that they should be investigating the unsuspicious disappearances too. But Madge had jumped in and done that for her: it would be a huge use — and possibly waste — of hours, but they owed it to the Ashford victims to establish everything they could about the possible murderer. Stoke-on-Trent; West Bromwich; Taunton: they had a lot of ground to cover.

'And, with Tom's assistance, we're checking all the other Ashford mispers of the relevant period to see if any of them might have been the killer and simply scarpered,' she added, suppressing a yawn. 'Ma'am, how much longer will the press embargo last? I'm feeling really bad that we've not notified the parents of the ones we've identified. And worse that the tests on the others have been postponed.'

The whole team echoed her frustration, which of course Fran shared.

'Only till Monday. And I have to admit that though I promised I'd go and talk to the bereaved families myself, I can't see me being able to, not until the Livvie case is solved.' She could hardly explain that she'd been ordered to investigate the whereabouts of one of their colleagues on top of everything else. And then she realized they were all waiting expectantly. 'Oh, and the embargo? It'll hold till tomorrow, and I'll ask the chief constable to press for a further extension, but—' She shrugged, but wished, as her shoulders creaked, that she hadn't. 'Now, as you know, the overtime budget has been slashed. What little remains is being directed at the Livvie case — which is coming in at about a million a day so far. Personally I don't think it's being wasted. When she's found, I shall argue for more funds for this case. Since I can't pay you to work extra hours, I shan't ask you to work them. In fact, I'd say you all deserve a break. I probably won't say the same thing when the embargo's been lifted, of course. It'll be all systems go — and then some!'

It wasn't until they left the room that she caught Tom's eye. He fell into step with her, strolling casually down the corridor, just as a son might with his mother. 'You might have to pass some of your work on possible other victims to someone else,' she said quietly. 'I've got some news. Absolutely confidential. Seems we need to look for Sean Murray.'

He raised an eyebrow. 'Nothing to do with the rumour that a senior CID bloke did a runner? The word was, though, that although he said he was hightailing it to a wedding, it was something to do with a girlfriend. Though I also heard a rumour that the voice he spoke to on the phone was a man's. Some thought it might be Don Simpson's voice, in fact.'

They exchanged a quizzical look. 'What a strange rumour. OK, Tom, you report to me and no one else.'

'Report?'

'Report. The thing that worries me most,' Fran said, 'is that Murray once remarked that Ashford was the easiest place in the country to get away from. I know Maidstone hardly hits those heady heights, but once you reach Ashford, in what — half an hour? — the same applies. Or you could simply get a train from Maidstone to London and disappear.'

Tom wrinkled his nose, as if she'd asked him to choose between flavours of crisps. 'Hard to disappear anywhere these days, isn't it? He'll have his car reg picked up on all manner of CCTV and motorway cameras. If he tries to use his credit card — more data. Mobile phone traceable, too.'

'In that case it shouldn't take you long to run him to earth, should it?' she smiled affably. She might have been asking for cheese flavour, or salt and vinegar. Heaven forbid she'd ask for either, of course, with those inches to keep off.

'You really are serious?'

'The chief's orders, no less. And the chief wants me to update him at ten tonight.'

'Ten! Does he have any idea how many hours you're putting in on the Livvie case? Not to mention Don's skeletons?'

'I doubt it. Nor how much time off in lieu you're owed. But that's what folk like you and me do, isn't it, Tom? We get on with things.' She patted his arm, and headed off to Murray's goldfish bowl to check what he might have taken with him.

It looked as if he'd never meant to stay long. Other people personalized their space; Murray's was quite anonymous. Thumbing through his meagre and extremely tidy possessions unnerved her. It was like picking over the property of the dead. At least the paper files he'd been working on were safely locked away, and she didn't fear for one minute that he'd failed to encrypt any information on the laptop he'd walked off with. She should have felt reassured. But she didn't. Not wholly.

* * *

One way of easing her back and leg pain was to lie on the floor, head supported by a couple of books, with knees bent and feet slightly apart. The idea was to relax into the pain, which paradoxically had the effect of releasing it. It might be — was

— effective, but it was hardly the position to be found in by casual visitors to her office, especially when she had relaxed so deeply she actually fell asleep. At least Ray seemed as embarrassed as she was, though Mark, a pace behind him, naturally took little notice. She declined a joint offer to help her to her feet, rolling over and doing a quasi-press up to return to the vertical. What a pity she spoiled the performance by needing the desk to provide final leverage.

'Back bad again?' Mark asked, gathering up the books and searching for a vacant spot on the desk.

'Prevention rather than cure,' she lied. But it was Mark who'd asked, so she conceded, wishing she could just sob on his shoulder and ask him to make the pain go away, 'OK, it's not so good. But you suffer an injury in one place, it's bound to have repercussions in others,' she added brightly for Ray's benefit. 'Or should it be, *for* others? Anyway, you both look pregnant with news?' She had an idea that that was a quotation from something; if she cared to know from what, Caffy would be able to tell her off the top of her head. She gestured at the chairs: Ray cleared both of them, dumping files on the floor. Then she remembered her conversation with the chief, and sighed. 'I've got some news myself, Ray — and it mostly affects you, Mark. Apparently Zac and whatshername — his wife — wanted you both beside them at their next appeal: the chief's vetoed the idea of Mark appearing before it even got put to you. No civilians to sully our TV presentation,' she declaimed in a vague attempt to mimic Wren's precise tones. She raised and dropped her hands to signify the pointlessness of arguing about it. 'We had a high-level meeting at his golf club,' she continued ironically. 'Sene Valley, no less. Cut short because he had a meeting in the bar.'

'Why did you have to go all the way out there? When you're knackered enough to snore on the floor?' Mark demanded.

'Me? Snore? Never. OK, another issue altogether. One that demanded face-to-face communication. Absolutely between the three of us — OK, Ray? Not so much as a flutter of an eyelid to show you've heard a smidgen of a rumour?' Or he could wave his permanent promotion goodbye. 'We have a problem with Sean Murray.' She slid a look at Mark, who responded with the tiniest nod.

'Done a bunk, hasn't he? Everyone knows that,' Ray said, as if stating the obvious, which he clearly was, given what Tom had said. 'They reckon it was after some phone call. If he wasn't such a cold fish, you'd think maybe he'd got some poor girl up the duff. Or heard he'd won the Euromillions lottery. No? But I won't talk about it with the others if you don't want me to,' he added with a seraphic grin. Clearly there was more to Ray than she'd realized.

She spread her hands, helplessly. 'So long as you didn't hear it from me, talk all you want.' She grinned, her smile softening and warming as she caught Mark's eye. All the same, she felt even guiltier at having, however tacitly, sided with Wren on the matter of the TV appeal. She should have insisted that they consulted both Ray and Mark: the conclusion might well have been the same. And she would have felt cleaner. 'I can't help noticing,' she said to Mark, 'that you're wearing your tennis gear. But you and Ray arrived hotfoot together. Something, apart from young Murray, is clearly up. Your news, please.'

Mark got to his feet and patted the kettle, apparently deciding it was full enough. He ranked three mugs irritatingly side by side and plunged a hand into her tea-bag caddy. 'Oh, Tom's auntie's cake. And the crumbs still sticky on the knife.' He fished three tissues from the box on her desk to use as plates; his portions were regrettably generous.

She waved hers firmly aside. 'You've been exercising off your spare calories. I haven't. And I have to say you've pissed around quite long enough. Ray'll burst if he can't get it off his chest soon.'

He placed the mugs and cake delicately in gaps Ray managed to create on her desk. 'Do you want the long story of how I was apprehended by a PCSO as a paedophile?' He overrode her exclamation. 'Or the shorter one about what the girls I was talking to wanted to tell me?'

'The long one, of course. Hell, no I don't. And I don't even have time for the abridged version. We've got that CEOP briefing to take in two minutes flat, haven't we, Ray? Will you come along, Mark, and report to the whole team what you picked up? Bring your tea and cake, both of you.' She picked her mug up to set an example.

'You'll be an honoured guest,' Ray said promptly.

But Mark pulled a face. 'Would you mind if I just went and sat quietly in the car for a bit? I want to pick up the football results . . .' He could have watched them on the TV in her office, or even in the scaled down canteen, but she said nothing. Perhaps he needed some fresh air. Or perhaps he'd had enough of feeling an outsider for one day. Detained by a PCSO, indeed.

* * *

'So two girls who were helping Zac on Thursday went to the Portaloo together, found it unusable — no surprise there — and helped each other through the fence into the woods, where they stood guard in turn while the other used one of the trees as a loo,' Ray told the assembled officers.

Although the CEOP hierarchy would have been well within their rights to lead the meeting, they'd insisted on taking a back seat and letting the locals get on with it. That was fine by Fran, but she had a sense that Ray felt he was under an uncomfortable amount of scrutiny. His delivery was far from smooth; he needlessly consulted notes. 'While they were there, one of them was sure she saw the glint of what she thought at first might have been someone's glasses. Emily, that is. Apparently she screamed to Flora. Her friend. But then she, Emily, that is, thought she must be mistaken, because though they both listened neither heard so much as a twig cracking. They even looked round — but only a bit, as Flora admitted, since they knew Zac needed them. But as they ducked through the fence on the way back, they both heard what they insist was a jingle. Something metallic. So

I'd say this fits in with Mark's horse theory. Though neither of them heard any other sounds — no neighing or whatever other noises horses make. And no manure, shall we say, left behind — I've already had the scene checked. We're busy processing a lot of prints from horses' shoes.'

Fran nodded. 'Excellent. Aren't they all supposed to be as individual as human shoe prints? It'd be nice if they matched the estate manager's gee-gee — what's his name now?' She clicked her fingers in irritation. If Mark had problems with his ears, she had hers with names. Always had — and it was getting worse.

'The horse's or the estate manager's?' some bright spark asked.

'Oh, the horse answers to Snowdrop,' she said, one cell in her brain functioning at least. Everyone laughed, obligingly, as if she'd made a daft joke. 'The estate manager's, of course.'

'Thwaite, ma'am, Ross Thwaite,' someone more sycophantic than the others volunteered quietly.

Ray nodded. 'Someone's on to it — and under Snowdrop — even as we speak.'

'Let's hope that snow is all Snowdrop drops, then. Or not.'

They went through all the horse and pony riders contacted so far: it had obviously been a tedious afternoon for a lot of people, particularly as a lot of riders seemed to have missed the media requests for information and had, quite simply, gone off for a ride. Should they simply eliminate youngsters' ponies?

The CEOP superintendent, a man in his late thirties called Chatfield, shook his head. 'Not if they're big enough for an adult to ride. Very small ones like Shetland ponies, yes. Shit, I'm a townie. Motorbikes, I'm your man. Quad bikes, at a push. But apart from Black Beauty and Warhorse, I know zilch about the things. Anyone here know enough to take charge of this aspect of the enquiry? Or do I have to bring in someone from Mounted Division?'

Enough already. Fran could leave the rest of the briefing in his and Ray's hands, apart from one point. The appeal from Livvie's parents was to be recorded in something under an hour.

With a quick apology she cut short his updates. 'Everything is urgent, but this has the doubtful honour of being bloody urgent. In two minutes we need a decision on who fronts Zac and his wife's appeal. Ray's the obvious choice.' Taking a breath, she added, 'Zac would like both him and Mark Turner involved, but the chief's vetoed Mark.'

Chatfield looked despairingly round the room and then straight at her. 'I'd like you to do it, Fran. Provided you don't mind using those crutches again. Ray said you were due an Oscar.'

Ray nodded. 'For being a cross between Tiny Tim and Long John Silver.'

Managing a grin, and actually pleased that Ray had summoned enough confidence to crack a joke, Fran suppressed a groan. Not pain. It wasn't so much back ache as brain ache. Her gran had always said it was better to wear away than rust away, but just at the moment she wasn't sure. 'Would the family be happy with that? And the FLO?'

Ray turned away to make a call. He smiled, perhaps ironically, as he faced the room again. 'Zac and Bethany—' he might just have lingered on the second name, as if willing her to register it — 'know I can't be everywhere. They want me here with you CEOP guys. And Mark had already told them he wasn't allowed to do it.' He managed a cheeky grin. 'They say that if they can't have Mark, Mark's fiancée will do.'

'So they'll accept the organ grinder's monkey. Hell's bells, Ray, thanks for the vote of confidence.' She heaved herself to her feet. She had an idea someone muttered something about her being plucked from the subs' bench, but couldn't be sure. In any case she'd have been the first to laugh.

* * *

Mark was still with Zac and Bethany when Fran appeared. She made sure she and Mark kissed — not much more than a peck, but something for anyone who wished to report back to Wren. Then she shook hands more formally than she liked with the grieving couple. Yes, she was the professional officer: he was allowed to hug them both as he slipped out of Fran's immediate range.

Fran had only seen Zac from a distance, on the couple of occasions when, before her accident, she'd given Mark a lift to and from the club. As far as she knew, she'd never set eyes on Bethany before. Her recollection of Zac was of a six-foot sun-bronzed giant. Now he was pale, unshaven rather than sporting designer stubble. Bethany might have been made up by an Oscar-winning make-up artist for a role as a mourning wife, but Fran didn't think the pale cheeks and deep under-eye smudges owed anything to art. On the other hand, if she herself was doing some window-dressing by displaying her elbow-crutch, there was no reason not to engage in a bit more.

'I don't suppose,' she said with a thoughtful frown, aware she sounded more pensive than tender, 'that you've got one of Livvie's teddies with you?'

Bethany shook her head. Eyes and nose dripped tears all over again. And why not?

'What the hell—?' Zac asked, with disproportionate anger, if disproportion was possible in his circumstances.

Fran turned to face him. She did bracing better than soothing, so she asked briskly, 'Do you remember when Madeline McCann went missing? Her mother carried Maddie's toy cat with her everywhere, and kept snuggling her face into its fur because it smelt of Maddie. I want Bethany to try the same trick. Just an extra little nudge at people's emotions.'

'Wouldn't that be unfair?' he asked. 'I mean, misleading people—'

'On the scales of rightness and fairness, where would you put child abduction? Somewhere beyond a bad line call. OK?'

With a hint of defensive steeliness that told Fran she'd won her over, Bethany said, 'There's not enough time to go home and get Paddy. Livvie's cat. She loves it to bits.'

Fran squeezed her hand. 'Would you object to using something from our soft interview room? It won't be a total lie because when we find Livvie I shall buy her an identical one.'

Bethany wouldn't let go, as if she was clutching hope itself. 'You still think . . . is there any hope at all?'

'Bethany, if I have to walk barefoot from here to Great Hogben and back we shall find her. Alive.'

'But what Ray called the Golden Hour—'

'Is long over. I know. But we have so much technology to follow people — and a wonderful team of dear old-fashioned cops who all love kids. Part of their DNA, I often think. Now, how about that police-issue cat? White? Ah, Mark said Livvie liked pink; is that right? I'm sure there's a pink bear in there.' At last freeing herself gently from Bethany's grip, she caught the eye of the most strapping constable she could. He'd always been a bit of a thug: it'd do him good to carry a cuddly toy through the corridors. Especially a pink one.

CHAPTER FOURTEEN

'How long do you think you'll be able to keep this up?' Mark demanded.

He'd joined Fran as soon as the reporters had dispersed, embracing Zac and Bethany again as if he was their father. All four, plus their ever-present FLO, whose smile would have driven Fran to murder in an hour flat, walked to the waiting car. For half a minute Zac had played truant, taking Mark to one side while Fran thrust the pink bear into Bethany's arms as a furry talisman.

Now, hooking her arm into his, he escorted her back to her room.

'D'you really want me to be honest? The answer is, not much longer. Oh, Mark, I don't know where I ache most. And there's another three or four hours to go before I can consider stopping. I've got to report to Wren at ten,' she added, as he opened his mouth to protest. 'And tomorrow all hell is likely to be let loose — I don't think the press embargo on our skeletons will hold much longer. Monday's the last possible day, for sure. And all we want is for some venal soul to tell the red-top press we've lost Sean Murray and—' She spread her hands, lost for further words. Unlocking her office door, she said simply, 'I need a hug, Mark. Oh, that's better,' she sighed, surrendering her weight as they stepped inside.

He held her until she managed to push herself vertical. 'Five minutes on the floor for you, my girl; I'll make some tea.' As he busied himself with the kettle, he asked, 'Any idea where you have to report to Wren? It's too dark for the golf course — how about the bar in the Hythe Imperial? Seriously, I know you have to check up with Tom, and I know Wren wants you at ten. But between times, do you have to be here physically? Can't you come and get a bite of proper food and then come back? I'll chauffeur you. And back. And back home after that.'

'Get thee behind me!'

'I don't see anything wrong about wanting a decent meal. You can't go on drinking green tea and refusing cake all day, can you? OK, talk to Tom first. See what he's come up with. And with luck you can brief Wren and simply come home. Go on, lie down: I'll get Tom to come down here. Floor or no floor. OK?'

Floor it was. 'Give me five minutes here with a painkiller first.'

'No can do. You have to have it with a meal, remember. I'm not sure that even cake as rich as Tom's auntie's constitutes a meal. A steak and salad might.'

'Is there any cake left? I'll risk a painkiller with it, phone Tom and nip out to the nearest quiet pub.'

'Maidstone? Saturday night? There's no such thing, sweetheart. Hell!' he responded to a scratch at the door. 'I'll get it. Ah, Tom! You can come in so long as you don't fall over your guv'nor.'

Tom squatted beside her, as if checking an accident victim. 'You all right, Fran?'

'Like the rest of us, shattered. Only don't tell Wren. He'll have me at the knacker's yard. I might even see that bloody Snowdrop there.' She eased herself on to her elbow, thence, with a struggle he could see she did her best to disguise, to her feet.

'I don't think he will. I think he'll tell you what a good detective you are,' Tom declared, picking the cherries out of the remaining cake crumbs. 'This didn't last long, did it? Good job I've got another one back at the house. Under lock and key, that one.'

'Or that I've got a team of good detectives. Take the weight off your pins and tell me what you've found. Apart from what would have been my supper,' she said with mock bitterness. She sat, clearly cautiously, and reached towards a pen and paper, which Tom passed her.

Mark tried not to sound reluctant. 'I'll just shove off and see if I can buy some sarnies or something.'

'I wouldn't bother, guv. OK, ex-guv. Not with the canteen the way it is. Truth is, Murray's disappeared into the same thin air as Livvie. He picked up his car, which he'd have known was under the gaze of the CCTV camera, and headed into the town. CCTV everywhere in Maidstone, of course. He parked in the Chequers Centre — made no attempt to conceal his face or anything — and spent half an hour milling round. At one point he bought a rucksack which he wore straightaway. More shops — Waterstones, Boots, average shopper stuff. The CCTV clocked him when he left the car park. Shopped at Sainsbury's — we've got all their footage and computerized till receipts. He bought a couple of ready-meals for two, not one. Best steak. Baking potatoes. Salad. Fruit. Three bottles of good Rioja. Fair Trade chocolate. All of this went into his rucksack. And he remembered to get his Nectar points.'

'Which suggests at least that he intended to live long enough to cash them in,' Mark observed.

'Then he drove to Maidstone East station, parked, and took a single ticket to London. St Pancras. And the single's the bit that worries me, guv.'

'Quite,' Fran agreed. 'And any CCTV sightings in London? Or at the Eurostar terminal?'

Tom grimaced. 'The funny thing is, while he was quite open in his movements down here, in London he managed to lose himself once he'd got off the train. No sightings at the Eurostar terminal yet.'

Mark said, 'But then, with all that food? And wine? If you're heading to France, why buy ready-made food?'

'Quite,' Tom agreed. 'Lastly, since he left Maidstone he's not used a cashpoint. Or his phone. Which I'd say is now probably in several pieces on the railway line.'

'It was a top of the range one too,' Fran mused. 'OK, I'll report on what you've done so far to the chief. I don't know how far he'll want this pursued: would he want the Met to know one of their own's become a loose cannon?'

'That sarnie, Fran — shall I go and get a few packs after all?' Tom asked.

'I'll come and help choose,' Mark agreed with alacrity.

She didn't argue. Wren absolutely wouldn't have wanted Mark to know anything about Tom's activities, and she — she preferred not to have conversations overheard and possibly misconstrued. At this level at least.

'News on Sean Murray, sir,' she said as soon as Wren picked up.

'I thought we agreed ten o'clock.' Perhaps the phone made him sound pettish.

'We did. But Tom Arkwright's gone as far as he can without assistance from the Met, sir. And I wouldn't let him seek that without your express permission.'

There was a very long pause. At last, Wren said slowly, as if he was still considering, 'Leave it with me. Where did this Arkwright — oh, he's your other temporary upgrading, isn't he? — lose Murray?'

'St Pancras. And there can't be stations with more CCTV coverage than that one.'

Another very long pause. This time she would swear she could hear the little wheels turning in his head. 'Are you sure that this Arkwright's checked everything?'

'There's no one I'd trust more,' she declared. 'Now, with respect, sir, Tom and I have both been working since six this morning. I'd like to send him home so he can come in fresh tomorrow — when the news of the skeletons might break.'

'Not if I have anything to do with it,' he said with surprising speed. 'I'll get on to the media myself. Though it may be too late,' he admitted, surprising her for a second time. Another pause. 'Any response to the Livvie appeal? I thought you did well there,' he added grudgingly.

'I'm just about to check, sir. And then, provided the CEOP team have everything under control, I shall go home too.'

'Oh.' He sounded genuinely surprised.

'But,' she added, hating herself for being so supine, 'I shall leave my phone on.'

'Very well. And report back to me on any Livvie developments. I need something to offer the media instead of the damned skeletons.'

* * *

'Leave it. Let it go to voicemail,' Mark said, as he was being signed out of the building. 'Oh, I knew you couldn't,' he added, as she reached for her phone. 'Pavlov's dogs, that's what we all are.'

'But this one's from Caffy,' she said, smiling, though she'd thought her face muscles would never work again.

He stood with his arm round her shoulders, and she moved the phone so he could hear too. Neither of them had time to argue with what Caffy proposed before she cut the call.

Each supporting the other, it seemed to her, they staggered to his car.

'She says she's bringing us food! I don't know whether to scream or to be grateful,' she managed, as she strapped herself in.

'I know. But she does need to return my watch — you never even noticed I wasn't wearing it, did you? Without her, we'd have had to get a takeaway. And the thought of Caffy delivering to our door what she calls iron rations — I'm salivating even to think of it.'

'Now who's a well-trained dog? Tell me about this watch of yours . . .'

* * *

'Fran: go and lie down,' Caffy greeted them as Mark opened their front door to her a mere minute after they'd arrived themselves. She carried two old-fashioned wicker baskets, their contents swathed in tea-towels. 'Mark, you can lie down too, or sit if you insist. If anyone knows her way around your kitchen, it's me — didn't I help design and install it? I'd give you a drink only you both look as if you'd fall asleep on me before you could eat, and alcohol's better with a bit of blotting paper. I'll wake you when everything's ready.' Caffy bustled off.

Neither argued. Neither slept either, for fear that a catnap would destroy their chances of dropping off later.

Within minutes, pâté and toast had appeared on the kitchen table, with a glass of wine apiece. The table was laid for two, the kitchen light glare reduced to candles.

'You're not joining us?' Fran expostulated.

'You don't want to talk to anyone, Fran, do you? Admit it. And in any case, I've got a date. Yes, the lunchtime guy, Mark. Would you mind if I kept your watch a bit longer?'

He grinned. 'Oh, this food was a bribe all along, was it?'

She responded. 'Or a thank you present, in advance. The pâté's home-made, so no E. coli or anything else nasty. Bread's some of Paula's best — she sends her love, by the way. Now, the casserole's in the oven with the potatoes alongside — I know they're only microwaved, but I'm crisping their jackets so you think they're the real thing. There's salad in the fridge. Cheese and biscuits ditto.' She whipped off an apron they'd not even registered. Dotting a kiss on first Mark's and then Fran's cheek, she was off. And back. 'Switch your phones off, please. Until you've eaten, at least.'

They heard the door close behind her. But even though she'd gone, they did as they were told. They didn't talk much: it was a companionable silence, though, she hoped, not one that suggested that his earlier unkindness had caused a major rift. They'd agreed, in any case, to forswear rifts: life was too fragile, too dependent on so many factors, to risk wasting a minute with a row. When they did make the effort to converse, pushing back from the table after the casserole and silently eschewing the cheese, they speculated mildly — they didn't have enough energy for wildly — about the new young man in Caffy's life, important enough for her to shed the watch they'd never seen her without.

'I've got it here,' Mark said, fishing in a pocket and laying it on the table.

'Pretty. But not exactly Caffy.'

'Which more or less describes the young man who gave it her, as I recall. I'd better put it in the safe.'

Was there a slight edge to his voice? There wasn't all that much in there, bar what little — but good — jewellery she'd acquired from time to time, mostly bought by herself for herself. There was also a very expensive watch, one his late wife had bought him not long before she'd died. Fran had only seen it a couple of times, and had never seen him wearing it. Assuming it had painful memories, when his old everyday one had abandoned any pretence at regular timekeeping, Fran herself had bought him the replacement Caffy was now wearing soon after they'd moved in together. She knew what he wanted — needed — to ask. But after their near-spat last night and again this morning, she knew he wouldn't want to risk hurting her, any more than she'd want to upset him. So she'd better say something herself.

'Sweetheart, I'm not going to be able to hurtle into Maidstone tomorrow, even less go to that nice shop in Canterbury. I know it might be a . . . a problem . . . that you might feel . . . but there is that other watch in the safe. The one Tina . . .'

She couldn't quite read his smile, though she did suspect there was a certain amount of relief mixed up with whatever else was there. 'The one I never wear? It's not . . . not actually a very good watch. I mean, she paid through the nose for it, and while she was alive I wore it. Of course I would. But it kept losing time. Or stopping. And when she died I went back to that old one, which you replaced. Do you remember afterwards? I thought you might! So I might have to wear Tina's for a few days and keep my fingers crossed it won't go wrong yet again. After that, I wondered about giving it to Dave, in trust for young Marco.'

She smiled. 'When you've had it repaired.'

He pulled himself to his feet, and kissed her hair. 'You finish your wine: I'll go and stow one watch and bring the other out. Anything you want while I'm there?'

'When all this is over, when I can think of putting on nice clothes and going out to the theatre and . . . doing things that merit a few diamonds . . . Leave everything where it is, will you?' And then — was it too late? Had his face fallen? — she remembered something. 'Except those lovely earrings you bought me in Paris. Just within the uniform code. I'd love to wear those again.'

CHAPTER FIFTEEN

'There's absolutely no need for you to get up too,' Fran insisted, as Mark struggled to a sitting position. 'One of the pleasures of a Sunday, remember — being able to lie in!'

'Not if you're offering the prayers of intercession at a nine-thirty service,' Mark said. 'Especially if you haven't written the prayers in question. I'd completely forgotten. I've asked Zac and Bethany to come along to the service, and then we — Zac and I — are going to knock up for half an hour.'

Despite herself Fran frowned. 'What'll the media make of that? Grieving father plays in sun?'

'They've got to find out first. The poor lad's stir-crazy — I think the FLO's more intrusive than she should be. And we thought that no one at the club would snitch if he got some air there. We can both change in the clubhouse.'

She nodded as she headed for the en suite. 'Actually that's quite a good idea from your point of view, too. There may be all sorts of rumours flying round after your encounter with the hyperactive arm of the law yesterday, and it'd be good to scotch them.'

He reached for the notepad that always lived beside the bedside phone and started to jot and cross out. In the old days, he'd been meticulous preparing official reports for his fellow senior police officers in ACPO; now he was addressing an even higher authority, he gave his words correspondingly more thought.

'You'll add one for Livvie, won't you?' Fran asked, emerging from the shower to find him still writing.

'And one for all of the team searching for her,' Mark affirmed, 'but not for the families of your skeletons — right? Unless the news breaks between now and nine-thirty?'

'Absolutely right. I just hope Wren's got more clout with the media than I suspect he has. Though I suppose he's done all right so far. Look, sweetheart — this tennis club business: are you sure about brazening things out?'

'Zac's idea, as it happens. He's going to meet me there. Fixed it last night while you were organizing that pink teddy bear.'

'Excellent. It's not just him trusting you but him showing the world he trusts you . . .'

'We've always got on well. And I think his going the extra mile might owe something to your getting that vile crap about him killing Livvie himself pulled off the internet. And after your bravura performance he's not going to pull out, is he? Heavens, is that the time?' He leapt out of bed and grabbed at clothes.

'No need to get dressed. I've decided today's the day I start driving again, and sod the medics.'

He shook his head. 'You can't. I mean, medically you probably could. But you've got to maintain your crutches charade for the media, haven't you? And before you go, you're having something in the way of breakfast or you can't take your painkillers. And I don't see you managing without those, do you? What we'll do is this: I'll drive and dictate the prayers for you to write down . . .'

* * *

To her amazement, since Wren wasn't known as an early riser, Fran was greeted on her arrival at work with a summons to the chief constable's office — the nest, as it was obviously going to be called.

He eyed her. 'I thought you were walking unaided, but now I notice that you still need elbow crutches some of the time,' he said, by way of greeting. The cup of coffee on his desk smelt exquisite. 'Have you cleared this with HR and the medics — insurance, of course?'

'The crutches? Never use them.'

'With due respect—'

'Sorry, sir. Of course, you saw them on TV. It was just that someone thought they would play well with the media out at the crime scene on Friday night, and I could hardly have staged an overnight recovery to manage without them for the press conference last night. I shall phase them out for the media, just as I did in real life. And I shall be delighted to do so — the angle they make me walk has really hurt my lower back.'

He surprised her again. 'Are you better sitting or standing?'

'Best lying flat on the floor, sir. But it's hard to maintain discipline from that position, isn't it?'

Lips compressed, he gestured her to sit.

'What sort of pressure did you put on Murray?'

She allowed herself not so much as a blink at the swift change of subject. 'The usual. No, actually it was slightly less than the usual. When I had to take time off after my accident, I got back to find that in my absence he had contrived to find an office some way away from mine.' She paused, but he didn't react. 'This meant that rather than simply pass jobs over to him, I often did things myself I'd normally have decanted straight away. But he did have to take on tasks like writing reports and minuting meetings to which he'd gone in my stead.' She patted her leg. 'All good preparation for the upgrading you agreed we could offer him.'

'Would you say he was bullied in any way? By his colleagues?'

She didn't think there was anything to gain from hinting that he wasn't the most popular in the team — well, not a team player at all, of course. 'To the best of my knowledge, no. He certainly said nothing to me. But, as I said, he actively chose an office as far from my base as he could — at least, that was how it appeared to me. I said nothing because to change what was by then a status quo would have made me appear more critical and carping than I actually am.' He didn't respond to her self-deprecating grimace. 'And it would have meant a further upheaval for the members of the secretariat, who've already had their working practices turned upside down and inside out.'

He leant forward almost confidentially. 'OK, that was your official response. The sort I'd expect. Off the record, I know you've got your ear closer to the ground than most. What rumours have you picked up?'

'Only those concerning the phone call that appeared to precipitate his departure. They involved anything from a demanding girlfriend upwards. But someone did note a call from a man, who was identified as Don Simpson.' This time he did pull a face. 'There will always be gossip that never reaches me because of what — rather than who, I hope — I am. My own feeling is that far from being cold and withdrawn, as some saw him, he was actually full of unexpressed anger. I was surprised he passed all the routine medical and psychological tests, to be honest.'

He looked taken aback, then ready to be outraged. 'But you said nothing?'

She spread her hands. 'He was your protégé, sir.' His face was almost carefully blank. She continued, 'I had — have! — no evidence of anything. I only intuited.'

'They say detective work is ninety per cent intuition and ten per cent evidence.'

'In the old days, maybe, sir,' she countered, thinking in any case that he was confusing the quotation with something about perspiration and inspiration. 'But with all today's technology—'

'Which still hasn't succeeded in tracking him down, Fran.' Wren did the most human thing she'd ever seen him do: put his head in his hands and tugged at his hair. Then he sat upright, and changed gear. 'Very well, any news on either of our other major investigations?'

'CEOP's Missing, Abducted and Trafficked Children Unit, in conjunction with our own team, are working their socks off to establish the identity of a horse two new witnesses now believe might have been present at the crime scene. As a matter of fact, that confirms something Mark suggested.' Wrong!

'I want him kept well away from all this, remember.'

She shook her head. 'It was he whom the witnesses approached, sir. He immediately directed them to Ray Barlow, who came and met them and did the necessary — by the book, of course. Parents in attendance, everything.'

'Why on earth did they approach Mark? And where, for God's sake?'

'At the tennis club, sir,' she said, wide-eyed with innocence.

'What the hell was he doing there?'

'Playing tennis.'

'That's preposterous!'

She almost choked: she would have expected the old chief constable to have used such a word, but not Mr Modernity here. 'Why would you think that, sir? He's not a police officer any more. Just Joe Public, who happens to have done us a favour by alerting us so early to Livvie's disappearance. Zac's been coaching him for months, as I've told you. They're good friends.' Perhaps now wasn't the moment to tell him that within two hours Zac and he would be seen playing together. And she certainly hoped Ray would keep his mouth firmly zipped about yesterday's paedophile moment. Ninety-nine per cent of her colleagues would laugh their socks off. Wren would see it as an incident with potential repercussions.

'I thought you might have suggested some restraint was in order. I was clearly mistaken.' He paused for a few moments, perhaps waiting for a contrite apology, which he did not get. 'Now, the youth centre skeletons. What progress can you report there?'

'Very little. We've allocated some staffing to see if our prime suspect may have committed any other murders in towns where he also worked; he himself is dead.' Something started to fizz in her brain. She raised a hand, either to stop him speaking or like a schoolchild asking permission to leave a classroom. 'Sir, you spoke earlier about police intuition. Can you spare me — I'll get back to you the moment I can.' She didn't wait to hear his permission or otherwise.

* * *

She'd more or less instructed the team working on the Ashford skeletons to stand down over the weekend, but wasn't surprised — or in any way displeased — to find several of them at their desks. Madge Stewart, halfway through a huge muffin, was so engrossed in what she was looking at on her computer that she didn't clock Fran's presence until Fran coughed gently.

'No, don't get up. You're not officially here, are you, Madge, any more than I am. What I want is the pictures of all the kids who disappeared. One of them, at least. Christopher thingy.'

'Christopher Manton, ma'am?'

'That's him. The scary one.' She almost tore the photo out of the younger woman's hand. 'Thanks. Sign this out for me, would you? Thanks. Back as soon as poss . . .'

* * *

'I want your permission to do something very sensitive, sir,' Fran said, once more in Wren's office. 'You may not like it, but I think it's necessary.'

He nodded. She was to continue speaking.

She laid the photo of Manton on his desk. 'Do you recognize this young man, sir?'

'No. Why should I? Wait a moment, he does look familiar. No, I'm imagining it.' All the same, he lifted it and turned it one way and another again.

'I'd like your permission to get the boffins to compare this with another photograph, sir.'

Wren froze. 'Why would you need my permission to do that?'

'Because it would be one of Sean Murray. To see if they're one and the same person.' She touched the photo. 'This boy was one of the kids involved in the Ashford youth club project. Christopher Manton. And it matters because if Malcolm Perkins doesn't seem to have killed anyone else, our other suspect is Christopher Manton. The other kids, some of whom were reportedly scared of him, said he was idle, both on the football pitch and on the site before he disappeared — which is what a lot of other people did from there, of course, so I'm not jumping to any conclusions. If he's Sean Murray, then he can't have been a victim, can he? But it's just — just — conceivable that he was the killer. Who somehow or other took on a new identity, got qualifications and joined the Met.' She interrupted herself, speaking slowly: 'It does seem a big leap, from a fully signed up dosser to someone with three A levels, a degree, a postgraduate qualification . . . What would change one's motivation so much?'

Wren's face was a study in incomprehension: clearly he'd always been highly motivated.

'Love? Religion?' she persisted. 'So he joined the Met and came to us — and then ran away the moment he heard Don Simpson telling him that human remains had been discovered.'

He never had much colour, but now he was ashen. 'You're saying that Sean Murray could be a mass murderer?'

'I'd rather say I'd like to eliminate that as a reason for him to disappear off the face of the earth,' she said steadily. And, as it happened, truthfully.

Fingers so tightly interlaced that the knuckles gleamed white against the purpling flesh, he stared at the desk. Then he looked her straight in the eye. 'Do it. You have my official permission. But if any word of this gets out—' He was about to bluster threats he almost certainly wouldn't be able to fulfil.

'It won't, sir,' she said curtly, and left the room.

CHAPTER SIXTEEN

'Start low, finish high! Come on, Mark, take that right hand up higher. Think Excalibur! You're leading a charge!' For the moment, for no matter how short a moment, Zac seemed to have forgotten his pain by concentrating fully on the coaching session.

As for himself, Mark had never worked harder on his backhand. He started low and finished high as if his life depended on it — more, as if Livvie's life depended on it. He wasn't so engaged, however, that he was unaware his presence was causing comment, if not some consternation. News of yesterday's incident had clearly got around. Perhaps it had been a mistake to come here after church, but, as he'd told Fran, it had been Zac's idea. He was glad he'd included the whole family in the prayers of intercession he'd said earlier. Zac and Bethany, who were christening, Christmas and Easter churchgoers — heavens, was Easter only last week? — had arrived a little late and flustered, with young Jack clutching a cuddly dinosaur, of all things, and although they were a different generation from the elderly congregation, they must have felt the glow of sympathy that enfolded them.

Casually Zac called him to the net, as if to demonstrate a bit of technique that he'd missed. 'Are those guys planning to set up a lynch mob?' he asked, pointing to the centre of his racquet head, but indicating with pointed glance an animated group of young men.

'You might have to cut me down from the hanging tree,' Mark said, not quite joking.

'There was some kid over by your car. Tell you what, I'll stroll over as if I'm getting something out of my boot. I'll see what he's up to. And you can work on your serve. Remember what I said about taking the ball as high in the air as you can reach?' He jogged briskly from the court, as if heading for his car, but swerving at the last moment and disappearing from view with a huge bellow of rage. The players stampeded towards the source of the noise. Mark abandoned all pretence of trying to achieve topspin and joined them.

Zac had the junior captain pinned against the side of someone's Chelsea tractor — with luck, the young man's own, since all he would be able to see was his face getting nearer and nearer the paintwork, which was nicely smudged where his sweaty face repeatedly hit it. Any moment now the sweat would be diluted by blood: the thuds of flesh and bone against metal were getting decidedly louder.

'Hold it, Zac.' Once he'd used that voice to carry across a swarm of hooligans. And here it was again, surprising everyone, not least himself. 'Zac, stop. It won't bring finding Livvie any closer. Zac, I said stop it.' The poor bugger's rage and terror, all those hours of viciously painful and frustrating waiting needed to be vented somehow, but not like this. 'Grab him, for Christ's sake!' The tall guys who'd guarded Mark himself the previous day obliged.

Mark had a chance to glance at his Audi. It now wore the legend PEDAPHIL SCUM scratched into the side — it looked like a bunch of keys job.

At last Zac turned sobbing from his target. Mark shoved his way through the melee to gather him up into his arms, as he'd held Dave when Tina had died. If only Fran were here — she'd know what to do or say. Over Zac's shoulder, he projected his voice again. 'Some of you know there was trouble here yesterday. Some of you may know what it was, and why. Whatever your own feelings about my playing here today, for God's sake consider Zac's. Does he need this sort of shindig? Use your heads, for heaven's sake.'

There was muttering. He'd no idea how things might go. But at last the A team captain, a young man whom Mark had only met a couple of times, since their games were literally leagues apart, caught Mark's eye, as if wanting permission to say something.

He coughed: speechifying was clearly not his thing. 'Harry Mansfield, sir.'

Expected to smile and nod in acknowledgement, Mark obliged. He tried not to show how tickled he was by the courtesy, which reminded him of Marco, always being far more polite with his *Sirs* and *Ma'ams* than any English boy.

Mansfield cleared his throat again. 'If Zac wants you here, sir, we want you here. And we don't want little shits like Toby around the place. Mark, I give you my word that that damage will be sorted. I'll talk to Toby's dad about paying. If he doesn't come up with the goods, the club will.' Reddening to the ears, he shoved towards the two men and held out a conciliatory hand.

Someone started to clap. Mark held his breath. Would the pace increase to real applause or continue to sound as if he was being given the bird?

Zac pulled away, his face still working. Then he actively man-hugged Mark. The clapping was definitely applause.

Mark blushed. 'Look, we're still looking for that poor child.' Damn, that slip of the tongue again! 'Like I said in church this morning, the police need information, any tiny snippet, some scrap of what could be nonsense. Yesterday afternoon those girls came up with what may well be a real gem, though they were almost too embarrassed to mention it. Please, search your memories. I know you're not Golden Oldies, but something might have occurred on Sundays just like this one that might have struck you as odd but without a context meant nothing at all. I've already put the senior investigating officer's contact details on the noticeboard. Please — copy them down and use them, whatever time of night or day anything occurs to you.'

'There was a rumour about horses,' a woman with a Sloane Ranger voice said.

'There still is. And we — *the police* — would be more than grateful if you would check any stabling to which you have access. As I told the girls yesterday, it's not grassing someone up. It's literally helping the police with their enquiries. It could be the difference between a life saved and a life lost. Livvie's life saved and Livvie's life lost.' He'd hoped to use that as an exit line, not to resume his coaching session but to go and retrieve his things and head home in the scarred Audi.

'What about search parties? The villagers helped in that case in North Wales, didn't they?' Sloane Ranger continued. 'I know most of us are weekenders, but that doesn't mean we can't help.'

It was hardly the spontaneous upsurge of community spirit the police might have hoped for, but it was an offer, and would do poor Zac no harm.

'Of course it doesn't. But I'm only a club member like yourself. The person to contact is DCI Ray Barlow. He'll know about search teams.'

'What about that woman who was on TV last night? She looked as if she'd got her head screwed on.'

That's no woman; that's my fiancée. 'Detective Chief Superintendent Harman?' Who would welcome an uncoordinated barrage of well-meaning offers like a hole in the head. 'She's in overall charge of the Kent team, which is working alongside a unit from a national police organization called CEOP. But Ray Barlow's your man. He was the one who came out here yesterday to talk to Flora and Emily. He'll know which of his team is organizing search parties. For Zac's sake, for Livvie's sake, please do all you can.' Another exit line, surely to God.

'So what would your advice be?' The same woman.

He smiled at her. 'Get the names of everyone here prepared to make up a search team. Or who can offer other skills.' If only one of them could pilot a chopper with thermal imaging equipment. 'Do it straight away, and then call Ray. The sooner the better, I promise you.'

He and Zac withdrew to the sidelines. 'Thanks for saving my bacon, not to mention the poor old motor.'

'Bastard. Yeah, it was touch and go.'

'Do you think this lot'll be able to organize themselves?'

'Dot, the one who spoke: she's a barrister. Saul over there is a brain surgeon. Sadie works as a dinner lady. Alastair's a civil servant.'

'I'd back Sadie,' Mark said. 'Look, you should be back home with Bethany and Jack.'

'Not to mention Ermintrude,' Zac said, with the nearest thing to a smile Mark had seen from him for days.

'Ermintrude?'

'The family liaison officer. It's her smile. Always there. Just like the cow's on *Magic Roundabout*. Not that she's a cow in any other sense. Nice woman. Emma Poole. But I shall be so glad to see the back of her.'

'The moment Livvie's back, you will. No, actually, she may hang on a bit longer to keep the media at bay, of course. But you should be getting back home anyway.' He flicked a look at his watch — Tina's watch. It had stopped. 'Must be almost lunchtime — don't want to miss your Sunday roast.'

'Come too. Beth always cooks too much. Likes bubble and squeak the next day.'

'Zac, I'd love to. But you know that the media are watching your place like hawks. What rubbish would they make of me popping into your house?' He slapped him on the arm. 'Home, Zac — for Bethany and Jack's sake.'

As he waved him off he couldn't resist drifting towards the knot of players, all, it seemed, talking and gesticulating at once. Of its own accord, his thumb found Ray's phone number. He explained briefly what was going on, was passed to a CEOP man, Sergeant Terry, who was running the search today.

'After yesterday, I don't want to be an intermediary,' he said.

'Fair dos. Put me on to their leader.'

He handed his phone to Sadie.

* * *

Sitting at her desk biting a knuckle didn't seem very useful, so Fran lay down on the floor and bit the knuckle instead. She really did not want Sean Murray to be a killer, reformed, presumably, or otherwise. Ought she to contact Tom to see if there was any trace of him yet? No, that was Met business, thanks to Wren. What about the locations where Malcolm Perkins had worked? Was it too early to chase the officers who were looking into possible incidents in West Bromwich, say, or Stoke or Taunton? Probably: after all, they were supposed to be working the minimum of overtime.

What she really, really wanted to do was check with the technical team. She wanted news of the photo. After lunch, the young woman had said. In other words, join the queue, which she'd explained was longer on Sundays because there was only, of course, a skeleton staff. Pause for ghoulish laughter.

Fran had a brief, nostalgic yearning for — could almost taste! — a good old-fashioned Sunday lunch. The sort her mother had cooked, with the meat roasted in too hot an oven, so it was always cremated outside and bloody inside.

One day, one summer's day, she ought to go up to Scotland to see her mother. Her sister said she was still her old self. Which meant that Fran was hardly overflowing with enthusiasm for making the journey.

The phone rang. It took painful moments to lever herself up, but she reached the phone before the line died.

'Ray Barlow, Fran. Mark's visit to the tennis club.'

Her stomach clenched. 'What went wrong?'

'Oh, someone vandalized his car, but apparently the club are picking up the bill for that.' Ray sounded very offhand.

'But Mark — is he all right?'

'Why shouldn't he be? Anyway, the incident elicited a lot of support for Zac, which Mark naturally put to good use: he rounded up all the Sunday crowd, which is apparently quite different from the weekday players, and got them involved. You might want to come along to the next briefing and hear all about it.'

Might indeed. If she wasn't very careful, she'd defuse her anxiety for Mark by losing her temper with the messenger. But she couldn't completely rein in her sarcasm. 'Were you by any stretch of the imagination expecting me not to be at the briefing, Ray? Good. I might be doddery but I'm not senile yet, thank you very much.'

'No, guv. Mark'll be there, by the way.'

'And I rather think I ought to hear of any new developments before the briefing, don't you? The phone'll do. Sod it, there's someone knocking at my door.' Time to get off her high horse. 'See you at the briefing, Ray. Come on in!'

The door inched open, to reveal the face of the young technical support officer to whom she'd entrusted the two photos. Perhaps she'd laid on the need for absolute discretion a bit too thick: the girl, who might have been twelve, no more than thirteen, looked terrified. But at least she was wearing her ID; Fran could greet her by name.

'Micki! Come along in. I was just on my way to see you.'

'Ma'am, I've done the work you asked. Only took a moment when I got to it.'

Fran opened her mouth to snarl. Hadn't she asked for it to be given absolute priority? But then, she probably wasn't the only officer with urgent demands, and after lunch was the time Micki had given. She transformed the snarl into a weary smile. 'Thanks, Micki. Is that a written report? Excellent. But sum it up in a word for me: are the photos of the same person?'

* * *

There was no reply when she knocked on Wren's door. His phone was switched to voicemail, but she felt the most revealing message she could leave was one simply asking him to call her as soon as he could. She sent a similar text. And then she did the only thing she could: she staggered back to her office and lay down on the floor, carefully setting her phone to give her an alarm call. Not that there was any need to. There were some occasions when you couldn't switch off your brain and this was one of them.

CHAPTER SEVENTEEN

Although she was laughing as she came into the room for the six o'clock briefing, Mark had rarely seen Fran look so tired. Not so much tired as old: this was how she'd look in ten years' time. The strong sunlight angling across her face didn't help, of course: it was no wonder that celebs of her age were always lit full face, much kinder to wrinkles active or latent. Then she spotted him, lurking amongst Ray's team, and her smile blew him away all over again. It was all he could do not to go across and wrap her protectively in his arms. But, as she valiantly pulled herself upright and squared her shoulders, he knew she'd hate that. She was here to do a job and nothing would stop her, bar an earthquake or a lightning bolt.

There was a little courtesy tussle: who would lead? Ed Chatfield, the CEOP super, gestured to Ray, who looked under his brows at Fran. Nodding and smiling at Ray encouragingly, she leant back in her chair, folding her arms, like a casting director not expecting to be entertained but hoping nonetheless.

'First of all, we have a development from the tennis club. A different group of players,' Ray explained. If only someone would take him to one side and teach him how to present information coherently to a large group. He was fine one-to-one, but this was all over the place. 'Some of them confirmed actual sightings of a horse. And suspicions that the rider might have been stopping to perv at the players — at least, that's what one or two of the women allege. The men just thought they had an audience, and probably raised their game accordingly. The horse in question is confirmed as being large and black. All over. And no, we don't know what name it answers to,' he added, sliding his eyes in Fran's direction.

'Not Snowflake?' she obliged, scratching her head like the class dunce. 'Or was it Snowdrop?'

'Not even Snowstorm. As to the rider, he was wearing a helmet, so any description is bound to be vague. But one of the men — Harry Mansfield, who's the A team captain — says he's sure he's come across him in the park and been reprimanded by him for not getting off his bike quickly enough. Which would suggest that it might be our friend Ross Thwaite.' He said the name with the flourish of someone who has laboured long and hard to tug a recalcitrant rabbit out of a particularly tight hat, and considers he has earned the ensuing gasp of admiring applause.

Probably most of the team were simply too tired to react with much more than relief.

With a final burst of bravado, Ray asked, 'So when do we pick him up?'

The CEOP super put out a warning hand. 'I don't know much about gee-gees, Ray, but I do know it's not a crime to own more than one.'

Ray stuck to his guns, probably unwisely. 'On the other hand, it wasn't particularly helpful of Thwaite to let us assume he only had that dear little Snowdrop in his stable. He's got stuff to explain.'

Mark knew who his money was on in the debate; the only question was how Fran would handle the issue.

'What do the rest of you think?' she mused slowly, as if they were all equals. 'Is this the best moment? If he really has abducted Livvie, you know, I'd like to find her before we interfere with his movements in any way. There's no point in having him in for questioning if he's going to clam up and refuse to tell us her whereabouts. It has been known.'

There was a short silence: they could all think of cases where their colleagues had nailed an abductor, but not found the victim till too late.

Ray shook his head. 'And risk losing him? No, let's get him.'

'Put him under surveillance,' Chatfield overrode him. 'Make sure we know to the inch where he is by night and day.'

Fran nodded. 'But we do it with the maximum of discretion. And maybe even mislead him a little, though that might of course be against his human rights,' she added ironically. 'How about the next media update suggests we're working with our colleagues in Europol? Which has the benefit of being true,' she added, with a limpid glance first at Mark then at Ray. 'But, as Ed says, we want every sneeze, every scratch of his head recorded. If he sleepwalks, we want to know if he raids his fridge and what he takes out of it. Understood?' It was clear that everyone understood: people tended to when Fran spoke in that voice. Belatedly she turned to the CEOP super. 'Sorry, Ed. Is that how you'd want it done? I keep forgetting this is supposed to be a shared enquiry. With your team doing the lion's share just now,' she added with a disarming grin.

'No problem. We're in total agreement here, Fran.' Was there a slight emphasis on the pronoun that Ray would pick up as a rebuke or a slight? Perhaps. 'In this case the victim's safety — assuming the poor child is still alive — must be paramount.'

Poor Ray: he took it as a public bollocking. But he was wrong, the others right, surely to goodness. Mark wished he could find some way to limit his loss of face. Perhaps he could. Even if it meant drawing attention to himself. 'By the way,' he said, 'some of the tennis players Ray was talking about have set up a collection for a reward for information received. They've already got quite a large sum pledged.'

He tried desperately — and at last succeeded — in catching Ray's eye. He willed him to pick up the idea and run with it.

'Thanks, Mark, for that and for all you did this morning.' He took a minute to brief the rest of the team, who clearly did not like one of their own — even an ex one of their own — being treated so badly. 'Guv'nor, how would you feel about leading on that at the press conference? Especially as it was Mark who was instrumental in getting them on side.' He rightly looked at Chatfield, but was no doubt desperate for Fran's backing. And was going the wrong way about getting it.

Bother protocol. Mark spoke up again. 'I'd rather you kept my name out of it, if you can. Internal politics, Chatfield, as I'm sure you've heard.' He caught Fran's eye. If Wren had vetoed Mark's appearance at a press conference once, as sure as hell he wouldn't like the idea a second time, even if it was just as a bit player, or a passing reference. Which it probably wouldn't be: he'd bet some reporter or other would want to ask searching questions about an ex-ACC's involvement. He would, in their position. 'Personally,' he continued slowly, 'I think it might have more resonance if the Sunday players were said to have responded directly to Zac's grief and distress when he turned up to work. They made the point that they wouldn't be much use in local searches, but did have other resources. And yes, Ray,' he added with a swift, comradely smile, 'it was Sadie who suggested they raise a reward.'

'The dinner lady,' Ray explained. 'If you don't have much money I guess you're more likely to know its value than if you've got loads. Will you mention the other horse, guv'nor? At all?'

Chatfield and Fran exchanged a glance. 'Let's just go with the French connection and the reward.'

'Agreed,' she said. 'Ladies and gentlemen, it's over to you for this one. Unless I hear from you, I'll see you all bright and early in the morning.'

Even as she left the room she was checking her phone. That wasn't like her at all, any more than her abrupt exit was.

Mark followed at a discreet distance, so there was no question of him listening in if she were on a confidential call. But she shoved it back in her pocket with obvious exasperation and turned to him, putting her hand on his. 'Are you sure you're all right? All that stuff about your car? They didn't have a go at you as well, did they?'

'For a moment it was touch and go — I think it could have gone either way. But in the end they did what Ray said they did: they came to my rescue and promised to deal with the damage. The car's tucked up in the garage at the moment: I didn't fancy everyone in Maidstone getting an eyeful of the graffiti. In any case, it was time yours had an outing. Are you ready to come home? There's plenty of Caffy's casserole left, remember. And I promise not to ask what's troubling you at the moment — which has nothing to do with the Livvie case, I gather.'

'You gather right. And I truly can't say anything. Except yes to the lift and yes to the casserole. Hey, is it warm enough to have a drink on the terrace?'

He shook his head reluctantly. 'The sun's been wonderful, as you probably didn't even have time to notice, but there's been a strong breeze all day, and now there's quite a nip in the air. I'd recommend a nice hot bath while I reheat the food. And a gin and tonic while you soak.'

'Sounds like bliss,' she declared.

But it didn't sound as if her heart was in it.

* * *

Fran had still had no response from Wren by the time the alarm clock rang the next morning. Since Mark didn't so much as stir, she tiptoed around in the hope that he'd sleep on: it must be safe for her to drive after all this time. But as she munched her muesli, he appeared, fully dressed if fashionably unshaven. Then he insisted on driving her in.

'I'm worried about that repair to your car,' she said, as he set off carefully through thick mist. 'You only want one person in the body shop or whatever it's called to tell his mates and it'll be all over the press, willy-nilly. Mud sticks. So do scratches.'

'Quite. I'd thought of that. So did Harry Mansfield. He texted last night to say he's going to make the damage far worse with some piece of farm machinery, so no one can read the letters. And the lad who did it is going to pay for the whole lot — him, or as seems more likely, his dad. Don't worry about it. It's a car. Full-stop. And you can't say you don't have other things to worry about.'

She took his hand and squeezed it. 'I'll tell you — all this stuff — as soon as I can. Thanks for not asking.'

As she let herself into the building, she checked the car park. No, no sign of Wren's car. Half of her wasn't surprised: it was unlike him to be in so early. On the other hand, most bosses, faced with at least two crises, and bombarded with the number of messages she had sent, would have been waiting on the threshold like a Victorian father, timepiece in hand, ready to confront a tardy son or daughter.

She'd no sooner switched on her kettle, however, than a text arrived. Tom. Telling her to take a casual stroll past the CID offices and keep her eyes open. A text? Tom? Not his usual modus operandi.

But stroll she did, and her eyes weren't just open but agog by the time she'd finished.

She didn't think it was necessary to knock as she walked into Sean Murray's goldfish bowl.

'DCI Murray. My office, now.' She added, 'We won't have the conversation I intend to have here, in case your colleagues can lip-read.' Turning on her heel, she strode off, yes, the old Fran stride, she noted triumphantly, even as another part of her brain was wondering what on earth to say. Correction: she had so much to say she didn't know where to start.

At least he had the nous not to try to fall into step with her, or, worse still, to try to engage her in conversation. However, as she turned to face him in her office, and nodded at him to close the door, she got the impression that he was at least as angry with her as she was with him.

She sat. She toyed with the idea of making him stand, but thought that it would be petty — too like a Wren move. So she nodded at a chair. Her hospitality didn't extend to offering him coffee, however, though she sipped at her half-cold mug.

She decided to resort to the interviewing method she'd used when dealing with low-life criminals: start with small, manageable accusations, and move up to the serious matters that really needed to be examined. Like, in his case, being someone other than he was claiming to be, and, perhaps, being a murderer. Mass murderer.

'How are you getting on with the files I asked you to check?'

'No pattern has yet emerged in the care home deaths. After all, you'd expect a few deaths amongst wrinklies, wouldn't you?' He ignored the height to which her eyebrows had risen and ploughed on. 'Come on, I'd have thought this was more a job for a bog-standard DC.'

'What a shame they're all engaged in work on an active case, which meant leave was cancelled and your colleagues were working double shifts. A case I'd have wanted you to work on, given your expertise and experience. And the fact that the head of MIT, Don Simpson, personally invited you down to see the scene and assist him in what promises to be a very complex enquiry — just the sort of case on which an officer with your record and potential would have been expected to shine.' She paused, not just for breath, but to give him time to respond.

He did, but only with what her dear old sergeant in her salad days would have called dumb insolence.

'You made a trivial — and as it turns out — spurious excuse and quit the premises as soon as you took the call, although you knew that MIT was short-staffed and must have suspected that all leave would be cancelled. Your phone was switched off and you didn't respond to my calls.'

'Not exactly a hanging offence.'

'Not exactly a hanging offence, *ma'am*,' she snarled, she who cared little more than a snap of the fingers about rank. 'For God's sake, Sean, I was calling to offer you a career-changing promotion — only temporary, but to detective superintendent. And you didn't return my calls.' She thought that had penetrated his carapace, but still he said nothing. 'There was so much concern for you — were you having some sort of temporary breakdown? — that we then wasted valuable time and resources trying to locate you.'

'You mean check up on me? How dare you? I was taking quite legitimate Time Off in Lieu.'

'But you hadn't cleared it with me.'

'Because you aren't my line manager. Ma'am.'

'Not yet. But you hadn't cleared it with your Met line-manager, either. Don't look so shocked. We have such things as phones, Sean. From lucrative and prestigious promotion to a disciplinary, I'd have thought. What a waste.' As she geared herself up for the next stage of her tirade, the internal phone rang: Wren's line.

'Your messages, Harman?'

'May be redundant, sir. Some of them. But I believe we need to have a very urgent conversation, sir. Before or after the rest of the one I'm currently having with DCI Sean Murray.' She eyed him coldly. Eventually he had the grace to drop his eyes.

'Murray! I was just going to tell you that we can stand down the search for him,' he declared. 'My contact in the Met has located him. Even as we speak he's probably on the train back here. I've made clear to my contact that I'm far from happy with his gross violation of discipline, and that I want him under my jurisdiction in future. So as and when he returns, send him directly to me. I may, of course, have to consider the temporary promotion you wanted to offer him.'

There was no point in correcting his use of pronouns. She had something more important to say. 'I would be delighted to discuss that with you. Meanwhile DCI Murray is here in my office.'

‘Send him to me.’

‘With respect, sir, I would prefer to have a confidential conversation with you myself before he is involved. And furthermore I would like you to take measures to ensure he stays on the premises, preferably incommunicado, while that conversation takes place.’

Murray was on his feet.

So was she. She held the handset away from her mouth, but Wren would almost certainly hear her as she barked, ‘Sit down. You know running will only harm your case. I said sit. Now. And make yourself familiar with those files.’ She pointed to a pile in the corner: let his back and legs deal with the tottering and undistinguished heap. ‘We’ll discuss the contents when I return.’

* * *

She was still shaking with fury when she presented herself in Wren’s office, moments later. He took a swift look at her, told her to sit and produced, wonder of wonders, a cup of coffee.

‘We have problems?’ he asked, also sitting down, but behind his desk. In his place, she’d have pulled her chair round to a less formal position, but that was Wren for you.

‘We do indeed. Thank you.’ Perhaps he thought she was expressing gratitude for the excellent coffee; in fact, she was acknowledging the change of pronoun. *We* was a hundred times better than *you*. She kept the word in play. ‘We actually have more than we expected. A DCI going AWOL is one thing; a DCI changing his identity is another.’

‘Changing—’

‘You’ll recall that I asked you to authorize the comparison of two photographs? Here is the report.’ She laid it on his desk. ‘The evidence suggests that Christopher Manton and Sean Murray are one and the same. I’ve not yet had time to check the possibilities of an official change of name by deed poll — it struck me as almost an irrelevance at the time — but I should imagine it won't take long. Probably the Met noted it and forgot all about it when they lent him to us. What matters far more is that in the Ashford case—'

'The skeletons in the youth club?'

'Exactly. We have two main suspects. By far the stronger is the youth worker, Malcolm Perkins; the other is Christopher Manton. Perkins is dead, that's for certain, but I have officers checking possible activities in the other towns where he worked. On the other hand, assuming my suspicions are correct, Manton is here. In fact, it is just possible that we have to arrest him on suspicion of the murder of at least eight young adults, currently being identified.'

'And you realize the implications of that?' He looked more troubled than she'd imagined he could.

'On him? On us? On the media embargo? On the ongoing publicity for the Livvie case? I do indeed, sir. The last thing we wanted was to have to go public now with the Ashford case but if there's the remotest chance of this getting out—'

The phone rang. 'Ah, that'll be the Home Office. Nothing to do with this case. But I have to take it. We'll continue this in half an hour or so. Meanwhile, get everything out of him that you can. Informally if possible, Fran.'

Fran, eh? Any moment now they'd be best buddies. Or not.

CHAPTER EIGHTEEN

As she returned from Wren's office she intercepted Tom Arkwright, just about to make his breezy way into her room. He always knocked, of course, but increasingly his tap was perfunctory and he would pop his head in simultaneously. Today she would have to freeze him out, having a conversation in the corridor.

'Morning, guv. I've got a bit of news for you. Not about Murray.' He registered her frown and the lack of invitation. 'I guess I'm not allowed to talk about that, am I?'

'No. And I'm afraid I'm flat out just now — rush job for the boss, Tom.' Which had the virtue of being true. Almost. Even though he didn't seem to expect frankness, she hated fobbing him off. She just hoped no one else had clocked Murray's early appearance. She made an effort. 'Do I gather you were working yesterday, despite what I said?'

Tom clearly picked up on something in her manner, but continued, 'Well, I always was a bit pig-headed, according to my auntie. So, yesterday I joined in with the little team checking on yon Malcolm Perkins.'

'As anyone would, if they were bored. Unless the sun was shining and they should be enjoying life while they're young. Oh, Tom . . . Very well. Bollocking over. Not that

I meant too much of it, except the bit about the sun. We should have been breathing in fresh air, getting some dear old vitamin D for free.' Her sigh was genuine.

'Sunshine or not, I found stuff I wanted to tell you first. Only to find you'd just gone home.'

'In other words, you were working till well after eight o'clock.' She shook her head sadly. 'And you didn't phone?'

He pulled a face. 'I reckoned if you'd called it a day, it was only because you were dead on your feet.' They exchanged an understanding smile. No one else would have dared say anything like that, and they both knew it. 'In any case, a mate was on to me for a couple of jars and a game of pool. No vitamin D in pub lighting, I'm afraid.'

'Too true. OK, what did you find?' She shook her head. 'No, tell you what, give me half an hour — maybe forty minutes — and then come back. With cake, if possible,' she added with what she hoped was her usual grin.

He looked at her steadily. 'Fair enough, guv. Though I'd say it was right important.'

'Half an hour, Tom?' But Tom never exaggerated. 'OK, if you don't need fresh air and birdsong, I do. We'll talk outside now. I'll just get my jacket.' And make sure Murray was working his socks off.

* * *

'West Bromwich is the most interesting,' Tom declared, turning his face to the sun and closing his eyes against the glare.

She did likewise. 'I bet that's the first time anyone's ever said that!'

'Unless you're a Baggies supporter, that is,' he said, picking up her change of mood.

'Or you're a fan of the M5.'

'Or interested in the activities of Malcolm Perkins. Now, just as you can't get much more rural than Kent, so it's hard to find anywhere nearer the industrial heartland of England.'

She must show interest, not relief. 'That might be a euphemism, young Tom. Or an oxymoron.'

He bridled. He must have misheard.

'*Oxy*moron,' she repeated. 'Figure of speech, meaning contradiction in terms. I'm not suggesting you're an idiot.' She started to walk: good physio for the leg, after all, which was always frighteningly stiff in the morning.

He fell into step beside her. 'I like a bit of industry, myself. It's not all *Last of the Summer Wine* and cricket up my way, Fran. A few mills, the odd canal — that's me happy. They call them cuts in the Midlands, did you know that? And there's some town up there says it's got more canals than Venice.' His face might have been as straight as a pallbearer's, but his eyes were twinkling.

So were hers. 'OK, spare me the *Rough Guide.* What's Perkins been doing in West Bromwich?'

'Youth work, as you'd expect. Particular speciality, the school drop-outs, the NEETs and so on. All the same, he doesn't stay long at Sandwell — that's the council that runs West Brom and a few other towns—'

She raised a finger. 'Also spare me the administrative details.'

He put on his pained expression: Eeyore without his tail. 'Just a couple of years, and he's off. Career path, they call it, don't they, going from one employer to another. Not like us in the police. Any road, during his period in West Brom, West Midlands Police have to register quite a number of mispers. As you'd expect: poverty, job market poor, lots of cuts to jump in. Sorry, Fran — but you should see your face when I wind you up.'

'To use your strange lingo, any road,' she prompted.

'I believe,' Tom said primly, 'that they actually say, *any road up* in the Black Country — which is the generic name for — OK, OK! No fewer than five of these mispers disappeared while they were supposed to be attending one of Perkins' schemes. Like in Ashford, they were all dossers and no-hopers anyway, to use the highly technical language of my contact up in Sandwell. So no one takes any more notice than they should. But I tell you what, Fran, it's all systems go up there now.'

'And in Taunton and Stoke-on-Trent, I should imagine.'

'Which my gran always used to call Smoke-on-Stench. I don't know about Taunton and Stoke, because I wasn't working on them, and I didn't want to tread on anyone's toes.'

'You've done enough work for three here. You know that. All incredibly valuable stuff. I'm proud of you, Tom. Well done. Meanwhile,' she added ruefully, 'your TOIL must amount to several weeks, by now. Where are you going to spend it all? South of France?'

'South Yorkshire, more like. Or Tunbridge Wells, swanning round with my new rank. My housemates are asking when I'm moving out. But I'd rather stay where I am. I think.'

She looked at him shrewdly. 'You're as overtired as I am, Tom, and that won't do for a brand-new inspector going into a brand-new job. Soon as this is over, I really want you to take some of this time off. Get some rest. Spend time with your mates. Get yourself a girlfriend for me to gossip about.'

He grinned. 'You sound just like my auntie. Thing is, Fran, attitudes to settling down and such are different these days. People meet later, settle down later—'

'And the women leave it so late to have babies they need IVF. I know, Tom, I know. But you could buck the trend. Think on it, as your auntie might say. Now, what time are your mates investigating Taunton and Stoke-on-Trent likely to come in?'

'They both said eight at the latest.'

'Excellent. The sooner we can pull all this in the better: we've got parents to face, not to mention the media.' And Sean Murray to let off the hook. Angry and insolent and disobedient he might be, but at least he didn't need to be questioned as a potential mass murderer. She hoped. It was time to get back to the office and talk to Wren. Fast.

* * *

Luckily his phone call was over when she tapped at his door. But Wren was adamant. Just because Malcolm Perkins was ruled in as the prime suspect, that didn't mean they could rule Murray out. Not yet.

'Murray or his alter ego, Christopher Manton?'

'Manton. I want this information to be ours and ours alone, Fran. And I want him investigated.'

Which was probably chief constable-speak for *I want you to investigate him.* 'But what if he's implicated in nothing more than a change of name?'

He seemed to be thinking about something else, however. At last he said, as if unaware he'd changed the subject, 'Fran, it occurred to me a few minutes ago that you could honestly say he's not our problem. He still insists he's answerable to the Met, remember. And they pay his salary. It's their appointment procedures, not ours, that are the problem. They should have checked he is who he says he is. We just took him on as a fully-fledged DCI.' She'd never seen him smile so broadly. A mistake that couldn't be chalked up against him as his career path led onwards and upwards! But then he looked almost furtive, staring into his coffee cup as if to read the runes. Another change of direction. 'So he might not figure in the Ashford investigation at all?'

She let her eyes drift to what looked like top-of-the-range biscuits next to his coffee machine. Just one wouldn't harm, not after the virtual starvation over the weekend. Would it? Well, it wouldn't hurt Wren to offer one. 'I think he'd have to, sir, don't you? At the very least as a witness — once his ID is confirmed, and not before, of course. He might even have information that would confirm Perkins as the killer.'

Uninvited, she sat down, making a show of easing her leg. 'Sir, a simple phone call to the Met would establish he's done everything by the book, wouldn't it? We don't want to overreact on this and have the Met laughing at us. And to be honest, though he's been a dratted nuisance and I shall have him doing the nastiest jobs for weeks to come, you've seen him in action. He's got so much potential we both wanted to promote him.'

With the barest of nods, he leant forward and pressed a button on his phone. 'Get me John Fraser of the Met, will you?'

What had happened to common courtesy and addressing his secretary by name?

While they waited for the connection, she continued, 'Just as important, sir, and we — *I* — keep losing sight of this, Murray might have information about other kids who disappeared from the same site. Kids whose parents have been waiting for years for news . . .'

'Have you a team on hand to inform the families?'

'There is one, of course. All trained. I need to brief them thoroughly before they deal with what's turned out to be a tricky situation. Some skeletons were ID'd almost immediately. We had to wait to process the others since we didn't have permission to fast-track the DNA tests. So while some families could be told today, others will have to wait in limbo. And I can't see that sort of difference being kept out of the media.'

He frowned. 'That's unforgivable.' She knew he wasn't referring to his refusal to allow the budget to do it. 'Everything should be properly synchronized. Even,' he added with less assurance, 'if it means that those who could be notified may have to wait.' Even *he* seemed to recognize the problems that this might cause as he returned to bluster mode. 'However did this arise?'

'You'll recall that the SIO was rushed to hospital: Don Simpson?' He'd have flouted every budgetary constraint necessary, and blow the consequences, to get the remains of the other victims ID'd post haste, but she'd better not point that out. It would be wiser to give Wren the chance to have that idea himself. 'He's on the mend, by the way — he was due to come out of hospital yesterday, but to tell the truth I forgot to phone to see how he was.'

'A Human Resources job, that. Not yours.'

'He's a colleague I've known for a long time, sir,' she corrected him more gently than she meant. So gently that unfortunately he didn't even realize it was a rebuke. 'Don Simpson's the most efficient and hard-working of officers, absolutely on the ball. And don't forget that it was he who put us on to the fact that Murray — if that's his name — knew about the Ashford case before he did a runner.' She added, 'When Mark visited him in hospital, he told him then.' She could have kicked herself. Why had she said that? Something to do with the fatigue she'd picked up on in Tom, no doubt. But stupid, stupid, stupid.

'You and Turner — you're like bloody Velcro! What the hell was it like when he was ACC here?'

She must bounce back. 'As strictly professional as you'd expect, sir. As it is now, when it comes to work. So before you ask, he knows nothing of my reservations about Murray. He's too busy,' she said limpidly, going on the pennies and pounds principle, 'being copper's nark at the tennis club. But he is exemplary about drawing the line between what people tell him personally and how the professionals deal with it.'

Wren grabbed the phone as if it were a lifeline. He wafted a dismissive hand at Fran, mouthing, 'Ten minutes.'

She nodded.

Ten minutes to be nasty to Sean Murray. But far from rubbing her hands in glee, she felt herself dropping. She needed the energy for more important things. To give herself breathing space, she headed for the loo.

She'd barely had time to check that he still had his head down working when Wren summoned her again. To her surprise he gestured her to a seat.

'Curiouser and curiouser,' he said, betraying an unexpected depth of reading. 'The Met tell us that Murray had already and quite legally changed his name from Manton by the time he joined them. In fact, he took all his qualifications in his new name. But he quite specifically asked for his family not to be questioned when the usual background checks were made.'

'Did he give a reason?'

'It wasn't recorded if he did. A good candidate with good college references and outstanding qualifications — why look a gift horse in the mouth, eh? I'm afraid the Met have had to tighten up their recruitment procedures, Fran — once or twice they've quite publicly been found lax.'

'Would you be happy for me to talk to him about this family problem, sir? It must have been serious for him to change his name at that age.'

'Talk all you like, Fran. But if I were you,' he added, with what seemed a genuine smile, 'I'd make him sweat. Carry on as normal. Make him work doubly, trebly hard — after all, his colleagues have had to in his absence. Should he complain, you can assure him you have my total support and trust. And then, when you feel the time is right, question him as formally as you like. And report your findings to me, of course.'

Fran returned his smile. 'Thank you, sir. I will. Meanwhile, if you'll excuse me, I ought to go and check with the officers investigating other aspects of Malcolm Perkins' activities. Taunton and Stoke-on-Trent, for the time being.' She could see him reviewing the geography of the UK: no, neither of those would impinge on his budget. 'Would you like me to update you?'

He looked at his watch, an even more upmarket one than either of those Mark owned. 'I'm involved with an ACPO venture for the rest of the day.' The sort of jolly Mark had always loathed. 'But perhaps you could text me. Yes, I'd appreciate that.' He nodded as she rose to her feet.

CHAPTER NINETEEN

Monday morning was Golden Oldies time at the tennis club, of course. Mark was tempted to miss it, lest there was a repeat of the previous day's incident. But he gave himself a man or a mouse talk, and headed off, though he felt anxious about exposing Fran's car to possible hostility.

There was a sort of reception committee waiting for him when he arrived, but it was led by Dougie, who initiated a round of applause. Mark could feel a blush rising: even if he'd done something to deserve being greeted as a hero, it would be embarrassing enough.

'Now, lad, what's the best way we can help sort out this bad business?' Dougie demanded, his arm casually but quite firmly around Mark's shoulders, to remind them all that he was a mate. 'Just give us your orders.'

'Heavens, I hardly gave orders when I was in the police,' he responded. 'But I suppose if I had a *Crimewatch* hat on I'd say we should play in the same groups as last Thursday, and see if anything odd clicks in anyone's brain.'

'Oh, a reconstruction!' Dougie rubbed his hands. 'That sounds good. Are we all up to it? Those of us who can remember back as far as last Thursday, that is. And even if we don't recall a single thing, I don't suppose running around on this gorgeous sunny morning will harm us. Now, Mark, do you want us in the fours we started in or were in when you realized the poor little lass had gone astray?'

'Let's start with the original ones, shall we? Now, I think Jayne wrote down for the police a record of who was partnering whom. Right, Jayne? Let's go.'

'We're missing a couple,' she said, consulting her iPad. 'So we leave gaps or get someone else to join in?' she looked around. 'Silly me: I don't see any spares. OK, threesomes then. So long as we're just knocking up . . .'

'There's no reason why we shouldn't play round games, two against one — those of us who like a bit of competition, that is,' Dougie added innocently. 'Five games for those in a foursome, as many as you can manage for you trios.'

The whole thing was going to be a complete waste of everyone's time, wasn't it? He should never have suggested it. It would have been better for everyone to enjoy another magical spring day — the sun already warm, but with an easterly wind to keep it cool to the point of cold: one or two who'd stripped off their tracksuits were already putting them on again. A cow was mooing fit to burst in one of the nearby meadows. A couple of horses, sharing a field, tossed their heads across the electric fencing that separated them. The whole scene was as idyllic as it had been the previous Thursday.

Now there were no kids to drown them out, you could hear the usual shouts: people apologizing for a bad shot; a ball called out. A double fault. Timeless. Ought to be in a Noel Coward play. At least they were all getting fit while they wasted time.

They finished the first five games. Consulting Jayne, they took up their places for the next five. Jayne reminded him that they'd been playing together: she'd grumbled when he'd broken up the game when he realized there was no sign of Livvie. They really needed to make up the foursome with George and Dan, but there was no sign of them: they played a languid game of singles, until the welcome appearance of Dan, who took in the situation at a glance and joined in.

When each foursome had completed their five games, he was just about to apologize and ask Dougie to resume the usual card-taking method of selection when Alex, she of the erratic serve, spoke up.

'I know this is probably a waste of everyone's time, but didn't someone use a phone round about this point, just as Dougie dropped all the cards?'

'Did I? Don't remember that. But if you say I did, I must have done.'

'That's right,' Dan said. 'But you dropped them at the end of the first set. I remember the ace of clubs blew away. We found it up against someone's bag.'

'Which wasn't away from the playing area, where it was supposed to be, but here by the net,' Alex said. 'I was going to remind whoever it was that it wasn't how we did things, but I didn't want to say anything in front of everyone else.'

Mark felt himself stepping forward. 'So whose bag was it? Just to clarify things? Could you just identify your bags now? Just to your neighbour — nothing official. And Alex, could you just see if any of the bags jogs your memory? And then perhaps we could come back here to Dougie.'

Off they trotted, like the obedient kids Zac had been coaching. He joined them, of course — he was one of them, not an officer. And back they all came, Alex shaking her head. 'We go in for some battered old specimens, don't we?'

'Quite appropriate, considering,' Dougie said. 'So, just to make it clear, it wasn't anyone here who left their bag at the net, rather than round the periphery or on the clubhouse decking?'

'So who was it?' Alex asked. 'Mark, any ideas?' Then she flushed, vividly. 'Actually, that phone call — it wasn't between sets even. It was as we changed ends. Really bad form. But I'd never seen the guy before so—' She covered her mouth with her hand. 'Does that mean it was the man with the red car? He said something about a dentist — perhaps he was just calling to say he'd be late or something. Or perhaps the dentist was calling to offer a cancellation. Had he lost a filling and needed emergency treatment?'

Mark had a very strong recollection that Stephen Harris was having routine treatment, all confirmed by the dentist involved. His pulses were racing, but he tried to sound calm, disinterested. 'Does anyone else recollect this phone call?'

'Must have been outgoing,' Dougie said, 'or we'd have heard it ringing. Or whatever these posh new phones do. Wouldn't we?'

But Dougie was as deaf as he was, so Mark prayed for corroboration.

'It was very noisy. Would we have heard anything except those kids?'

'Let's try it,' Dougie said. 'I assume two of you have phones? Go on, one of you call the other and we'll all make a noise.'

They obliged. Beethoven's Fifth, pretentious or what, announced a call. Even Dougie and Mark nodded. So there was agreement. No ringtone, conventional or otherwise, had sullied the courts. Dan said, 'He must have had the number on speed-dial if he made the call and had time for a conversation in the time it takes to change ends.'

'It was a very short call,' Alex declared. 'Just a few words before I caught his eye. He didn't argue with me, just cut the call and put the phone back in his bag. I've said something, haven't I, Mark? My God, what have I said?'

'I don't know, Alex. I really don't. Have any of you said anything about this call to my ex-colleagues?'

'How could we have done, if we'd all forgotten?' Dougie asked with some asperity.

'Quite. Now, with your permission I'm going to call this information in. I'll tell the guy who came last week, and let him decide if it's relevant. And then — let's not waste this lovely weather — it's over to you and your playing cards, Dougie.'

* * *

Fran had barely opened her mouth to check Murray's progress on the files when her phone rang. Media relations. They needed to talk to her urgently. Telling him, as if he was a cross between a half-trained dog and a recalcitrant school child, to stay where he was and continue poring over the files, she scooted. It sounded as if what she and Wren had feared had come to pass: someone had broken the news of the skeletons.

They had. It was damage limitation time. And who was to be the little boy jamming his thumb into a great big leaky hole?

Naturally, she suggested Wren. It was what he was paid for, after all. But he'd already left the building and of course there was no ACC in post. All fingers pointed at Fran.

The first question, before she could even give a statement to the rightly horrified media pack, was the worst.

'Is it true that the police have only identified half of the poor kids left behind that wall, and that the other half lie in some lab awaiting tests?'

'Yes,' she said flatly.

'Could you explain?'

When she didn't respond, someone supplied the answer in another question. 'Is it lack of manpower or lack of money?'

She gave a horribly Wren-like answer. 'I'm sure you're all aware of severe constraints in the present economic climate.'

'So you're prepared to put money before suffering families?'

She wasn't going to put her hand up to that one. So she took a huge risk: she went into confiding mode. 'The enquiry's had its problems. In fact, we've known about this horrible crime since Friday.' Raising her voice, she overrode the hubbub. 'So, ladies and gentlemen, have your editors.' She waited for the uproar to subside of its own accord. 'We — and they — decided to throw all our resources at raising consciousness in the kidnap case. Livvie's kidnap. We had to make a terrible, terrible decision: should we prioritize justice to the dead or try to find the living? Did we make the right one? Who knows? As far as we know, Livvie is still alive. If we find her in time, the decision may have been the right one. If not, the only thing I can do — the only thing any of us can do — is apologize to the families who are all still in limbo. None of them yet knows whether to hope that their child is about to get a decent burial or that he or she isn't among them and is still walking in God's fresh air.' She braced herself for a decent moral question: would all eight families wait together or would the four be told straight away? But she didn't get it.

'So you've all sat around doing nothing about this case all weekend?' some idiot asked.

'No, I've had a team of officers working round the clock, many of whom weren't scheduled to work this weekend and are giving freely of many long hours of their time,' she retorted. 'Thanks to them we are very close to confirming the identity of the man we believe to be the killer.' She fed them a few geographical crumbs: after all, their provincial colleagues needed local news. 'Naturally, as soon as we have hard information we will make a further announcement. You have my word on that.'

She was about to draw the conference to an abrupt halt when she saw a familiar face, that of a TV reporter whose life she had once saved. Dilly could ask a really useful question if she had a chance. Fran caught her eye. Dilly nodded.

'Detective Chief Superintendent, a few minutes ago you mentioned that dear little lost girl? Is there any news of Livvie?'

What a good woman.

'I wish there was. Ladies and gentlemen, every hour is now critical. However much you want — need — to cover this truly horrible story, I implore you to keep Livvie before the public eye.' She suddenly recalled the decision to move the focus away from Kentish horses and stables. 'As you're aware, we're now following leads on the continent. So any digital media cover that reaches expats in France and Spain helps us. Without your help, without their help, we may not find her in time.' She swallowed hard, moved by her own emotion. Only then did she get to her feet. Her stagger on her weak leg was genuine, not stage-managed, though it could scarcely have happened at a better moment. Even as she limped out, she wanted to scream and shout a telling postscript: that if the government imposed even deeper financial cuts, a poorer police service would inevitably ensue. But as long as she was in the team, she had to be a team player. She zipped her mouth.

She couldn't face going back to her office, not with Murray still there. And she had a terrible suspicion that her emotional appeal for news about Livvie had made her mascara run. The loo again.

As she headed that way, Ed Chatfield almost literally ran into her. He didn't give the impression he'd noticed anything amiss; he was positively pulsing with energy.

'Progress, Fran. I wanted to tell you myself. Progress. No, we've not got her back. Sorry if I raised your hopes. But we're a step nearer. Ray's on to it now.'

Was that how you got to be a superintendent these days? You got to give the good news while someone else did the legwork? But she liked him too much to bark, and she was afraid Ray would sense a snub if anyone else took over what he saw as his territory.

'Excellent. Now, I could do with a coffee, but someone's sorting out a glitch on my computer so I can't use my office. Can we grab something from the machine and take it to that shoebox they've allocated to you?'

He looked surprised, but walked with her to the nearest dispenser, pulling a face as he looked at what emerged.

'It's not exactly top of the range. Hey, have you seen that hi-tech machine that Wren uses?' He let her into his office and pushed forward a couple of non-matching chairs.

She eased herself into the more upright one. 'You've been favoured with admission into his nest, have you? Whoops, forget you heard that word. His sanctum, I mean.' She felt obscurely irritated that she hadn't known. When had this happened? Why? Was Wren trying to undermine her authority?

'Only the once. When I was summoned I felt like a naughty boy called to the head's office. Then I didn't. He's such a politico, that man, isn't he? He just wanted to find out how one of his old muckers was getting on — he was dead chuffed to hear he was still just a DCI. He likes a bit of status, your guv'nor.' He paused, looking at her sideways. 'Talking of status, are you going after the new job?'

'Depends which new job you mean,' she said carefully. Was it something she'd want to discuss with a comparative stranger, anyway?

'Running the combined Kent and Essex MIT?'

'Oh,' she asked casually, 'is that official yet?'

'Not yet. Any moment now, I'd have thought. I might just give it a go. But not if it's yours for the asking.'

'Absolutely not. And to be honest with you, Ed, it's a job for someone younger than me: someone with five or six years of their life to devote to that and nothing else. You'd need to build a team full of resentful potential rivals; you've got the geography to worry about, with our dear old friend the M25 getting in the way of everything; you've got major cuts when you need expansion — oh, and you've got to factor in the new crime commissioners and their budget preferences, not to mention new chief constables.' There: she'd just signed her resignation letter, or near enough. 'But don't,' she added with a suddenly cheerful grin, a weight lifted from her shoulders, 'let me talk you out of applying — you're just the sort of person who should be leading it. If I had any influence, which alas, I don't, I'd put in a good word for you.'

'You mean that, don't you, Fran? Thank you.' He sounded more emotional than she'd expected. Poor man, thinking he was going to have to tackle an old dragon. 'Anyway, I'm going to burst if I don't tell you this, Fran, bad coffee or not. Your Mark did some sort of reconstruction exercise with those elderly tennis players this morning. And one of them remembered Stephen Harris making or taking a phone call.'

She narrowed her eyes. 'Which wasn't disclosed at the time.'

'Quite. Mysteriously he's lost the mobile in question — yes, we've got that far. We've talked to him again. He conceded he'd maybe taken a call. Something about loft insulation, he said. But we're nosy buggers, aren't we, Fran — so we're checking with his phone company. Someone's on to it now.'

'We've already got an account of his movements, haven't we? All confirmed by CCTV, as I recall. Thanks for this, Ed. It's nice to have good news for once.'

'You're sure it's good?'

She looked him in the eye. 'You are, aren't you? The trouble is, despite all our efforts, the story may have gone off the boil after this morning's announcement.'

His face was ludicrously blank. Carefully, tactfully blank. Wouldn't even utter the words *Ashford* and *skeletons*, would he?

'Oh, we know it wasn't Kent Police's finest moment, admitting we'd only ID'd half the poor little buggers. A total balls-up. At least we could fob them off with that stuff about Somerset and Staffordshire. A genuine mass murderer. They lapped that up. Actually, I ended up plugging the Livvie story.'

'Thanks.' His phone went. 'Do you mind if I take this?'

Of course she didn't. Especially as it was very short, and the moment he cut it, he asked, 'Do you fancy a walk to the Incident Room?'

CHAPTER TWENTY

Mark ought to have felt something, surely — exhilaration, maybe, for having helped conjure the memory of a simple phone call that might help the search for Livvie. The thrill of the chase, albeit at second hand. Instead it was as if someone had pulled an invisible plug, all his emotion draining away. What was the point of playing on? He knew better, however, than to go back into — he almost called it work! He certainly knew better than to intrude on Fran's territory just at the moment: MIT would be going round like headless chickens, and Ray and Ed Chatfield would be too busy with the information that Alex was giving even now.

Belatedly, when he thought it would all be official, he'd texted Fran with the news: all she'd had time for was to send a couple of XXs.

As if equally weary, the rest of the Golden Oldies played in an increasingly desultory manner until their usual session time was up. He'd been a focus of attention, but as he'd rightly protested, all he'd done was float the idea of a reconstruction, and in any case he'd never dealt well with admiration. Now he was afraid that people were letting him score points he hadn't entirely earned.

He dragged himself back home, Fran's poor car protesting at the indignity of being bounced around the track potholes, showered and then did what he'd promised himself he would do — he made an appointment with the practice nurse to have his ears syringed. Tomorrow, please? Not for another week, the receptionist declared with unnecessary fierceness: he had to undertake to put drops in his ears every single night, something he'd loathed ever since he was a child.

Now what? He looked at his watch, but it had stopped — again. He was almost tempted to nip into Maidstone or Canterbury to buy another, but he thought of Fran's chagrin if he did. Caffy's too, of course — she'd feel guilty if she ever found out.

The kitchen clock told him it was time to stare at the contents of the fridge to decide on the options for lunch. Surely by now he ought to be used to having time for such choices, and time to eat in a civilized manner without sharing a table top with half a dozen folders, the contents of which he should have mastered a week ago. It was time to stop feeling guilty about being free to relax. He'd have to have another talk with his therapist about it all.

Meanwhile, and his heart lifted as he saw who was phoning him, here was the next best thing to a therapist — or, come to think of it, a better shrink than anyone with letters after his or her name he'd yet come across. 'Caffy?'

'Hi, Mark. Are you OK? Bored enough to share some of that food you bought during your supermarket run on Saturday? Great. I'm on my way.' End of call. That was Caffy for you.

A flan warming in the oven, he was still mixing salad dressing when she arrived. She washed her hands and laid the table, one of the family — and soon, of course, to be his best woman. He was aware of being under scrutiny as he tossed the salad.

'Are you OK? You're so deeply involved in this abduction case but haven't any power: how does it feel?'

Trust her to go for the jugular. 'It's weird. Very weird. But I can't say I'd want to be back in my old job. An assistant chief constable is so remote from real people, which was why I joined the force in the first place — and I should imagine that when they finally appoint a replacement, whoever picks up the poisoned chalice will find it overflowing with budgets and redundancies. Not my thing at all.' Nor Fran's.

'You'd need to be a Manager, with a capital M,' she agreed, sliding easily into her next question. 'And how is Fran, with all this business about the skeletons hitting the media? Didn't you know? Oh, of course, your tennis morning. Well, as far as I can see, every radio news bulletin is leading with it. And presumably all the TV cameras in Kent will be zooming in ghoulishly on the same bit of Ashford.' They exchanged a grimace.

'She'll cope. She always does. But then, she's always had a supportive boss in the past — the old chief constable was a fully-signed up member of her fan club.'

'That guy who wanted to usurp my position as best woman, and ended up offering to escort Fran up the aisle instead?'

'The same. He's off helping to organize the police force in Mali or somewhere, but he's promised to be back in time.' Is that what Fran would want to do, when she had to leave Kent Police? Go and sort out some unsuspecting developing country? Or would she really want to hang up her handcuffs finally and for good?

'Lucky Mali,' Caffy said dryly. 'And Fran had you, of course. To support her when you were her boss.'

'I suspect I spent as much time bollocking her as being kind.'

'That's not how she tells it — and why would a woman like Fran want a sadist as a husband?' She fetched plates and set them on the table. 'Now, before I forget, here's your watch. Wow, that's a posh one,' she added, eyeing his wrist.

'Posh but useless. It keeps stopping. Now I've got the other one back I'll get this repaired. I'll just get yours from the safe and then we'll eat, shall we?'

She raised a hand to stop him. 'If you don't mind, it can stay where it is. I can't see myself ever wanting to wear it again, but to get rid of it seems like tempting providence. Meanwhile, I bought this classic timepiece at a garage.' She dug it out of her bag and put it on with a theatrical flourish. 'Ta, da!'

'So things are looking good with this new young man?' He took the flan out of the oven and put it on the table. 'Sit and dig in while you tell me. Alistair, is it?'

She blushed vividly. Caffy, blushing? 'I wouldn't tell anyone else this, especially Paula, but every time I pass an old ruin I eye it up to see if we could rescue it together. Pathetic or what? Hey, is this some of your home-made bread?'

In other words, end of conversation about Alistair.

* * *

'So the media still think we're following up leads in France,' Ray was saying as Ed and Fran slipped into the incident room.

'Those of them that aren't high as kites on theories about our serial killer and our failings in that regard,' Fran cut in dourly — better it came from her than anyone else. 'Hell's bells, what a cock-up. Let's see if we can do better with this one. Let's have that good news, Ray.'

He didn't need any more prompting. 'Thanks to Mark Turner,' he said, 'we now have information that Stephen Harris, the man with the cleanest teeth in Kent, may not be the lily-white boy all the way through. He made a phone call halfway through a tennis match. He's since "lost" his phone, of course, but his provider's records show exactly when and to which number he made it. And three guesses who owns the phone with that number. Right: Ross Thwaite. According to the surveillance team, he's working on the Livingstone estate this morning, just as you'd expect. He arrived in his four by four; Snowdrop is still safe in his stable.' He looked from Fran to Ed, and back again. 'Are you happy to leave him there — Thwaite, I mean, not the horse — or are you ready to start talking to him now?' If he'd had his way, Fran thought, he'd clearly have had him in for questioning, preferably under the cosh with a bit of waterboarding thrown in.

Fran watched Ed evaluating the response of the joint team. Although she outranked him, she knew she'd let him make the decision, and she'd back him, against vocal opposition if necessary. He was the one who spent his professional life chasing paedophiles; she was just an old Jill of all Trades.

But he was looking to her — not for guidance, surely, but more for approval. 'My feeling,' he said slowly, 'is that we let him be. Still. I know it goes against the grain, but there's still just an outside chance that she's OK, and he may yet lead us to her. If he goes anywhere out of the ordinary we're tailing him. If he simply goes home and gets his supper like any normal man and puts his feet up to watch the telly, perhaps then it's time to call on him. In fact, I'd say it is. Wouldn't you?' He turned to Fran.

'Absolutely. Surround his cottage completely and silently. Get him. Oh, and make sure the RSPCA are on hand to look after Snowdrift.' She smiled ironically. 'In the meantime, as before: the man so much as sneezes and we know. Hard if he takes to the woods, of course,' she mused.

One of the CEOP team shook her head. 'Not if he goes in his 4×4. Tracking device,' she added briefly. 'And there's a listening device in place in the cottage. Just trying to get permission for a phone tap even as we speak.'

'Excellent.' There was nothing else to say, was there? She'd better go and check on those skeletons. And maybe — she checked her watch — pick up a sandwich.

* * *

The media team were in overdrive, involved in damage limitation, drafting statements and making encouraging noises about interviews. Fran longed to phone Don Simpson, to see if he was up to fronting a press conference, but she restrained herself: the man was entitled to his sick leave. But she phoned anyway, just to let him give his trenchant opinion on the situation. Predictably this involved a satisfactory stream of invective directed at anyone involved in cost cutting and putting budgets before the needs of victims' families. All highly un-PC, but if she'd wanted a polite conversation she'd have spoken to Wren, wouldn't she?

'Who's going to talk to the media in tonight's briefing?' he paused long enough to ask.

'Wren, if there's any justice in the world. Better still, our beloved government for slashing funds. Or more likely me. Trying to defend the indefensible.'

'Tell you what, Fran,' Don said, dropping his voice conspiratorially, 'tell them where to put their press conference. Wren's problem. Let Wren deal with it. It should be an ACC, not just a Chief Super like yourself. You're not paid to put your head above the parapet.'

'Wren's tied up with ACPO for the rest of the day.'

She pulled the phone from her ear as he snorted. 'What a surprise. Tell you what, then, Fran — if you have to do it, you take those crutches, right? That stumble of yours was brilliant this morning: yes, it was on TVInvicta. Something like that reminds Joe Public just how much we do for them. Except we can't walk on the sodding water — even with crutches,' he concluded.

CHAPTER TWENTY-ONE

With mispers at every location where Malcolm Perkins had worked as a youth leader, which now appeared to include temporary placements in Portsmouth and Rotherham, where Fran was strongly tempted to send Tom, given his hankering after Yorkshire, the media were leaping up and down with morbid hysteria. They particularly relished the fact that Perkins was some sort of social worker, always their favourite scapegoat. Heads of Social Service departments all over the country were being dragged out for interviews. Her turn would almost certainly come later, as yet another example of policing failure.

Meanwhile, after his day in the sin bin, perhaps she should go and talk to Sean Murray, though it would leave her hard pressed to prepare for the early evening media briefing about the latest on the skeletons case. On the other hand, perhaps she shouldn't be the one to do the briefing. Not for the tempting reasons that Don had put forward, but for a quite professional one. If she wasn't thoroughly up to date on all the developments, she'd mess up. It ought to be someone with the very latest news to offer. Young Madge, for instance. She'd been on media courses recently: how would she cope with the real thing? It would be more than a baptism of fire, of course, but she was so attractive, with an air of what Fran hoped was totally spurious vulnerability, that a few hacks might be disconcerted enough to miss a stride or two. She wouldn't summon her to her office, but go down to the incident room and no more than float the idea of her fronting the bun fight. One nanosecond of hesitation from the young woman and Fran would make the decision for her.

'You're the one who's done most of the work, Madge — you're far more up to speed than I am. If you have a moment's misgiving, tell me and I'll be there instead. I promise. But I really think the investigation would move forward more quickly if I followed up another lead. There's just a chance someone's run Christopher Manton to earth. A contact from the Met,' she lied hurriedly, 'wants me to deal with it.'

'That's one person whose DNA is on record — should be a doddle to prove that,' Madge declared.

'Excellent. So all we need is a sample of this guy's. Now, you'll have gathered that this is someone else's case at the moment. Something quite different. But if you wanted to battle with the media scrum this evening, you could truthfully say I'm pursuing a lead. Of course,' she continued slowly, 'there's no need to do this on your own. The three of you who investigated Perkins' other youth placements could appear.'

'Like wise monkeys. Or Macbeth's witches, except Tom wouldn't quite fit that scenario.'

'Quite. But you could all talk about how you went about your searches — the meticulous, time-consuming work. Lost Saturdays and Sundays. Cancelled dates — no, maybe that's going too far. Say how easy it would have been to assume that Perkins' death wrapped up everything. Heavens, you've all been on media courses: I'd trust you more than I'd trust myself at the moment, and that's the truth.'

The sympathetic look Madge subjected her to seemed to confirm the worst. 'Look, ma'am, can I go and have a quick word with the others? See what they say?'

'Of course. I've got stuff to attend to back in my office. But remember — if one of you has the slightest reservation, it's back to me.'

Madge shook her head. 'Ma'am, we know you work miracles. But even you can't be in two places at once.'

So now it was Sean Murray time. The confrontation she'd put off all day. She just hoped he was as knackered as she was.

* * *

Mark was in front of the fridge again. He felt guilty about not waiting for Fran, but an afternoon spreading compost over the garden had left him with what he told himself was a healthy appetite. Before he could choose between a slice of the lunchtime flan or a hunk of his bread — a bit crumbly, this particular loaf, not easy to slice neatly — and some cheese, the phone went.

'Caffy! Can you see into my kitchen? Every time I'm looking in the fridge, tempted by the unhealthy option, you phone.'

'In that case close it now and grab yourself an apple. Are you busy?'

'Just about to have a shower.'

'I want to show you something. In good light. It's called Abbot's Croft. The nearest village is Westry. It's east of Stone Street. You know what it's like out there — all lanes, no real roads.'

It wasn't like Caffy to be so incoherent. He grabbed at his old professional calm. 'Give me the map references and I'll be there. What am I looking for?'

'Just a PACT van at the moment. It'll take you — oh, about half an hour to get here. Maybe a bit longer. No, don't bust a gut. I won't go away. I've got something to read.'

'As if you ever didn't have. OK. Pen and pad ready. Fire away.' He wrote to her dictation. 'Caffy, you're being sensible, are you?'

'I'm parked too far away from what might be a crime scene to draw attention to myself or to compromise it.'

His ACC voice returned, this time the stern version. 'This really is something serious, isn't it, Caffy? So you can show me what you've found — but from a distance. If necessary I'll call for back-up. If I do, I want you to get the hell out of there. Understood?'

'But it might be nothing, Mark — and I know how resources are stretched. They've even got three substitutes for Fran on the evening news.'

'If I take you seriously, I know a man or a woman who will too. Just shoot, Caffy — we're wasting time here.'

'It's a deserted farmhouse, partially ruined, with recent four by four tracks and a horse's footprints. I'd say the horse is still at home.'

'OK. I'm on my way. Half an hour, you said.'

'But Mark, what if someone turns up?'

'Did you trust me over that watch? Well, then, trust me now. Pull back to at least half a mile — no, a mile away. My car keys are in my hand. Start your engine and scoot. And then we can make a decision.'

* * *

Sean Murray was no fool. He must have been all too aware that Fran was interested in far more than a minor disciplinary defence, the way she probed the reasons for his precipitate departure. All the same, he stonewalled until he must have been bored almost to tears.

'Why did you change your name, Sean?'

'That's like asking me when I stopped beating my wife.' To Fran, there was less charm than anxiety behind that smile.

'Don't be ridiculous. It's asking a question I'd like an answer to. I'm happy with your name: you can go on being Sean Murray. But you were once Christopher Manton, and that's why I want to know why you became someone else. Come on, we can check your DNA if you prefer.'

'I don't see the point.'

'A police officer has to do a lot of things he or she doesn't see the point of. I don't see the point of sitting here pretending that we're just talking about you bunking off for a perfectly innocent weekend in the Smoke when you should have been investigating a horrific find in Ashford. That's bad enough, of course. Actually, as I'm sure you've heard, there have been equally grisly discoveries in other towns and cities. What do you know about them?'

Fran would swear he was completely nonplussed.

'I don't know what you're talking about. Why should I know anything about them? The skeletons in Ashford—'

'If you'd rather talk about them, fine. Let's do that.' People who had known Fran longer would have been worried at this sudden burst of affability. 'The fact you changed your name at about the same time as those kids were being murdered and bricked up raises the odd eyebrow, you know. The files other people had to read while you were skiving reveal you weren't popular with your mates then. You had the reputation of an idle bully, as you could have seen if you'd spent the weekend working with your colleagues who had to come in and work instead.'

'OK, you've made your point. I'm sorry. I should have asked you before I left.'

'You're not getting this, Sean. Knowing that Don had found what he had you shouldn't even have asked for leave.'

'After all the work I had to do in your stead I'm owed weeks rather than days.'

She stared at him and raised her right eyebrow. It never failed.

Dropping his eyes, he gave a grudging shrug. 'Actually, I suppose it was quite useful.'

'Yes, it was. For one thing you got access to the level of meetings a DCI wouldn't normally go to. And your reports, which were excellent as I said at the time, put your name in front of all sorts of influential officers. But this is nothing to do with what you are or are not owed. And as I said earlier, this is really very little to do with the fact that you bunked off. It's *why* you bunked off that interests me. Sean, was it because you knew some of the people who were now walled up there dead, and you couldn't bear to look at what was left of your old mates? Or, Sean, and I really want you to think carefully before you answer this — was it because you'd put them there?'

CHAPTER TWENTY-TWO

Perhaps it was love that had addled Caffy's brain. To call her calm and efficient was usually a masterpiece of understatement. He'd never known her as panic-stricken and downright flaky as this. So he made a point of calling her every few minutes as he drove, firstly to reassure her that he was on his way, secondly — and possibly more importantly — to make sure she stayed put and didn't attempt any sort of heroics.

The location, in a tangle of lanes miles from an A road and with no major towns, or even villages apart from the hamlet that she'd mentioned, Westry, was considerably further south-east than the parts of Kent he knew like the back of his hand — better, since he didn't spend all that long staring at bits of his anatomy he simply relied on to do their job. Silly image altogether: how many people did? They looked at their palms, perhaps, if they were holding something.

On his fourth call he tried to displace some of her anxiety by eliciting her thoughts about the hand cliché. There were few things she enjoyed more than discussion about words.

'It's a terribly narrow lane,' she responded. 'I know I said it was urgent, but you won't take any risks, will you?' She gave a familiar gurgle of laughter. 'I wouldn't want anything to prevent my being your best woman. Sorry. I'm being such a pain. I keep thinking how obvious I must be parked up here.'

'Or not. White vans, even clean ones like PACT's, are not unknown. In fact, surveillance teams find them very useful. OK, I'm hitting traffic — need to concentrate since this is Fran's car — so I'll call you back.'

By the time he'd negotiated a couple of awkward staggered crossroads, he knew he was almost there. However, the deep, winding lane meant he really did have to drop speed — it wasn't just Caffy being nervous then — and he was almost on the PACT van before he had any warning. Caffy had parked amazingly well in a really tight space; he had to find a gateway sixty metres further on before he could park and walk back to her.

'No blues and twos?' she asked quizzically as he let himself in.

'What the hell brought you down here?' he demanded by way of greeting. 'There's even grass growing down the middle, for heaven's sake.'

'Large scale OS map. No, I'm not joking. It's a very good way of finding out all sorts of things you didn't know about a place you think you're familiar with. And a woman on that course said she'd located several disused places worth developing just by scanning a map. If she can, I can. I didn't bargain on this lane being quite so narrow, to be honest.'

'So which way is it? This Croft?'

She pointed forwards.

'So you've driven past, turned, come back here and turned again? On a lane this wide? Hell's bells, Caffy — what if someone had come hurtling along?'

'They'd just have cursed me for being another White Van Man — or Woman, of course.'

He raised his hands in despair. But there wasn't any point in arguing with her when she was in a mood like this. In fact, to be honest, there was very rarely any point in arguing with Caffy. 'I thought we'd do a nice quiet walk past first,' he said. 'You've hidden this well, and mine's tucked out of harm's way. Any problems, anything dodgy, we simply turn and walk back here. Agreed? Or we forget it.'

She jutted her lower lip like a five-year-old. 'And you'd come sneaking back on your own.'

'Of course. Maybe me and some mates in a helicopter.' Except he didn't see Fran getting away with that a second time. 'Are you coming or not?'

Anyone spotting them would have taken them for father and daughter taking an evening stroll, albeit in a slightly unlikely location. Had she been wearing dungarees at any point, she'd shed them and was now neat in jeans and fleece, as he was. They both wore serious trainers. She rapidly engaged with his thoughts about the backs of hands and other clichés, picking up and running with them as he'd hoped she would. What would this Alistair make of her mind? She must be Mensa level, not bad for a self-educated painter and decorator, who'd once been a drug-taking prostitute. He hoped he'd appreciate her, value her, as she deserved. And if he didn't, Mark would personally eviscerate him. Or maybe her adoptive parents would beat him to it.

'Over there,' she said quietly.

'It's just a Victorian farmhouse,' he objected. 'Not the sort of place you'd want to rescue, surely. And though it's run down, I'd scarcely describe it as a ruin. However, that's not the point, is it? It's the deserted bit and the horse that matters. Look, we'd best keep walking, just in case anyone does see us, but we can sort of drift, the way folk do. Could you have a problem with your trainer — needs retying or something? So I can walk back to you?'

'OK. It's when you turn back you'll see what excites me,' she murmured, adding more loudly, 'Drat this thing!'

As if he hadn't heard — he only just had, to be honest — he walked on, and then feigned surprise mixed with irritation and walked back, holding out a hand to help her to her feet. Unlike Fran, of course, she didn't need assistance, but sprang up with enviable agility and resumed her stroll.

'Well?'

'Was that really a Tudor chimney at the back of the farmyard?' he asked.

'Looks like it to me. It's as if someone simply gave up living in the original building, and built a more fashionable one. But waste not, want not — another of those damned proverbs — and they decided to use the old entrance hall as their stables. I'd say there's quite a lot of it we can't see from here — perhaps it was used as a store or a barn. Who knows?' They were now well clear of any eavesdropper. 'Did you hear the horse?'

'With *my* ears? I'm having them syringed next week, by the way.'

'And how would you feel about hearing aids? You wouldn't see them as some stigma?'

Right question, of course, but definitely the wrong time. 'Let's just focus on the house. And any moment, we'll have to turn round and walk past it again. No, I didn't hear the horse. But I did see the manure heap, which looked fresh, if you take my meaning. And I did see hoof prints — I don't know much about horses, but I presume they're like humans: the taller the animal, the bigger the feet. Right? And I saw the tracks of a fairly heavy-duty vehicle. On the other hand, I saw no evidence of any activity in the house itself. The curtains must have been the original ones, or near enough. The paint ditto. Real neglect. What would you do with it if you bought it so you could resuscitate the Tudor part? Pull it down?' He turned them round and set them in motion again.

'Let's be quiet — see if you can hear the horse too.' She strolled on casually. 'There? Did you hear it? Though the birds were trying to drown it out.' She stopped dead and looked him in the eye. 'Mark, you can't even hear the birds, can you?'

He couldn't deal with the depth of pity. He smiled grimly. 'No, but I can smell a rat. As soon as we get back to the car, I'm going to call it in. And just so that we're clear about this, Caffy, you are going home to Alistair—'

'We're not — I mean, we're just seeing each other. Nothing more.'

And yet she was besotted enough to trawl round unknown parts of Kent searching for ruins they could turn into joint projects.

He touched her cheek. 'Yet. At any rate, for now, go safely home to Andy and Paula — I shall phone to check, you know, so you better had.'

She pulled a little girl's face. 'They're in Mustique.'

'And Fran's in for a dead busy evening. Let's go and find a pub — didn't I see one on the last main road we crossed? — and I'll shout you some food. After all, when I've made a few calls from somewhere some way distant from here, I'd probably just have to make myself scarce as well. Not being a cop anymore,' he added with a trace of pathos, some of which was genuine.

'Bugger,' she said. 'Poor you, too.'

'I couldn't have put it better myself. Now, you drive off first. Have you got enough space for a U-turn?' he asked so seriously she missed the joke.

She pulled a face. 'It'll take three goes. Why not just drive straight down the lane?'

And drive past Abbot's Croft yet again? 'You know exactly why. I'll see you out if you need me to,' he goaded her.

'Over my dead body.' And she turned the van in three precise manoeuvres.

He resisted the temptation to drive past Abbot's Croft himself, and, yes, even to call Ray from where he was. He turned slowly and carefully — thank God this was such a quiet lane — and headed back towards the pub.

* * *

Murray was saying nothing yet. Then he looked coolly at his watch. 'Chief Superintendent Harman, would it be possible to have a comfort break?'

'Of course. But don't think of leaving the building again, lest we take it as a sign of guilt. Would you like a cup of tea when you return?'

Fran sat back. Had she gone too far when she'd accused him of murdering the kids? He'd have been within his rights to ask for a formal interview at that point, and possibly legal representation. And what was the point? There was no indication he was ever anywhere near Taunton or Stoke or West Bromwich, was there? Not if his college records were accurate. He'd not reacted to her earlier reference to other killings. And Perkins certainly was in those locations, and doing just the same sort of work in the same sort of situation as he was in Ashford. Was she letting her dislike of the man get between her and best professional practice? Was wanting to shock something out of him justification enough? She didn't think it was.

She stretched her leg and hip. She hadn't eaten enough recently to risk taking another painkiller, and there was a griping throb in her right buttock almost severe enough to make her call it a day. But that would be to give in, something completely alien to her.

Returning quietly, Murray sat down, apparently more relaxed, but still looking disengaged. He was no fool: he must have known the weakness in her position. Which made her look all the more unprofessional.

His shrug — he had the shoulder vocabulary of a Frenchman — was dismissive rather than apologetic. 'I would say I've committed what the Church would describe as a sin of omission, rather than a sin of commission. All the qualifications I've gained, from the Access course that got me into University, my degree, my Master's — everything, in short, that enabled me to become a police officer, were gained by Sean Murray. All I failed to do was notify you that until the age of eighteen I was indeed, known as Christopher Manton. Needless to say, the Met saw and accepted the evidence of my change of name by deed poll. All legal and above board. But I admit I should have told you who I was as soon as the investigation got under way.'

She didn't want to help him with a prompt, even an acknowledgement, but eventually decided to retreat in order to further advance. 'Let us agree that as Christopher Manton, you spent some time working on a youth project in Ashford, from which, then as now, you skived, which has since thrown up a number of skeletons. What does the man formerly known as Christopher Manton have to say about that?'

'That if there are the remains of my contemporaries on the site, they were put there after I left the project. Skived off. Or walked away. There must be any number of less pejorative synonyms. I began, as they say, a new life. Quite successfully, I'd say. Wouldn't you?' He produced his superior and irritating smile. 'If you want corroboration about dates, I suggest you contact the person who rescued me from my old life — from my old self, you might say. Unfortunately he is far from well, and I should imagine the sudden arrival of a whole load of my colleagues would do him no good at all.'

A sick friend? That would fit all the things young Tom had seen him do in Maidstone — the rucksack in which to put food, the meals for two. Yes, it would fit. And as for bunking off to London on Friday, presumably that was where this man lived. For once Murray was doing what any normal young man would do. In a crisis, he was going home if not to mother, at least to a substitute dad.

'And who is this man? We won't send in the cavalry, I can promise you that. Anyone who can turn around the sort of dosser your Misper file depicts so that he ends up in your position must be someone extraordinary. The sort of person whose hand I'd want to shake,' she added with a dry smile.

To her amazement, he responded with one of his own, the first that didn't remind her forcibly of a crocodile. 'Anyone would.'

But she wasn't going to get a chance yet because a barrage of texts was tumbling in: Mark, to say that something interesting had come up; Ray, to say that something very interesting had come up; Ed Chatfield, to ask if she wanted to be involved in something very interesting.

Wouldn't she just, if she wasn't involved in something very interesting herself? But in truth she simply could not sit still any longer, and she didn't want this cold man to see her wince with pain and hold her desk to support her.

'Very well, Sean, what I suggest you do now is take yourself downstairs to the incident room and read through all the files there. I want your written opinions on the effect losing their child had on the families concerned. I want your written, reasoned opinion on who might have done these terrible killings. And then you can take yourself off home and ponder what your disappearance did to your parents. You may have wiped your feet of them very thoroughly, and good luck to you, but maybe, with the wisdom of hindsight, you might want to find some way of letting them know you're not dead.'

Another smile. 'That's what my friend in London said. But I'll say to you what I said to him: I'm not ready to, now or for the foreseeable future. As for all this written work — you make it sound as if you're keeping me in detention like a naughty schoolboy.'

'And you have a problem with that?' She watched him leave. It was time to see what was — what was the word? — *interesting*. What would Caffy say about the three of them all choosing the same uninformative word?

CHAPTER TWENTY-THREE

When she reached the Incident Room she was greeted by an ironic cheer. She responded with a flap of the hand and an enigmatic smile — not for anyone was she going to report on the needs of her bladder, which had caused a three-minute delay in addition to the time spent wrapping up the conversation with Murray.

'Well? What is it that's so interesting?' she demanded. Ed and Ray were looking cock-a-hoop, but there was no sign of Mark. Nor should there be, of course, but her heart bled for him, especially as Ed greeted her with the words, 'Mark's had what looks like a breakthrough. A remote farmhouse in the middle of nowhere — between Stone Street and the east coast.'

Obligingly the map reference appeared on the magic screen, immediately replaced by an OS map and then by Google Earth's view.

'Abbot's Croft,' Ed said, touching it.

A red circle appeared on the map, which had reappeared. No other cottages for miles. No other anything. A hamlet called Westry was the nearest to anything like civilization.

What the hell was Mark doing out there, when he'd promised himself an afternoon's gardening to wind down after tennis?

'So to get to it from Upper Hogben you can go cross country, meaning you can miss out all the nice CCTV and number recognition cameras on the M20,' Fran observed, thinking it was time she said something useful. 'You'd only be able to do it slowly, wouldn't you? But it's horsey country out there — no one would remark on a horsebox picking its way through the lanes. And no one would check if there was a child inside the horsebox . . .'

'Quite. But we've taken no action yet,' Ed Chatfield said. 'Not until we could consult you. After all, we've absolutely no evidence of any wrongdoing connected to the farmhouse and the stable. It's just a hunch.'

'And not even our hunch,' she added. 'Just Mark's hunch. Upstairs won't like it at all if we call it wrong, will they? Trouble is, the place is so isolated that it isn't as if we can knock on the neighbours' doors and talk to them.'

'Seems to me the horse is the answer,' Ray said.

Someone jeered, 'You're going to have it in for questioning? Check its ID?'

Fran snapped, not least because she should have come up with Ray's idea herself, 'We've got a good description. We know its shoe size; we've got casts of the prints it leaves. We start from there. So we'd need to access the farm and its buildings.'

'And to catch and examine the horse,' Ray observed quietly. 'For which we need experts. After all, I don't imagine it'll just stand still and raise its legs for you.'

Fran nodded and spoke to the young man who'd mocked Ray. 'Check out someone from Mounted — and the vet who Mounted use. Someone with experience and discretion. Now. OK?'

It was very clearly going to be OK from the minute she opened her mouth. 'Ma'am.' He sprang into action.

She continued, 'All this is going to take time — time we may not have. I think we should take a big and expensive risk. Let's assume Livvie's at that farm. Hang the budget. I want her out alive. And just this once we'll throw everything at it. Even a search dog — the sort they use in earthquakes. So long,' she added in her most dulcet tone, 'as we don't frighten the horse.'

It was hard to do everything at the double when the lower half of her body protested at every move, but hard it would have to be. Grabbing her jacket, she rushed to the waiting car via a snack machine, texting Mark as she went: he needed to know she was backing his judgement. Even if he didn't respond — and she had a multitude of other things to do as she was ferried to the site — she'd bet her pension that though he'd never for a moment interfere with the operation, he'd not be far away. He couldn't bear to be, any more than she would in his situation.

* * *

It was another lovely clear evening, with bright stars but no moon, and was as bitterly cold as the previous ones had been. The uniform sergeant in charge of the site flagged them down some five hundred metres from their target, then gave an embarrassed and general salute. 'Park over there, mate, with the others,' he whispered to Fran's driver — not Dizzy this time, but a constable from Ray's team, a lad called Jay. 'We're keeping a clear run just in case we need an ambulance — right?'

'Good work. Better have an ambulance on standby, actually, even though their budgets are as badly hit as ours,' Fran said, forcing herself to get out of the car without assistance. At least now she didn't have time to worry about the pain, which was as bad as it had been for weeks, or the consequences. She slipped on the regulation brightwear and accepted a hard hat.

'It's a bit of a step, ma'am,' the sergeant warned her. 'Would you want to wait till the DCI says it's OK to bring in wheeled vehicles? He arrived five minutes ago, ma'am — scooted off as if the devil himself was nipping his heels. Or if you prefer, I could get someone to offer you their arm, as it were? I don't see your crutches, ma'am,' he added, half in, half out of the car, burrowing behind the front seats.

'Don't tell anyone, but I've given them up.'

'Very glad to hear that, ma'am.'

He sounded so sincere she added a sop to his pride. 'But I would be grateful for a torch — starlight's all very lovely, but a few streetlights would have been more useful. Or a moon.'

'No problem, ma'am.' He proffered one. 'But I could detail someone to accompany you anyway.'

For goodness' sake, did he think she was the queen? But why kick such thoughtfulness in the teeth, especially as it was quite a good idea? 'That would be more than kind. Thanks.'

Her escort turned out to be Ginny, a bright-eyed young woman, quiet until spoken to, and then happy to brief her.

'So how many people have been deployed round here? There were enough cars back there for twenty-odd,' Fran breathed.

'That's right, guv'nor.' The response was equally quiet. 'And a personnel carrier's down the lane the far side of the farm — so another dozen, I suppose.'

'They've done very well — even though I know they're there I can't see anyone — or hear anyone.'

'Total blackout — though they've got night glasses and cameras. Oh, and radio silence, guv'nor. No talking rule, of course — until you give the word and things kick off.'

'I'd better observe it too then, hadn't I?' And it was a good idea to concentrate on where she was putting her feet.

Perhaps the horse could sense her colleagues' presence, however: even from fifty metres away it sounded as if it was moving around a lot, and it whinnied from time to time. She hadn't a clue what that indicated. Hard hat in hand, Ray was lurking under a tree and flapped a hand to attract her attention, so she asked him quietly, 'Any sign of the mounted officer yet?'

'On her way — but now she's caught in a six-mile tail-back on the M20. Fatal RTA.'

'Sod it.' No time to feel sorry for the victim or those dealing with it. Not yet. 'What about that tame vet?'

'We're on to it now, guv'nor,' Ray whispered, pointing at another bright-jacketed figure, who was apparently doing a square dance until he settled for a far corner. 'Poor mobile coverage.'

'So I see. Search dog?' she asked.

'Also on its way — the Fire Service were very helpful,' a woman's voice responded, almost inaudibly. She wasn't sure who it was, but thanked her anyway.

Ray continued, 'We're rigging up lights too. We won't switch them on till you ask for them, but they're focused on both the house and the stables.'

'Excellent. This place is a bit of a dump, isn't it?'

'The farmhouse? Yes — it belonged to a Mrs Dyer, who became something of a recluse after she lost her husband. And now she's so far gone with dementia they had to section her.' He added grimly, 'When she goes, I dare say her relatives will be down like vultures. The house'll fetch a bomb when it's been done up a bit. Don't know about those ruins at the back, though.' He pointed at the stable area. 'They'll probably accidentally on purpose run a JCB into them and bring the whole lot down. And worry about planning permission later.'

'That'd be a shame. Mark assures me they're Tudor. It'll be easier to tell when we risk switching the lights on.' What did Mark know about Tudor architecture, come to think about it?

Ray turned to speak into his radio. 'Everyone's in place. How much noise do you want when we go in?'

'We're not on some drugs raid in the back end of Canterbury filmed for TV. We know we've got a restless horse with sharp bits at the front and metal at each corner, and I very much hope we've got a terrified child. So very little noise, in other words. Check the house first: though it's boarded up, there may be some unofficial way in. And then we approach the stable area. But, I repeat, I don't want anyone getting in the way of those hooves.'

He spoke into his radio again, almost immediately turning back to her. 'Shall I get them to take the bolt-cutters to the chain round the gate? Actually, the gates themselves are in remarkably good condition. You can see the oil on the hinges. See, open sweet as a nut, don't they?'

'Excellent. Now, where's that young woman who played the Girl Guide and got me down here without falling over? She's got a nice voice. I'd like her to call out to Livvie. Better than a man, I'd say. Ginny,' she recalled at last. 'And Ray: we all need to observe Elf and Safety regs, all the time.' She patted his unworn hat.

'Sorry.' The hard hat went on. 'I'll get her over here and brief her.'

Meanwhile, a small van drove up, and two men emerged, freeing a bounding, bouncing spaniel from the rear. 'You're sure that that's child-friendly?'

'She's not just any dog, remember,' Ray said, as the new arrivals retrieved equipment from their van. 'She's the one on loan from the Fire Service — she sniffs out bodies in collapsed buildings. She's done service in Japan and Italy.'

'Live bodies or dead bodies?' To her own ears her voice sounded hollow.

'Live, as it happens.'

'OK. House first!'

The moment Ray gave the signal, a detail of a dozen black-clad officers surrounded the house, most tearing down the planks from a front window and piling in. The rest deployed themselves to the rear. She could hear voices calling from room to room. Soon they emerged from the same window, like giant chickens from an ugly egg.

'Zilch,' their leader reported. 'The place has been stripped back to the floor boards — no furniture, no soft furnishings, nothing at all in the kitchen — not so much as an old milk bottle. At least the old woman's executors will have an easy time.'

'So nothing at all?' Ray's face fell comically. 'Shit. And I wanted lots of items dripping with DNA. OK. Plan B, then guv'nor? We get Ginny to call the girl?' He made a swift cutting gesture — and got absolute silence.

She was sure she wasn't the only one holding her breath, willing her ears to pick up the slightest sound coming in response. Nothing, except more noisy activity from the damned horse.

If only there was something to raise the team's spirits. Anything. 'I don't suppose there's any news from Ed about picking up Thwaite?'

'You'd be the first to know, guv'nor,' he said reproachfully. 'You want us to go back into quiet mode?'

She nodded. 'Unless Thwaite turns up here and things kick off.'

'But we'd still like him taken alive, eh, guv?'

Was he joking? Just at the moment she didn't care. 'Quite. Get that dog in there.'

The taller of the hard-hatted handlers, whom Ray identified as Gavin, Simon being the shorter, peeled off with the dog and headed briskly to the stable. Within what seemed like seconds came the sound of shrill barks. 'What the hell? We warned you about the horse!' Ray snarled at the remaining handler. 'It's not supposed to be some crazy canine that barks for the pleasure of it.'

Fran put a hand on his arm, trying hard to catch Simon's eye apologetically. But no doubt he'd seen a lot of het-up would-be rescuers, so he nodded coolly and resumed his study of the night sky.

But Ray was still frantic. 'Maybe it thinks the horse is human. Shit, I'd better take this,' he groaned, fishing out his radio. But he turned back, beaming. 'Guv — Thwaite's left his house. Ed's got a tail on him. And we, of course,' he added grimly, 'have a reception committee here.'

Probably no one heard his last words. The woman officer — Ginny — was calling. 'I think I can hear crying. A child.'

'A child? You're sure?'

'Yes. And I'd say it's a girl. But I can't see where the noise is coming from.'

Fran was at the stable door before she knew it. 'Let the dog show us.'

'Sod it!' She fumbled her phone from her jacket pocket. 'Bloody Wren.' She switched it to voicemail.

The spaniel was barking at a solid stone wall. Helpful or not. At least it was a solid stone wall some ten feet from the loosebox. The horse looked increasingly frantic — and they hadn't even brought in the sledgehammers yet. Where the hell was the vet?

She stepped inside, raising one finger, like an umpire giving a particularly firm verdict. Silence, that was what she wanted. 'Everyone out,' she said. 'It looks to me as if that horse is spooked. Let it calm down. Meanwhile, let's see if we can find an alternative way in. Time for all those lovely lights to be switched on, I'd say. And hard hat time for anyone venturing into the more dilapidated section — understand? And in the yard generally. For everyone's sake. And get that bloody vet here. Any bloody vet, if the regular one's done a disappearing act. And make sure there's an escort for him or her to speed things up.' She turned to Gavin, a disconcertingly elegant young man with beautiful almond-shaped eyes. 'How would you feel about taking it—?'

'Her. Flo. Short for Florence.'

'Sorry. Flo. How would you feel about taking Flo into the rest of this — this ruin?'

He smiled serenely. 'It's what we do, Chief Superintendent. That's why they're called rescue dogs. Not a lot of neatly standing buildings left after an earthquake. Just a nice lot of — ruins. We've got all we need in the van — lights, digging equipment, first aid, ladders. A few dog treats, too,' he added.

'She looks as if she needs one,' Fran observed. The dog was desperate to get back into the stable, its feathery tail working harder than a wind turbine. 'Hey, she really likes that bit of wall, doesn't she? Soon as we get rid of Dobbin here, she can tell the team where to wield their pickaxes.'

'Uh, uh. Best leave that to me and Simon. Generally speaking it's best not to whack fragile structures. They don't take kindly to it. First we'll take Flo in through any other access points and see what she picks up. Come on: good girl.'

'I take it you don't need company.'

'We don't, if it's all the same to you. Concentration apart, the structure doesn't look too clever. It's our job to read the danger signs. We know when and where to scarper.'

The team waited, in varying states of impatience. But there were people with even more right to be impatient. 'Ray, has anyone called young Zac yet? I know we can't be sure it's Livvie. But if it is, the one thing that'll keep her going while we demolish the place around her ears is the sound of her parents' voices. Oh, give me the phone. I can't bear doing nothing. Thanks.' Fran gave a thumbs up — Zac had picked up. But it wasn't Zac, of course — it was the family liaison officer. 'Fran Harman here. Put Zac on please.' She rolled her eyes. 'I know you can give him a message — I know that's your job. So first tell Zac we've found a child and I believe that it's Livvie. Alive. Right? And then tell him I need to talk to him now. For God's sake!' There was the sound of a phone being dropped. My God, at this point they drop the phone! 'Zac?' But it was the FLO again. Fran had a special voice for underlings doing their job well but misguidedly. 'I repeat, this is Detective Chief Superintendent Harman here, constable. Now, I just want you to forget your training and the rule book — especially the rule book — and get Zac to the phone this instant. Yes, Zac or Bethany.' She gave the news with as much caution as she could.

Zac's voice was disconcertingly pleading: it was as if the FLO had taken so much responsibility in recent days that he was almost institutionalized. 'Can I come over?'

'Yes. Absolutely. So long as you know that there is just an outside chance it may not be Livvie.'

'But it may?'

'It may. Now, you won't have to drive because I'll want to keep in touch with you. So your FLO will bring you over. With a blue light escort.'

'What about Bethany? And Jack? Can they come too?' He still sounded plaintive, unsure — the strong and authoritative young man having to ask strangers for permission.

Fran snapped her fingers in irritation: what sort of woman was she not even to think about the rest of the family? 'Of course. Wrap Jack warmly — the temperature's dropped very sharply. And warm clothes for both of you as well — it could be a long wait and there's no point in false heroics. Oh, and Livvie too — most important. They'll need what she's wearing for forensics. Her favourite cuddly toy. The one Bethany said she loved to bits.' She must make sure she got Livvie that pink teddy before the case was closed. 'Now, keep your phone on. With luck you can help even while you're being driven along. OK? Oh, which of you is closer to her? You? Yes, it's you I need then. Give me that FLO again . . .'

That felt better. Now what? Would a KitKat and a packet of crisps crammed down during the car journey over here constitute a meal in the eyes of the painkillers? In her eyes they would. But the last time she'd risked popping a pill on a semi-empty stomach she'd thrown up. On one's hands and knees retching into a ditch wasn't a good look.

The dog handlers returned. 'She's not so interested in that side of the wall,' Gavin said. 'But in any case, neither of us can see any access points in there, either. Nor anything concealing one — we moved everything we could.' He turned to look over her shoulder. 'Someone's in a bit of a hurry.'

Someone was. Blues but no twos. Her radio crackled.

'Vet's on her way, ma'am. A Dr Webb. Expert in equine medicine, as it goes.'

Perhaps the dice were beginning to roll her way.

First up, Dr Webb, a disconcertingly petite woman in her thirties, wanted the yard completely cleared and the main lights off. She also wanted a horsebox. Red faces all round. Presumably no one had fully explained the situation to her.

'A field?' asked Fran to break the silence. 'We've got plenty of those.' She spread her hands. 'OK, send for a horsebox. Any preference as to size?'

'There's no need to take that tone with me, inspector,' Dr Webb objected.

Fran hadn't enough energy to argue. 'What size, Dr Webb?' She summoned Ray. 'See Dr Webb has all the equipment she needs, will you? Including safety gear. Pronto.' She turned back to the vet. 'The animal's well and truly frightened. I can see that. But we really, really need to get at the child we believe is in there. Can you hear? She's crying again. And who can blame her? The thing is, with the horse in there needing quiet we can't get anyone in to reassure her, which currently means bellowing at the top of one's voice.'

'Her? Is it that missing child? Livvie? My God, why didn't anyone tell me? OK, I'll go and talk to the horse. Do we know its name?'

Ray said, 'My colleagues think it might be Thor.'

'Nothing unpretentious there, then,' Webb declared briskly. 'OK. No lights, no cameras, but maybe some action. And silence and a clear yard, remember. Oh, best make sure that field's horse-proof first.'

'Over to you,' Fran said with what she hoped was an encouraging smile. As she limped with all the others out of the yard, she fell into step with Simon and Flo. 'You really can see no way to get at the girl?'

Simon shook his head. 'I've tried shinning up on to the next level — there's a rough set of steps, not original and hardly deserving of the name — but really it's the same picture. Blank walls.'

'Not even a fireplace,' Gavin agreed.

Fran stopped so suddenly Simon nearly tripped. 'What would you normally do in a situation like this?'

'Find a builder? Or an architect?'

'Or someone used to restoring old buildings?' she asked slowly.

'Spot on, I'd say. But where would you get one of those at this time of night? And in this neck of the woods?'

'Keep Flo in treats and leave it with me.'

CHAPTER TWENTY-FOUR

Mark's lack of enthusiasm for his Cajun chicken and chips was matched by Caffy's for her prawn salad. Neither would accuse the food of being below par, which it wasn't, not for a quiet Monday night with hardly enough people in the bar to justify being open, let alone serving food. But both spent more time putting down their cutlery and eyeing their phones as if they'd never heard of the watched kettle principle.

'This is the part of being retired I hate most,' Mark said at last. 'Knowing there's important stuff happening yet having no part. Knowing I actually need to keep out of Fran's hair.'

'You're worried about her, aren't you?'

'Wouldn't you be? She's got too much to do and the harder she pushes herself the more pain she gives herself. And because she's skipping meals and grazing on rubbish where she can find it, she daren't take her painkillers. And no, until she's found Livvie, I can't possibly ask her to slow down. Who could? But the minute she does, I shall whisk her off to the GP and get her signed off for a week or so. Let the other buggers do the paperwork and go to meetings.'

'And will you really put your foot down so firmly, or would you just like to?'

'You know, I think I might. And succeed. After all, if there's one thing she loathes, it's paperwork. Another apple juice?'

'No thanks. But go ahead if — Mark, that's your phone. Yours, not mine.'

It was. Bloody, sodding ears. 'Fran?'

'The very same. Sweetheart, that sudden rush of architectural knowledge — where did it come from? You see, we've surrounded your Tudor ruin and can hear a child, we think—'

'Livvie?' he squawked.

'Please God, yes. But we can't be sure and we can't reach her. So this Tudor stuff: was it Caffy who told you? And if it was, have you any idea where she might be? We could really use her and that course of hers.'

'You got it in one. She's here. Do you want to speak to her?'

'Just bring her, love. And bring yourself. Sooner the better. I really need both of you.'

'Just a sec. Caffy, we've got an invitation. Your van or my car?'

'My van: all the safety gear's in there.' She was on her feet settling the bill at the bar.

'We're on our way,' Mark said. There was inaudible muttering. 'We'll be in Caffy's van. Can you make sure we get clearance?'

'You bet.' She ended the call.

Thank goodness for the tennis. He might be twice Caffy's age, but they reached the van at the same moment, throwing themselves in and fastening their seat belts as one. There was no argument about who was going to drive. Caffy probably suspected his night vision might be as bad as his hearing. Of her own she clearly and terrifyingly had no doubts at all.

* * *

As they all huddled silently in the lane, feeling the cold far more now they weren't busily doing things, they heard a reassuring sound: the clatter of hooves on cobbles. The sound went away from them.

'That woman's a heroine,' Ray observed, 'calming that bloody great nag. Now what? No, no one's to move till she gives the OK.' He held out a warning arm, an umpire delaying a bowler at the end of his run-up.

'What indeed? Watching and waiting aren't our strong suit, are they? Ah, she's waving now. Get Ginny back into the stable to see if she can establish any sort of contact with Livvie.' Fran made herself keep pace with Ray, as everyone returned to the yard.

'Still assuming it is Livvie, and not some cat stuck up the chimney,' he growled, his voice gravelly with emotion.

She gripped his hands. 'Ray, we've got this far — hold together a bit longer, lad.'

He nodded. 'Just a minute, guv, that's my phone.' He pulled his mobile out, listened briefly then turned to her. 'It's the chief constable — wants to know why your phone's switched to voicemail. And, more to the point, wants to speak to you right now.'

What the hell could he want at this time of night? He should have been roosting by now. 'Tell him I'll call right back.'

'He says now.'

She dug out her mobile. 'Keep yours for urgent calls. Tell him I'm dialling even as we speak. Sir,' she added in her standing-to-attention voice. She moved away from the group in her search for a signal; it wouldn't be good for her team to hear her being bollocked for whatever she'd done to upset the boss.

'HQ now, Harman.'

'We're trying to rescue Livvie.'

'I don't care if you're trying to arrange tea with the Queen. Delegate. My office. Now.'

'Sir, with all due respect, I cannot leave this scene. Cannot. Can we not discus whatever is needful over the phone?' Why should she think *cannot* and its variants sounded more authoritative than the usual abbreviation? 'Our suspect is on the loose, and Livvie trapped out of reach . . . In fact, sir—'

'Are you refusing an order, Harman?'

Of course she bloody was. 'In fact, sir,' she continued as if he hadn't spoken, 'it would be a brilliant media opportunity if you came here. The moment the press and TV get hold of the story, and it's far more complicated than you've been told — the child's trapped in a dangerous building, and her father's on his way — they'll be here like wasps round a glass of beer.' OK, incoherent, but surely he'd get the gist. She took a breath. 'If my place is here, yours is too,' she declared. That felt better. 'Though of course, Acting DCI Barlow's doing brilliantly,' she continued, knowing the response, but choosing to sacrifice Ray this once.

'Acting . . . Ah, Acting DCI Barlow. Of course. But where's the CEOP superintendent?'

'He's detailed to pick up our suspect.'

She could hear his hierarchical brain ticking. 'Of course,' he admitted at last, 'it's operationally appropriate that a senior officer be present. Very well. Give me your coordinates.'

'I'll pass you to DCI Barlow — he's more technologically competent than I am, sir, and I think the father's just arrived,' she lied.

Ray's conversation with Wren was surprisingly calm and succinct. Once the call was over, she opened her mouth to congratulate him. But his radio crackled. Turning from her politely, he spoke with some force. She was too preoccupied to feel sorry for the person at the other end.

He turned to her. 'It's Mark Turner and someone called Caffy?'

'Caffy, yes. Our buildings expert.'

'Right: you'd given them top-level clearance, I gather, Fran, but neither had any official ID, and . . . Anyway, they're on their way. That's probably them now.' He pointed to lights moving fast down the lane towards them. And some other lights coming much more slowly. 'Oh, and that must be the horsebox the vet wanted — I don't blame her wanting to get the damned thing inside. There's a nasty wind blowing across that field and she's stayed with it all this time.'

'Good.' He might be expecting a more positive response, but she didn't have the energy, especially as they all had to make way for the horsebox and then, of course, clear the yard all over again. There was a collective sigh of relief as the underpowered box struggled into action and off up the lane. 'Now, I don't want even a second's delay when Zac and Bethany appear,' she said, as if he didn't know already. 'Sorry.' She patted his shoulder. 'You're doing fine.'

'Thanks, Fran. I must say I'm a bit out of my depth, so it's good you're here. But you're not so good, are you? Shall I find you somewhere to sit?'

'Do you ever sit on the job? Well, then.' Her voice might have started bracing, but ended grateful. 'But thanks for the thought. I'll be OK. Don't start worrying about me in case you take your eye off the ball.' All the same, as the PACT van stopped, she had to wait for Mark and Caffy to run to her.

Ray pulled a face. 'Women builders, guv?'

'I hope I don't get a whiff of sexism there, Ray. Wait and see, that's all I'll say. Talk to Mark. He'd give her not just a medal, but a halo.'

To hell with what others might think, she hugged them both before, still holding Mark's hand, she briefed Caffy. Let Ray take his cue from her.

'I'd better talk to the dog handlers,' Caffy said, professional as always, dipping back into the van for boots, hi-vis jacket and a hard hat. Times two, it transpired as she passed Mark his kit. In an instant she was transformed from their quasi-daughter into the professional who'd rescued their rectory. She strode off in Ray's wake.

All Fran wanted to do was collapse in Mark's arms, but that was scarcely an option. For an instant, she rested her forehead on his shoulder. Almost as an afterthought, she said, 'Mark — would Livvie recognize your voice? She might, you know. Just might. Come and do the biz, for heaven's sake.'

She paused while he donned the kit Caffy had provided. 'Talk the talk, please, sweetheart, while we find a way in. She's behind that wall.'

She could see he had to say it: 'I'm not trained—'

'You're a grandfather — of course you're trained,' she said more crisply than she ought. 'Please, just talk to her,' she added, her hand on his arm. 'Imagine it's young Marco in there.'

Mark hunkered down; he even put his hand on the wall, as if to make better contact. 'Livvie? It's Mark, here, your daddy's friend. From tennis. We've come to take you to your daddy. Did you hear that? Be a good girl and tell me where you got in.' He raised an urgent hand — silence from everyone. Then he cupped his ear — he couldn't hear her reply, could he?

'She said something about Father Christmas!' Ginny whispered.

'Father Christmas?' Mark repeated, but to Livvie.

Ginny pointed upwards and mimed. What the hell? 'A chimney?' she whispered.

'Did you come down a chimney?' Mark ventured.

Everyone except Mark heard her sob. Actually, he might just have done too.

Fran murmured into his ear, 'Can you keep talking to her? Zac's on his way, tell her. And Bethany and their baby.'

'Of course.' Mark pressed to the wall as if hugging the child to him and shouted. 'Mummy's coming too. And Jack. They won't be long, Livvie. And I'll stay here till they come, I promise.' There was movement behind him. He'd been joined by Caffy and the handlers. The dog's tail might have been wagging the animal, it moved so fast. 'Livvie, we've even got a dog looking for you. Can you hear the dog? Listen quietly, now!'

Flo barked obligingly.

Mark turned to her. 'How about I phone Zac and switch the phone to conference? There's just a chance she'll hear him. And he her,' he added. 'But the rest of you might drown her out.'

They withdrew soberly to the brightly lit yard. If anything, it was getting even colder.

Ray stepped forward. 'Guv, do you want Ed and his team to stop Thwaite where he is and bring him over so he can tell us?'

She narrowed her eyes. 'Do you really think he would? Some men might, others would clam. Besides which, it'd be interesting to see where he's heading. And I tell you now, if it's to someone else's house, we need to bug it straightaway. I want that conversation on record. Right?'

Caffy and the dog handlers had taken Flo back into the upper reaches of the building: Fran could hear movement, but there was no sign of them. Peering into the stable, she checked again on Mark and Livvie. Mark was holding the phone as close as he could to where they thought Livvie must be. Zac could talk to the child, even if he couldn't pick up her replies.

'Any progress?' Mark mouthed.

'Only that Wren's flying in.'

'Maybe he does a good Father Christmas impression? I can't think of any other reason — Fran, you didn't?' His face fell comically.

'Didn't what? Invite him? Had to. It was either that or me being whisked off to HQ and put on the naughty step, by the sound of it. He can deal with the media — come on, he'll relish that, won't he? And no jokes about preening. Until Livvie's out of here I'm this close to hysterical giggles.'

Ray's face appeared at the door. 'Thwaite?' she asked, using Mark's shoulder to lever her up.

'Still driving. Not obviously in this direction. But Ed thinks he may have suspected a tail and he's pulled right back. After all, Thwaite's tracking device is still transmitting happily so there's no point in worrying him. And Zac and Bethany are only about ten minutes away now.'

'Excellent.' She passed the message on to Mark, still holding the phone to the wall as if his life depended on it. She took his spare hand and gripped it, dotting a kiss on it before she crept out again, straight into Caffy's arms.

Instead of a polite after-you dance, Caffy grabbed her and hugged her, asking quietly, 'Are you OK? Silly question, you've got to be, haven't you? Anyway, just to update you: we think we must have come across a priest's hole. If you think of it, there must have been staging posts for Catholics coming over from the Continent during Elizabeth's reign, and this place is old enough to have been one of them. Externally I know it looks Elizabethan, but I reckon it might be an earlier building with a facelift — you know how when Georgian became fashionable, loads of medieval houses had make-overs.'

Fran didn't, but nodded encouragement — the last thing she needed just now was a lecture on architecture.

'While they were installing panelling and so on,' Caffy continued, gesturing to the upper level, 'we think they must have constructed a hidden chamber. Trouble is, it's so well hidden we can't quite find it ourselves, not without tearing the wainscoting apart. For which we need permission, of course, technically from the owner.'

'Are you sure that's the only way in? The child's just mentioned Father Christmas: is there a handy chimney?'

'There's a whacking great fireplace. I'll get on to it. Or into it. Thanks for letting me do this, Fran. And Mark: he was so desperate to be involved.'

'I couldn't manage without either of you,' Fran said sincerely. 'Or your hugs.'

'You'd better have another one, then. And then I'll locate my reindeer.'

'Take care: we want two lives safe at the end of this, not one sacrificed in a fruitless search.' The two embraced.

Wren chose that moment to pop up. Hop up. Whatever. Fran couldn't read the expression on his face but introduced the two cheerily. 'My boss, the Chief Constable, Caffy Tyler. Sir, this is my honorary daughter, a historic buildings expert. Like I said, Caffy — be careful. Simon and Gavin — the guys with the search and rescue dog — they'll have loads of appropriate equipment. Cooperate with them. Anything extra, let me know.'

'On the other hand,' Wren objected, 'if our suspect got the child into the building without such extras, it might be presumed that we can remove the child without them. And without damaging the building, if possible. We don't want legal repercussions, do we?'

'Especially as you've not yet confirmed that I'm covered by your insurance,' Caffy rapped back, leaving Fran to take any flak as she clambered back to the upper floor. Pausing at the top, she called down, 'Assuming that I am, would you care to see the site, Chief Constable?'

'Chief Superintendent?' The wretched man made a courteous gesture. She was to go first.

'Sorry, sir. I could lie and say my job's on the ground here, but I'll tell you the truth. My back's so painful that in other circumstances I'd be on sick leave.'

'Back? I thought it was your leg that was broken?'

He sounded so offended that she was tempted to burst ironically into the old song about the connections between bones. 'Secondary injury, sir. So though I'd give my teeth to be up there, I might put others at risk. But Ray Barlow's already checking it out, sir.' She pointed as Ray, his hand firmly grasped in Caffy's, made a final heave and scrambled to elevated safety.

'She looks very young to be an expert.'

'Ray's already dismissed her as the wrong sex to be an expert,' Fran said cheerfully. She debated pointing out that he'd not followed Ray aloft, but dismissed it as dangerous point-scoring when no one knew how much weight the upper floor would bear. In any case, there was movement behind her. 'Mark? Problem?'

He waved his phone as if he'd like to commit violence either with it or upon it. 'The battery's given out. Ah. Wren.' Nodding coldly, the two men eyed each other in mutual distaste. 'As has Zac's,' he continued, getting back to more important matters. 'Can one of your people get in there and keep Livvie posted? You know my hearing's not up to it.'

Fran wasn't sure that hers was either. Where was that nice girl who'd escorted her down here? Jeanie? Ginny!

'Where are you, Ginny? Good girl, can you get in there and tell Livvie that the phone's gone wrong but that her daddy's getting nearer every second? Keep her talking. It may help Caffy and the others locate the opening. Thanks.' She smiled and turned to Wren, who still hadn't managed to speak to Mark. Out of the blue came a memory of an A level text when a woman called Mrs Moore knew she had to get warring factions apart. She tried her hand with Wren first: 'Sir? This is the other part of the site.' She led the way into the stable. 'You can see at first hand the challenges we're facing. At least we've got rid of the horse,' she added kindly as he slipped on some manure.

When they'd come in, Ginny was calling reassuring words, and turned, ready to pass on what Livvie had said. There was no need, however, to interpret what they all heard — and possibly those outside too. A piercing, terrified scream.

CHAPTER TWENTY-FIVE

Mark didn't think he could move so fast. He was up on the upper storey and in the huge fireplace before he knew it, and, elbowing Ray aside, peering down on his hands and knees beside the frantic spaniel and one of its handlers. Of Caffy and the other handler there was no sign.

'Gavin,' the young man said, offering his hand as if they were guests at some formal party. 'There's no problem. It's just that a panel gave way before we could warn Livvie and she was surprised, that's all. Nearly as surprised as we were, to be honest. Looked like solid stone and it just slipped sideways.'

'Mark. A friend of Livvie's father.' They shook hands formally. 'What are the chances of getting her out?'

'Look for yourself. No, wait. Clip this round you first. OK with heights, are you?'

Heights were the last thing in the world he was OK with, but he leant down anyway. 'Livvie? Livvie?' He'd have liked to wave but that meant releasing one hand gripping the edge of the hearth as if his life depended on it, not Gavin's safety line. 'I'm your daddy's friend Mark. Tennis? We were talking, weren't we, before you could talk to your daddy.'

'I wet my knickers.'

'We'll find you some dry ones.' He hoped to goodness Bethany had had the sense to bring a change of clothes for her. He should have thought of it — no way Fran would. Was there? 'Caffy, how soon can you get her out?'

'Soon as Gavin lets down the next safety line. And a dear little hard hat specially for her. Just move to one side, Mark, and let us get on with it. But don't go far: I think she'd like you to be the one to hold her when she pops up like a rabbit out of its hole.'

He did as he was told, but yelled down to the onlookers in the yard — no police radio for him, after all — to give the good news. Back to the hole, to reach for the arms lifted trustingly to him. Yes, the child smelt — knickers worse than wet — but she was alive and trusting him as two of his own grandchildren would never get the chance to do. Cradling her, he put his face down to hers.

'Everyone back. Flo's sensed movement!' Gavin yelled. 'Get her down now, Mark. Quick. Floor's collapsing!'

He did as he was told, propelled by Gavin.

Then everything happened at once. A rapid response vehicle erupted into the yard, disgorging Jack and Bethany. Fran hurtled forward, arms outstretched, to hold them back. Zac pushed past her. She gave chase. Zac was up the make-shift steps like a monkey, grabbing Livvie. There was an ominous creak. 'Everyone off here. Now. Go, go, go!' Gavin's voice was loud, authoritative.

Zac and Livvie first. Mark made sure of that. Someone — Gavin? — sat him down hard and slid him on his backside like a kid on a slide. Ray next. Lastly Gavin and his dog. But no sign of the other handler or of Caffy as the ancient wood and plaster that had supported them collapsed into a heap of dust and rubble.

He was on his feet before he knew it. 'Fran? Fran?'

'Over here.' She was, but was on all fours, as if someone had cut her off at the knees. But not a simple trip, or she'd be up by now, wouldn't she?

Dear God, not a heart attack?

Before he could reach her, before he could even waste breath on a scream, she pushed herself up from her elbows on to her hands, but no further. She let forth a stream of invective he'd not heard her use since they'd become an item. 'Leg. Other leg. Something's snapped. Not a bone, it's just the leg won't work. Bloody hell,' she screamed, as he tried to lever her up. 'No. Leave me be, for God's sake. Sorry!'

'I'll get the paramedics.'

'No, Livvie needs them more than I do.'

'But—'

'Don't waste time on me. Just leave me here. I'm not going anywhere. Find Caffy and whatshisname. Mark, promise me.'

'Promise you what?' he asked, crouching beside her in the chaos, now augmented by the blues and twos of an ambulance. Of course, Fran must have had one on standby and one of the team had reacted to her fall. Whoever it was deserved a medal. 'Ironic,' he added, trying not to let his voice shake, but not with laughter, 'that your forward planning gets you a ride to A and E.'

She didn't find it funny. 'No. Livvie first. And Caffy. Promise me you'll rescue Caffy.' One hand gripped his painfully.

'There's a team on to that now,' he said reassuringly, moving so she could see. The dog, which had always been vociferous, was now dashing back to the stable, pursued by Gavin.

'I'm not moving from here till I see them in one piece. Understood?' she barked at Ray and the paramedics. 'I said, understood? In any case, you need the ambulance for Livvie. She is OK, isn't she?' Her grip on Mark's hand was painful.

Ray leant over them both. 'Cold, guv. Dirty. Hungry. But her parents are sorting her out and Ermintrude's already taking them as a family to A and E. See?' The car was going back up the lane as fast as it had come down.

'Ermintrude?'

'Their name for the smiley FLO,' Mark explained, with an exaggeratedly toothy grin at Ray, who returned it in spades.

'Oh, her!' she snorted. 'Ray — time to call in the media. Get Wren to earn his corn. Oh, very well.' She submitted to the paramedics' insistence — wise kids, that was the way to deal with her! — that she was in the way where she was. She looked with loathing at a wheelchair they produced. One more quite convulsive grab of his hand. 'I know how much you love her, Mark — go and help.'

What the hell did she mean by that? 'Of course I love her. She's the daughter we'll never have together,' he said, and felt her fingers relax a little. 'But just now my priority's you. I love you,' he added, as they increasingly did to end every phone call.

'I love you too.' Did he detect a swallowed sob? Not Fran, surely. 'Caffy,' she said firmly, at last submitting to being carted off.

Where this fresh lot of tears came from he wasn't sure, but he did as he was told, stumbling up collapsed masonry until Ray grabbed him. 'You'll only be in the way. They told me to clear out. Gavin and that bloody dog are in charge. That poor kid. I told Fran girls shouldn't be builders. Or experts,' he added with the venom of anxiety.

'I've got to be there, Ray. Same as Zac had to get to his daughter.'

'And a fat lot of good that did. Brought the whole lot down in one nice, sentimental move.'

'It's called being a parent, Ray. Which is why I need to be near Caffy. Her own parents are out of the country.' No need for complicated explanations about their relationship. 'So she'll need me.' Already his mind was looping frantically round the problems of summoning people he hardly knew to her bedside. Funeral. Dear God.

'See if you can make contact through the stable wall, then. I daren't risk more people where it's collapsed in case more goes. Sorry, Mark. It's where Gavin is, after all — he'll maybe have time to keep you briefed but don't bank on it.'

'Of course. Sorry. The stable it is.'

Ray pushed him through the cordon, but he stopped on the threshold. What he feared most, he supposed, was silence from the far side of the wall. Or screams. Moans, maybe, assuming he'd have heard them. The dog was silent, staring intently at the wall. Gavin was probing gently, a millimetre at a time. He both widened and lengthened his little hole. Mark didn't ask any questions. Just prayed. The dog and Gavin froze: they must have heard something. Actually, yes, he'd felt movement.

Ray came bustling in: 'Gavin, there's been another slip. Lots of bricks and stuff. But it's good news. The rubble came outwards. We can see them now — Simon reckons he's broken a rib or two, but he insists he's fine. Caffy's trapped by her ankles, but says the boots saved her. She wants to wriggle free but we said not to till you'd taken a look. Do you want to come and supervise?' As an afterthought, he looked at Mark, and then sharply away, embarrassed.

'She saved my life,' Mark told him. 'Caffy. Saved it at a time when my own daughter had given up on me.' He'd wanted to do something in return. 'I need to be there,' he pleaded with both of them.

Ray sighed. 'She didn't strike me as a woman who'd want heroics, any more than your Fran. Once you know she's safe, do you want a lift to the hospital to pick up Fran? I reckon Caffy and Simon will need the meat wagon when it gets back — cuts, Mark, cuts! — we all have to share transport now, which means longer waits. Oh, there's a motorbike paramedic waiting to triage them, but no wheels to A and E. But we've got a couple of cars you can — bloody hell, now what?'

The noise penetrated even Mark's cloth ears. Cheering even from the case-hardened men and women who'd seen practically everything but still believed in justice and law and order. But try as he might, he couldn't be as excited as they were by the news that Ed Chatfield had arrested Ross Thwaite. Better still, they'd got his accomplice at the house they'd been tailing him to. It was icing on the cake for Wren, now plumping his feathers and standing tall, ready to face TV crews in the lane approaching the site.

'OK. Let me just talk to Caffy: Fran'll be worried sick about her,' he said. 'Then I'll take you up on your offer.'

Simon was being hauled clear by Gavin and reunited with Flo. He was obviously in pain, and Gavin's bear hug looked very tender — clearly they were partners in both senses. Why hadn't it dawned on him till then? Because they'd been as professional and discreet as he and Fran had been when they'd officially worked together, that's why.

But Caffy was still stuck. In other circumstances it would have been comical, like someone who'd buried her feet on a beach and was waiting for a wash of sea to set them free.

When she saw him peering down she stuck out a hand like an old-fashioned traffic cop. 'Don't even think of coming down. What with Fran's leg and my foot, we've got to have one of us in one piece for this here wedding.'

'Your ankle — it's as bad as that?'

'It's not as good as I thought it was — there's no way I can get it out of the boot, and equally no way I can get the boot out of this lot. I'll just have to be patient and wait for someone to make the place safe and then get digging. It'll need shoring up there and there, I'd have thought, Gavin?' she added, over his shoulder. 'Unless you can risk taking out a bit of the stable wall and letting all this rubble simply respond to gravity? That wouldn't take nearly so long.'

Gavin squatted beside him. 'I'm going to lower a foil blanket. We need to keep you warm. But if that foot's as bad as you say, it may need surgery, so no nice hot tea and bikkies. OK with that?'

'More than OK,' she declared, swathing herself.

'Pity Livvie can't see you like that,' Mark said. 'She'd think you looked like a fairy.'

'You're sure she's OK? Good. What about the guy they think kidnapped her?'

'Taken in for questioning.'

'Oh, Fran'll enjoy that. She won't? Mark, what haven't you told me? Is she OK? She isn't, is she? My God, what's—'

'It looks like a torn muscle or snapped tendon. But they've carted her off to A and E.'

'So what the hell are you doing here?'

He managed a wry smile she soon shared: 'Acting under her orders. Would I dare do otherwise?'

'Who would? Ah! They've started on the stable wall. Watch for the landslip. Don't worry — the rope's got me safe. See?'

He did see — the expression on her face as she tried to use her leg. But Gavin clearly had a system, and he was in the way.

'Mark — go to Fran. And tell her I'll be in the next A and E cubicle before she can say crutch. Go!' Her cheeriness didn't deceive him; she didn't want an audience for what promised to be a very painful manoeuvre. All their bloody stoicism: she and Fran might have been mother and daughter for all they liked letting their guard down.

'You're sure?'

'Sure. Fran needs you: go!'

He went.

* * *

Every other time he'd had to collect Fran from A and E, she'd been furious that he'd left her there so long. She'd been demanding clothes or shoes she could wear over her injured limb. Most of all, her freedom.

This time, on the hard narrow bed, she didn't stir. For a moment — and he forced back the bile brought up by his terror — he thought she was dead, she lay so still. Flat on her back; hands clasped lightly on her chest; feet supported by three or four pillows — apart from the angle of her legs, trousers rolled to the knees, she might have been a figure on an Elizabethan tomb. Except, he told himself with a rueful, affectionate smile, carved figures didn't snore. He looked down at her, ready to take her hand, but unwilling to wake her. If anyone could sleep in the chaos of a busy A and E, they must be very tired indeed. Or as Caffy would say, he or she must be very tired indeed.

He found a chair and sat beside her, ready to wait.

She opened an eye. 'Caffy?'

'Will be joining you soon. Her leg got in the way when the wall collapsed. Just her leg. She wouldn't let me rescue her because she thought three of us hobbling round on our wedding day would be a bit too much.'

'Seven weeks on Saturday. We've both got time to shed the sticks — again. They think I tore a muscle. Nothing much.'

He looked: judging from the size of her calf, it was rather more than nothing much. However, if it was just enough to keep her away from work till she'd caught up on some sleep he'd be grateful.

'They gave me some painkillers in triage. They seem to have made me a bit sleepy.'

'A bit! You were sending your pigs to market for five minutes at least after I arrived. Ah, a medic.'

He stood back to await fireworks as a brisk young woman with hair scraped back in an Essex facelift ponytail approached. He got a worryingly docile fiancée nodding sagely and obediently, even when the words *five days' complete rest* were uttered. 'Yes, a muscle tear. Just here, I'd say? Yes?'

Fran yelped obligingly.

'Could be worse. Could be a tendon. Could be a ligament.'

'Treatment?' Fran sounded humble.

'RICE, Mrs Harman,' the doctor said, as if to a child. 'Rest, ice, compression, elevation. A nurse will strap it up in a moment. Ice it the moment you get home. Keep it above heart height. Complete inactivity bar just a few very gentle ankle exercises every hour.'

Mark asked grimly, 'And if she doesn't? If she goes into work?'

'Simples,' the young woman declared in an irritating Russian meerkat advert voice. 'It'll take much longer to get better. Five days' total rest, Mrs Harman. The nurse will make you a follow-up appointment next Monday — then we'll see if you're ready for physio. Meanwhile, use the crutches we'll organize for you, all the time. Repeat, both crutches, all the time. The more heroics, the less progress.'

'Thank you, doctor,' he and Fran said as one. She didn't mention the ones left lying somewhere in her office.

He shot her a suspicious look the moment they were alone again. 'Am I to believe a single word you said?'

'Those were the first words I was planning to say to Sean Murray tomorrow morning. Doesn't look as if I'll get the chance, now. It won't even be light duties for a bit, will it?'

'Not unless you plan to run your departments from the elegance of that chaise longue we've always loved and never quite got round to using. Actually, if there was anything truly vital, you could Skype. Either that or this time the mountain will simply have to come to Mohammed.'

'I'll worry about that in the morning. Hello, that isn't Caffy, is it?'

Mark waved.

An obliging nurse changed course and steered her wheelchair towards them, promising to tell his colleagues where she was. Somehow they managed a three-way hug.

'Your foot. I let you get hurt!' Fran exclaimed.

'Not you. Gavin said it was Zac trying to reach Livvie that precipitated the collapse. And that you were trying to stop him. Actually, those nice paramedics think I couldn't move it not because anything was broken but because it was just so compressed by the weight of the rubble. Of course they'll want to scan it, but the paramedics said I needed a lot of ice, a bit of compression and a bit of rest. I shall dance at the wedding, never fear. Will you?'

'If I have to spend all day, every day, doing physio I will. I promise. Spend all that on a gorgeous dress and have the line spoilt by crutches? I think not.'

CHAPTER TWENTY-SIX

There was no problem getting Ed and Ray to update her on the abduction case: they needed her input into their joint report, and turned up mid-morning with embarrassing quantities of flowers.

'We'd have bought chocs and biscuits too,' Ray said, 'but your secretary vetoed them.'

Fran nodded: 'Price beyond pearls, that woman. Or is it rubies?'

They also brought a pile of files, a neat camera to video her responses and a capacity to drink large quantities of tea and coffee, which they had to make themselves since Mark took advantage of their presence to join the Golden Oldies on court.

'You should have seen the stuff we found on Thwaite's computer,' Ed told her. 'If only we'd had the remotest excuse, I should have taken it earlier and had it examined. Anyway, now we have it, with links to all sorts of equally unlovely men, including the one he called on last night. This sleazeball lives on the coast, so our guess is Thwaite wanted to cadge a boat trip to France. With or without Livvie. Actually, if we hadn't interfered we think he'd have taken her.'

'Kidnap to order?'

'Yup. Either — best scenario — a rich childless couple wanting a china doll of a daughter, or—' He stopped as if he didn't want to articulate the alternative.

'We're talking all sorts of video nasties, maybe even a snuff movie?'

'That's what I'd fear.' He took a deep breath. They all did. 'We'd still have got him, of course, but sooner rather than later is best, in my opinion.'

'Yes, indeed. So did he take Livvie to order, as it were, or just on impulse?'

'Fran, the planning that went into it,' Ray said, leaning forward so she didn't have to twist to see him. 'Goodness knows how many other actual or attempted abductions we'll be able to pin on him. The collapse of the stable block will have messed up most of our forensics, but from what Livvie says the priest's hole was a proper little Wendy house — her words. She's as bright as a button. Said there was a plastic barrel full of water. Food and packets of juice. Toys. Tiny bed. The only thing she didn't like was the loo — the old garde-robe, I think your Caffy called it. She was afraid she'd fall down the hole, poor little mite, if she used it. Anyway, the medics sent her straight home with her family — but of course there'll be constant assessments. Ermintrude will have to stay a bit longer just to fend off the media, of course, but once they've had their pics, I hope they'll leave the family alone. Including young Zac. What's the latest on Mark's car, by the way?'

'You don't want to know. OK, you do. The graffiti's been modified a bit so no one could read exactly what it said and it's booked in for repair later this week. The club will pay if the miscreant can't or won't. Mark thinks he probably will.' She eased herself up a little. 'There's one thing you could do for me, Ray. I promised Bethany I'd get her a pink teddy, as soon as she was found, like the one we used as a prop on one of the appeals. Zac felt unhappy, since it wasn't really Livvie's. I bet she's buried in teddies from thousands of well-wishers at the moment, but I'd really like to keep my promise.'

He made a note. 'It's a sort of touching wood, isn't it?'

'There is one thing, Fran, I'd like your advice on.' Ed shifted in his chair. 'While we were pounding round the countryside yesterday evening, some guy called the BBC and promised a reward of ten thousand pounds for information leading to Livvie's recovery. And there's the cash the club members have raised. That's near enough six thousand. The obvious person to get it all — well, it's Mark, isn't it?'

'Sometimes the obvious thing isn't the answer,' she said slowly. 'I mean, yes, of course he should have a reward, but one thing retired senior police officers aren't terribly short of is money. And it wouldn't look at all well in the media, would it? But I'm not the one to make the decision. If you want to nominate Mark, that's your business. But I'll bet you a fiver he'd be horrified.'

'Of course, there are the two girls who approached him. And then the Golden Oldies did their reconstruction . . .'

'You could always float the idea to Mark that the club as a whole might accept the money — they could use it to build some decent loos and strengthen their fences. Maybe a crèche for littlies, too. Of course, this is rather shutting the stable door after the horse — sorry. Really didn't mean to say that.' She shifted in embarrassment. But if their groans were ironic, hers was real. She really would have to stop being so bloody stubborn and take the full dose of painkillers. 'This here report: shall we make a start on it?'

* * *

Although by now everyone knew that Sean Murray had done a runner and crept back with his tail between his legs, neither Ed nor Ray knew any more than that.

'The idiot,' Ray grumbled. 'If he'd come out and said he had a problem with the case, I can't imagine you'd have chucked him under the chin and said, "There, there, diddums," but I'm sure you'd have worked round the issue. After all, some of the grieving parents desperate for news might have been his own — the ones they say he's disowned.'

'And he might have had to visit other families who recognized him,' Ed agreed. 'Not easy.'

'To be honest, I don't know how I'd have handled it,' she admitted. 'I'd have gone ballistic, probably. Then, belatedly, sympathetic. I'd have asked to have him transferred to a case he could work on and brought someone else in with immediate effect. And yes, I suppose I'd have found someone to refer him to so he could get professional help.' There was no need to mention the time she and Tom, not to mention Wren himself, had spent tracking him. 'And then I'd have questioned him as a suspect, I'm afraid.' She explained. 'So who's in charge of the enquiry now? Don Simpson's still on sick leave.'

They looked genuinely shocked. 'Won't you be coming back?'

'Not for at least a week. At the very least. Not until I'm off the painkillers. Maybe it was my being so irascible when I was in pain before that made Sean feel he couldn't talk to me.'

Ray shook his head. 'Everyone knows your bark's worse than your bite. I was terrified at the thought of working with you. I was only Acting DCI, for goodness' sake! Still am, of course.'

'The sooner they firm up that promotion the better,' she said. 'But I should have tried harder with him.'

'With due respect, Fran,' Ed put in, 'as an outsider, I could see the graft you expect of yourself. Could you have done any more with the time and energy at your disposal? I wouldn't have thought so.'

At least he didn't add, *at your age*. 'Maybe I expected more of him than I should.' She bit her lip like a guilty schoolgirl. 'When I was on light duties after the first accident I sent him to a lot of meetings. He did a lot of running around while I couldn't.'

'And gained invaluable experience and contacts. No, Fran, if the man's kept his secret for twenty-odd years, he's not going to open up to someone he thinks could slow down his progress up the promotion ladder. Let the shrinks work their magic on him: see what they can do.'

'And meanwhile his job and mine have to be done by people new to the case.'

Ed got up and wandered over to the window. 'It's not your job to worry about that, Fran. And it's not even ours, to be honest. I don't know any cops at our level who don't give a hundred and ten per cent. Now management asks us for a hundred and twenty, a hundred and thirty per cent — and we can't do it. You were doing the work of — what — three people? You work for weeks in pain; you're injured again.'

'Not exactly in the line of duty,' she protested. 'I could have pulled a muscle anywhere — even on Mark's beloved tennis court.'

'But you wouldn't have been playing tennis until you were fit. You were buzzing round like a blue-arsed fly and trying to stop Zac getting on to an unsafe building,' Ray said. 'Sorry,' he said, checking his phone, 'I'd better take this.' He headed for the window.

Fran smiled at Ed. 'So from CEOP to Kent and Essex MIT. Or will it be Essex and Kent? I bet even now there are top-level meetings to decide,' she said.

'No takers,' Ed said. 'I may not go for it anyway. My partner wants kids, Fran — what good am I to her if I move her down here where she doesn't know anyone only to find I'm spending my life on the M25? I might just stay where I am a few more years: CEOP is doing a vital job and I want to be part of it.'

'The trouble is,' she mused, 'the better the job the unit's doing, the more likely they are to axe it. Sod's law.'

Ray's call over, the two men checked their watches and prepared to depart, promising to lock the door behind them and post the key through the lock. Fran had a terrible feeling that this wasn't just sensible security for anyone in a house in such a remote location; she felt they were caring for Granny. After their short conversation about her sick leave, no one had mentioned her return. It was almost as if the two men thought she was never coming back.

* * *

Mark had to be back at the rectory in order to admit Wren, who was paying a state visit, complete with driver. He did everything a host should, providing drinks and nibbles, and then, as he recognized the driver as Dizzy, let Fran deal with Wren on her own while he jogged down the steps to ask the young man how his cricket plans were proceeding. He was glad he had: Dizzy was leaving Kent on Friday, and heading up to Birmingham. He seemed to be realistic in his expectations, coming to the professional game comparatively late, but was full of a hope Mark found touching. But he was still a professional police officer, casting an anxious eye at his watch.

'He's cutting it fine, the guv'nor, isn't he? He's due at Maidstone West in less than half an hour, and though I'm happy doing a ton on a motorway, I don't fancy my chances round these lanes.'

'Maybe I'd better go and flush him out,' Mark said without enthusiasm.

But of course, Wren was a clock-watcher. Though still talking to Fran, he was already standing at the living room door, ready to leave.

Trying to acquit himself of eavesdropping — he was in his own home, after all — Mark paused. He couldn't pick up all Fran said, but it was clear that what Wren would probably call an animated discussion was taking place. Wren's voice took on a pleading note; Fran's remained flatly implacable. Whatever he wanted her to do, she wasn't going to be persuaded, was she?

The voices got louder, clearer.

'Look, Mr Wren, I'm happy to retire — I've done well over thirty years' service after all — or to take redundancy. Whichever is better financially for your budget. But I can't come back and continue the job — jobs — I've been doing. Not now. Not when both legs are fully healed, whenever that may be. Not ever. Is that clear?'

Wren hadn't finished. Mark was sure he made out the words, *post of Assistant Chief Constable.*

But Fran hadn't finished either. He picked up, 'Put it in writing and I'll give it due consideration.'

Like a discreet butler, Mark coughed. Wren wheeled round. 'Yes, Turner, what is it?'

'Your driver tells me you're likely to miss your train.' He held open the front door, ironically. Or would Wren want Fran so much he'd stay and exercise his powers of persuasion?

Wren turned tail and flew out.

* * *

Fran was looking pensive when he came back into the living room. Pensive, speculative and — an expression he'd rarely seen recently — impish.

'We always said that when we retired we'd make a point of having drinks on the terrace, didn't we? Well, I feel like a glass of bubbly tonight. Out there. If it isn't too much trouble for you to heave me on to that lounger we've never got round to using, and to swathe me in blankets if necessary.'

'I'll just put out some extra cushions to raise that leg of yours,' he said, playing along with her mood. 'Actually, the wind's changed — it's quite balmy tonight.'

What was she up to? It only took a matter of minutes to pile the cushions and to find the champagne — it was her preferred tipple, so there was always a bottle in the fridge. He was surprised she hadn't heaved herself to her feet in her usual independent way, but she was waiting for him to pass her the crutches and to support her back.

'In its own quiet way, the muscle's as bad as the break,' she admitted as he settled her again. 'Another pillow under my head, please, unless you can find a straw for the bubbly. That's lovely. Thank you.' She squeezed his hand.

'Come on, Fran — time to stop winding me up. All the excitement of receiving Wren into our home has eroded my patience to a quite marked degree.'

'I'm sure it has. He wasn't a very happy little birdie when he left, was he? You might say he flew off in a rage. We could tweet it.'

'You wouldn't be so disrespectful of your boss, surely.'

'What if he's not going to be my boss much longer?'

His smile froze: what if she was going after that Essex-Kent MIT job after all?

'I've told him I'm taking every minute of my sick leave entitlement, you see, and that then — whichever way I do it, either with redundancy or with straightforward retirement — I'm quitting my job. I can't do this anymore, Mark. I forget names, I can't stop someone breaking through a cordon and risking people's lives, I get injuries. I can't be an operational police officer anymore. So let's give the irritating little man the bird.' She raised her glass to his. She spoiled the gesture a little by slopping a few drops — he had to raise her head to prevent a further mishap.

'What if he leaves?'

'Oh, he mentioned that. He certainly wants to go onwards and upwards. Today Kent, tomorrow Europol. That's why he made me an offer he really can't imagine me turning down. I played along a bit, told him I wanted to see the terms in black and white. As if that would make it any more attractive. He wants me for your old job. ACC.'

He felt his face going stiff again. 'What did you say?'

'I told him to put his offer in writing and that when my medical adviser said I was in a fit condition to make such a decision I'd consider it in due course.' She smiled. 'I suppose I should put him out of his misery and tell him tomorrow not to bother. After all, if I delay it's not just him I'm messing up, it's Kent Police, and after all these years . . . It's well over thirty, Mark. I just feel this huge loyalty.'

'Is it enough to make you take the job?'

'After what it did to you? And you're a good manager. I'm crap. No, the only thing I have to decide tonight is when I tell him. Is champagne fattening? You know they were going to bring me choccies and Alice stopped them?'

'Good for her. But to hell with calories tonight: once your physio starts you'll be walking miles and using the exercise bike and shedding inches left, right and centre.'

'You're OK with the prospect of my cluttering up the place all the time?' she prompted him. He'd not responded to her announcement, after all.

'More than OK. Fran, when I saw you keel over . . . I had this dreadful fear . . . You remember you once said you didn't want to try living without me. I sure as hell don't want to try now.' He managed his old grin. 'Not until we're properly married, at least.'

'So I won't pop my clogs for another few weeks. And after that? You didn't quite answer my question. What'll we find to do?'

'You want to help Adam reorganize Mali's police?'

'Heavens, no! You know me and organizing: the words piss-up and brewery come to mind. But you've got a really good life going, with your gardening and your tennis and your grandchildren. I don't know how I'll fit in,' she added, with a hint of a crack in her voice.

'Is that why you've stayed on so long?'

'To be honest, sort of. When you retired, apart from it looking really bad if so many senior officers disappeared all at once, I wanted to let you . . . find your level, as it were. And now somehow I've got to find mine without messing up yours. God knows, looking after a temporary cripple again is going to cramp your style. I'm sorry.' She gripped his hand.

Raising hers to his lips he said, 'Leaving something you've committed all your working life to is terrifying. It's OK, as my therapist says, to be scared. But if I can do it, you can do it. And more to the point we'll find things we can do together. First up is to find a short-term project we can share.'

Her hand now at rest in his, she smiled thoughtfully. 'There's one I'd love to do. If ever two people were meant for each other it's Caffy and Tom.'

'Pity she's so smitten with this Alistair,' he said, laughing. 'That may have to wait a while. But the first one, the really big one, is to get you walking again: agreed? With no limp?'

'Agreed,' she said, pulling his head down so that she could kiss him.

If either of them regretted they couldn't celebrate a major decision in their usual way, neither mentioned it. They sat hand in hand until it was time for him to help her back into the house.

CHAPTER TWENTY-SEVEN

Mark would have bet his pension that the wedding wouldn't go entirely without hitches, but so far the pluses outweighed the minuses. Adam, the former chief constable who'd demanded to lead Fran down the aisle, was stuck in Mali, having the time of his administrator's life at a top-level international security meeting: what was it with managers and meetings? Fran could scarcely conceal her delight. Secretly Mark hoped his son Dave would offer to take Adam's place. After all, Marco and Phoebe, augmented by Livvie, who cared not a jot for the pink bear Fran had organized for her, were going to be Fran's attendants. But Fran had other ideas. And Mark couldn't argue with her choice: it was young Tom Arkwright whom Fran asked to do the honours. He accepted with obvious pleasure.

What was meant to be a small wedding had grown. Once Fran had known that a lot of tennis club folk would be coming to the church, she'd spread her hands expansively. 'Why not invite them to the reception too? After all, they'll all know Zac and — by now — Livvie. And they've got all the improvements to talk about.'

'Are you sure? You wanted it all small and intimate.'

'Look, all this work you've done on the garden deserves the widest audience.'

'You too, don't forget.' Mowing the lawn had become her speciality, as part of her muscle-strengthening therapy.

'Your work,' she insisted. 'The marquee will hold another forty, if needs be, and the weather forecast's wonderful. Just tell the caterers how many more mouths to feed.'

He smiled, raising his cup of coffee in a toast. What Fran didn't know, of course, was that the Golden Oldies proposed to form a guard of honour, with raised racquets — he hadn't had the heart to veto the idea.

And so here he was, walking gently down into the village, his best woman beside him. The sun shone brightly, but not so hard people would squint at the myriad cameras, and the wind was almost non-existent. He and Caffy weren't alone in enjoying the day: it seemed to him that every bird in Kent was yelling its sweet heart out. He dawdled to a halt.

'Are you all right?' Caffy asked. 'Good God, you're not getting cold feet or anything?'

'Absolutely not. Just enjoying — all this. It's the first time I've heard the birds for ten years, give or take. The audiologist was right: the aids aren't as good as having nice young ears, and he said that it can take a year or more to get the full benefit. But even this — this is a minor, no, quite a major miracle. A good omen.'

She chuckled. 'Well done you for being so brave.'

'What's brave about seeing sense?' he countered, not entirely honestly. It had felt like a very big step at the time, but now wearing the aids was no more of a deal than putting on his reading glasses. Less of a deal. They went in first thing in the morning, and came out last thing at night, which meant that unlike the specs they didn't get hidden under the newspapers or under the day's post. 'Not brave. Just getting sensible. And please don't add, "In your old age!"'

'As if I'd dare. Can you hear the bells?'

'Imagine if I'd missed them. You know, there are some incomers who wanted them silenced. I won't say they got run out of town, but it was damned near it. And here the bells are, welcoming us. This is so special, Caffy, all this.' He spread his hands, as if embracing the whole day. 'You have — you have got the rings?'

'Of course I have.' She patted her bag, small enough to hide behind the posy she carried, which matched Fran's attendants'. She'd chosen not a mannish suit, as some best women might, but a simple, extremely elegant dress. She and Fran had chosen it together, when they'd picked out the little girls' outfits. They looked as pretty as pictures; Caffy looked stunning. So what had gone wrong between her and the young man she'd been so infatuated with, Alistair?

Miraculously she had had no lingering damage from being trapped under the collapsing ruin, apart from a foot so wild in hue she'd taken photos of it. But there might be damage of another sort. Unlike her he wasn't good at probing emotions, his or other people's, but if Caffy needed a shoulder to cry on, he must put his at her disposal.

'And how are you? Not the foot — there's no sign of a limp, is there? I mean, over Alistair?'

She shrugged. 'You win some, you lose some. It would have to be a very special relationship to survive working together. I don't think we'd ever have got to the stage you and Fran have reached. Anyway, that won't stop me dancing tonight. Point me to a handsome tennis player and you'll see. Or,' she added with a slight change in tone, 'to Fran's protégé, that nice Yorkshireman. They might be mother and son, mightn't they?'

'Tom? Yes, a lovely lad. She always insists that she'd have been a dreadful mother, always putting work first, and that the young people she mentors are her substitute kids. Tom certainly tells her home truths no one else would dare. Even me. Especially me.'

'What does he think of her decision?'

'To retire completely?'

'As completely as Fran ever will retire,' she said with a grin. 'How will she cope?'

'I don't know. I can't imagine her without some project or other, can you? She's not missed work too much these last few weeks because her task was to get well. And she had a lot of visitors popping in to tie up loose ends in the cases she'd been working on. CEOP have taken the lion's share in the Livvie case, and I know she likes working with the two guys in charge.'

'Ray and Ed? Good, old-fashioned, decent cops like you — the sort you'd stop to ask the time!'

'Time! That's one thing the poor buggers don't have now. She's not had so much to do with the skeletons case: they had to parachute in a woman from another MIT until the original SIO came back from sick leave. Meanwhile, the shrinks are still working on the man who went AWOL. But that's between you and me. At least he's back at the Met and no longer cluttering up our corridors.'

'Mark, I have to say that that's not a very kind sentiment from someone who had a breakdown himself.'

He couldn't imagine anyone else being as forthright as that without being offensive. 'Sorry. You're right. But it seems so strange to me for a man to refuse to let anyone tell his parents he's still alive. What sort of limbo . . .' He coughed, and deliberately tweaked the subject. 'You know Fran went to every single funeral for those kids? Spoke to every set of parents? That's what policing should be. That's what she expects of herself, and all who work for her. Sorry, that should be past tense. At least people like Tom will carry on the tradition.' He was conscious that the reference to Tom was rather dragged in, as his next comment would be. 'He's been well taught. And I can't imagine he won't be popping round here from time to time to use Fran as a sounding board.' And if he and Fran had anything to do with it, Tom and Caffy would pop round at the same time.

Whatever Caffy might have thought of his change of gear, she didn't have the chance to tell him. Their priest for the day had wandered out of the church, which was picturesque to the point of being tourist bait, but was the place where they worshipped every week. Seeing them, Janey moved into the sun, raising her arms as if not just to greet them but to give further thanks for being declared free of cancer. She was vicar of an ugly church in a run-down part of Canterbury, and though they both loved her dearly, neither of them had wanted to marry there. The sadness, the suffering of the regular congregation had seeped into the fabric. It was Janey herself who'd suggested they ask their own rector if she might officiate in their church. Even deafer than Mark, and without trendy new aids, he had been happy to let her.

'Come your ways inside: it's quieter in there,' she said. 'The bells are deafening, aren't they?'

'They are indeed,' Mark agreed gratefully, but looking behind him, wondering if he'd catch a glimpse of Fran.

'It's not that Fran's late,' Janey said reassuringly, leading the way down the aisle, 'but that you're early. Is she over her accidents? Truly?'

'She'd never admit it if she wasn't. But I'd say she is: she walks a couple of hours each day, uses an exercise bike someone in the village pressed on her, and we've hired a fancy rowing machine. She's having acupuncture and doing Pilates and goodness knows what else. She was determined to get into her dress without having to have it let out.'

'Have you seen it?'

'What do you think? She insisted it would be bad luck.'

Caffy smiled. 'It's a cracker. Take it from me. And more than that I will not say. I'll tell you this, though: you both look as if you've got lights switched on inside you today. Even if you weren't kitted out in posh clothes, everyone would be looking at you and knowing what you're about to do.'

* * *

'You know Dizzy wanted to drive you down to the church?' Tom said, checking she'd fastened her seat belt.

'Come on, you've done a couple of pursuit driving courses yourself. You could still get us down in less than no time and stop with a great spurt of gravel. If you were in a police vehicle, of course,' she added in her most ma'amish voice.

'And if it were a bona fide emergency,' he said, picking up her tone and grinning. 'You heard they bust a police driver up in Brum for using blues and twos so he could pick up his kid from nursery? Which reminds me, why no kids in the back?'

'Because Livvie's still very clingy, and her mum's driving her and Mark's grandchildren down. She's better at supervising kids than I am — she'll stop them howling and might persuade them not to eat their flowers.'

'And why should you have to get snot on that nice frock of yours? OK, Fran, are you ready?'

'More than ready. Let's hit the road. I feel such a fraud, you know, using a car. I've been walking ten times this distance against the clock every day.'

'It's not so much getting to the church, remember, it's getting back. You'll both need to be ready to greet your guests. I was wondering,' he continued ultra-casually, 'if I should give the best woman a lift back too? So we could compare notes for our speeches.'

Speeches? She'd never even considered there might be speeches. But that wasn't what Tom was interested in, was it? It was Caffy, and why ever not? She was looking totally beautiful; perhaps her heart wasn't broken by the break-up with whatshisname. And if it was, who better than Tom to mend it?

'Here we are.' He pulled on the handbrake. 'And I am going to help you out, whatever you say, because you seriously do not want to tear your dress. Silk, isn't it?'

She waited obediently, and, taking his arm, walked solemnly into the church. The kids fell into step behind.

Mark turned towards her, and smiled.

Bother the slow march the organist was playing, bother her injured legs: she hitched up her skirt and ran towards him, arms outstretched.

EPILOGUE

She comes here every year, the anniversary of the day she saw him for the last time. No flowers, of course. If he was the victim of a car crash, she could leave a bouquet on the spot. But there was nothing dramatic like that. He just walked away, hands in pockets, not even turning to wave.

All she can do is peer down the road. Most times she's had to cover her mouth to stop herself calling out because she thinks she's seen him there. But it's another lad in the same jeans and hoodie uniform walking away. In any case, he won't be a kid now. He'll be a man.

One last stare, one last sigh. She hunches away. She tells herself she'd know if he'd died — if he was one of the kids behind that wall. Is it wicked to envy their parents? At least they know, even if it is the worst that they know. At least there's been a service for each one; at each she's been part of the congregation, standing slightly apart at the back, not wishing to crowd the family or friends who were lucky enough to be able to say a last goodbye.

She even made a bit of a scene at one of them, when someone pointed out that the tall woman on crutches was one of the detectives. She grabbed her arm: 'Are you sure,' she wailed, 'that there weren't any other bodies? Are you sure you've identified them properly?'

The tall woman didn't flinch. 'The scientists promised me that each child — because they were no more than children, were they? — was properly identified. Promised me. There are no mistakes.'

'At least they can bury theirs!' she said, knowing her voice was carrying more than it should. 'And my son — when will I know what's happened to him?'

'I wish I knew, Mrs—?' the detective's eyes had dropped to her ring finger.

'I'm Ms now. It broke us up, losing him. We blamed each other. And I went back to my maiden name. Years ago. Oh, when will someone find him? When will I know what happened?'

The detective gripped her hand tightly. 'I wish I could tell you. I just wish I could tell you.'

Then a mourning mother claimed the detective's attention. But she swore that the detective looked back at her over the sobbing woman's head with extra compassion.

It's only now that she realizes she never told the officer her names, now and then. How silly. But perhaps it wouldn't have made any difference.

No, there's no sign of him today. And dimly, painfully, she comes to realize there never will be.

THE END

ACKNOWLEDGEMENTS

I could never have written this novel without help from the following people, to whom I am very, very grateful:

Paul Bethell, Senior Review Officer, South Wales Police. Although the novel changed radically in structure and content from our original conversations, it wouldn't have started at all without his invaluable input.

Keith Bassett, Food Standards Agency inspector extraordinaire and dear friend, who put his finger straight on to a horrible plot-hole and enabled me to darn it in time.

John Webster, Corinium PC Clinic, who rescued me when my computer died midway through Chapter Five and then, when the new computer deleted every last word of the text, retrieved it at a time when other men would still have been sleeping off their Sunday lunch.

Anna Chesson, who put me back on my feet after not one but two tennis injuries and kept smiling throughout.

Ivor Higgins, who meticulously spots typos and corrects my MSS before anyone else in the world sets eyes on them.

THE JOFFE BOOKS STORY

We began in 2014 when Jasper agreed to publish his mum's much-rejected romance novel and it became a bestseller.

Since then we've grown into the largest independent publisher in the UK. We're extremely proud to publish some of the very best writers in the world, including Joy Ellis, Faith Martin, Caro Ramsay, Helen Forrester, Simon Brett and Robert Goddard. Everyone at Joffe Books loves reading and we never forget that it all begins with the magic of an author telling a story.

We are proud to publish talented first-time authors, as well as established writers whose books we love introducing to a new generation of readers.

We won Trade Publisher of the Year at the Independent Publishing Awards in 2023. We have been shortlisted for Independent Publisher of the Year at the British Book Awards for the last four years, and were shortlisted for the Diversity and Inclusivity Award at the 2022 Independent Publishing Awards. In 2023 we were shortlisted for Publisher of the Year at the RNA Industry Awards.

We built this company with your help, and we love to hear from you, so please email us about absolutely anything bookish at feedback@joffebooks.com

If you want to receive free books every Friday and hear about all our new releases, join our mailing list: www.joffebooks.com/contact

And when you tell your friends about us, just remember: it's pronounced Joffe as in coffee or toffee!

ALSO BY JUDITH CUTLER

FRAN HARMAN MYSTERIES
Book 1: COME TO HARM
Book 2: DO NO HARM
Book 3: IN HARM'S WAY
Book 4: NO HARM DONE
Book 5: NO HARM, NO FOUL

DETECTIVE KATE POWER MYSTERIES
Book 1: MURDER THE BOYS
Book 2: MURDER BY THE CANAL
Book 3: MURDER BY ARSON
Book 4: MURDER BY FRAUD
Book 5: MURDER IN DEVON
Book 6: MURDER ON THE JOB

Printed in Dunstable, United Kingdom

78574178R00150